SOUTH ISLAND STOWAWAY

It was sheer accident — she'd stowed away in the wrong car — that had brought Julia to Adam Dare's sheep farm in New Zealand's South Island, and wrecked his engagement as a result. Julia felt it was her duty to repair the damage — but was that what she really wanted?

Books by Essie Summers in the
Ulverscroft Large Print Series:

SWEET ARE THE WAYS
WHERE NO ROADS GO
HIS SERENE MISS SMITH
SOUTH TO FORGET
THE LARK IN THE MEADOW
THE BAY OF THE NIGHTINGALES
A PLACE CALLED PARADISE
THE MASTER OF TAWHAI
THE SMOKE AND THE FIRE
THE KINDLED FIRE
NOT BY APPOINTMENT
MOON OVER THE ALPS
SOUTH ISLAND STOWAWAY

This Large Print Edition
is published by kind permission of
MILLS & BOON LTD.
London

ESSIE SUMMERS

SOUTH ISLAND STOWAWAY

Complete and Unabridged

19295

ULVERSCROFT
Leicester

First published 1971

First Large Print Edition
published July 1978

© Essie Summers 1971

All the characters in this book have no
existence outside the imagination of the
Author, and have no relation whatsoever to
anyone bearing the same name or names.
They are not even distantly inspired by any
individual known or unknown to the
Author, and all the incidents are pure
invention.

British Library CIP Data

Summers, Essie
    South island stowaway. — Large print ed.
    (Ulverscroft large print series: romance).
    I. Title
    823'.9'1F   PR9639.3.S/

    ISBN 0-7089-0156-5

Published by
F. A. Thorpe (Publishing) Ltd.
Anstey, Leicestershire
Printed in England

This book has been written for
Marion Estee
of Reading, Massachusetts, who has
been a source of much inspiration to me
across leagues of sea and it is dedicated
to Miss Emily Guard, granddaughter
of the famous child-bride Betty Guard;
to Helen Guard, granddaughter-in-law;
Elaine Guard, great-granddaughter-in-
law, and her small, enchanting Edwina,
for introducing my husband and myself
on a smiling Sabbath day to the delights
of their own small Eden at Kakopo Bay,
Port Underwood, New Zealand.

The author wishes to record her thanks
to A. H. Reed for his book *Marlborough
Journey*, and to Cecil and Celia Manson
for their *Pioneer Parade*, which were of
invaluable help in writing this novel.

1

JULIA simply couldn't believe her brother was saying no to her. She'd plotted this move for two months and had congratulated herself that for once she couldn't be accused of a wildcat idea. She hadn't rushed into it in the first poignancy of Noel's loss of his wife-to-be. Even though chafing at the delay, she had marked time, then told her chief she would be leaving in August, giving him ample time to get another clerk, and had thought she'd have nothing more to do then than stow her gear in her brother's station-wagon and drive back with him over the Rimutakas and across the Wairarapa to his farm near Castlepoint.

Noel said now, in a non-persuadable tone, "I might have known you'd offer to do this, Julia. I even thought of it myself when I knew Alison couldn't get better . . . that you'd want to come to keep house for me. I made up my mind then that I wouldn't allow you to do it. You've given up more than enough for the family now.

"It's been the constant pattern of your life . . . our little sister looked upon as the mainstay of the family. It's against nature and we'll allow you to make no more sacrifices. Robert is sure that if you hadn't gone up to Dannevirke to nurse Denise you and Murray might have been married by now."

Julia heaved an immense sigh. "I might point out we were not — when I left Wellington — even engaged, and in any case, if I couldn't leave him for that length of time without him falling for someone else, it proves there was no strong attachment, doesn't it? Noel, everyone thinks I'm suffering from a broken heart and it's maddening. Believe me, the writing was on the wall long before I went up to Dannevirke, but because everyone thinks I leap before I look, I was trying to make up my mind slowly, so no one would say I'd broken it off on a sudden whim. I don't blame Murray one bit. We'd just become a habit with each other.

"I've come to the conclusion it doesn't pay to act against one's nature. I wish I'd done it there and then, and now I'd not be battling against the pity of my friends. I've given up telling them how it was because they think I'm just trying to save face. Faith is the only one who knows how it was because I'd told her of my increasing doubts . . . and *don't* look at me as if you too think it was just pride! It was a darned relief when I came back to find Murray had fallen for the Australian girl and I wouldn't have to suffer any remorse when I gave him up. That was why I hesitated so long. . . . It seemed cruel to keep company with a chap so long, wasting his time, then ditch him."

Noel said, his eyes keen, "For the first time I'm beginning to believe you. But I'm still adamant about you coming up to the farm. I managed it on my own before and after I became engaged to Alison — oh, I admit there are times when it's just hell, knowing she's gone beyond recall, but it's not as if I'm living on my own. I've got the two single men and we all take turns at the cooking. I'm damned if I'll let you come up there, cutting yourself off from all the city doings."

Julia heaved a prodigious sigh. "What

you really mean, my dear brother, is that you think Wellington is full of eligible men and Omairangi isn't. You think it would be a sacrifice. It would be heaven. I'm not a city girl even if I was born and brought up in one. I'm like Grandma and Grandpa and you. Must be our genes. We hark back to our farming ancestry."

"Just the same, you aren't going to bury yourself up at my place. There's not even another woman for ten miles. It's time you began thinking of yourself, Ju. You gave up your teaching career when Mother was so ill — we've got you to thank that she made such a wonderful recovery — and then you wouldn't go back to Varsity when she was on the mend because she needed so much help for so long and you couldn't have studied and done that too, especially when Dad was branching out into politics. Gosh, when I think of all you did, always putting Mum and Dad first, and gaily, too, so that their scruples vanished, I feel you deserve freedom from responsibility now. I know you say you've given notice — wish you'd told me at the time and I'd have scotched that pronto — but Mr. Gibson would take you on again — he's always short of staff, so there'd be no problem there. And Faith hasn't a new flat-mate yet."

Julia's stubborn chin set even more mulishly. "I am *not* going back to the office. I've *had* the rat-race of the cities. I'm not tied to it any longer with Mum and Dad overseas. I'll — I'll go into the country as a housekeeper if you won't have me. There are plenty of positions advertised."

"Like heck you will! Look, Julia, why don't you go across to Canada to Mum and Dad? They've got another year of the Trade Mission still to go. You've enough saved to go by air and they'd love it. The only reason they'd not suggested you going with them was because of Murray."

Julia looked at him with sorrowful hazel eyes. "And leave you on your own? At least if I take a position near here I can come up to you for weekends, even if you won't let me come to stay."

They continued to argue till time ran out. Noel said: "Look, I've got to be off. This meeting starts early, so some of the chaps, including me, can get home before it's too late. It's mighty near lambing and I'd like to get home. I'm sorry you've got all your cases packed, but I'm not playing ball. Faith agrees with me that it's time you started thinking of Julia Merrill as a person in her own right and not the dogsbody of the family. You'd better give me that spare key to the car. I might need it."

Resignedly Julia went off to get it. She was just taking it out of her purse when the great idea struck her. And she *wasn't* going to have second thoughts about that one. It didn't pay! She slipped the key back, went through the motions of opening and shutting drawers with great vigour, slamming them each time.

Noel appeared in the doorway. "Can't you find it, Sis?"

She shook her cropped head. "It's just nowhere. I have a feeling I must have left it in my office-drawer yesterday lunch-time after I put the groceries in your car."

"Oh, not to worry. Post it up when you get my jacket back from the cleaners. I'll be off. Tell Faith I'm sorry I missed her. Good-bye, Funny-face, and don't worry about me. I promise you I'll never skip cooking vegetables, that I'll air my clothes thoroughly, even to the point of baking them, and I'll make my bed properly every day! I appreciate your gesture immensely,

6

but for once I'm putting my foot down." He aimed a brotherly kiss at her cheek and went out to the Holden station-wagon where his cases were already stowed.

He thought nothing of the fact that his sister said "*Au revoir.*" After all, he came to Wellington at least once a month.

A mischievous spark lit Julia's eyes, making them almost green. She went across to her cases and transferred one or two articles into a shopping bag. She had jeans and skivvies up at the farm anyway, and pyjamas, plus a couple of frocks and some undies. Toilet things and make-up would be all she'd need and in a day or two she'd ring Faith to ask her to put these cases on the local bus. It was as simple as that.

She'd noticed Noel had the back seat up and a rug on it . . . she could get on the floor between the seats and pull the ends of the rug over her. If he had anything else to dump in — though not likely — he'd put it on the tray at the back or on the seat beside him. It wouldn't be a joy-ride, swinging round the many bends on the Rimutakas, but it would be worth it.

Just imagine Noel's face when she walked in on him after he got into the house in the wee sma's! There'd not be a thing he could do at that unearthly hour and once she was there she'd talk him into letting her stay. Anyway, he could hardly bring her back to the capital by brute force. His men would back her up, too. They didn't like cooking. They were both getting married next year, and Noel would find it easier to get new hands if a woman was there to cook and clean.

Julia began to enjoy herself. She wouldn't go down to the hall where the meeting was till about half an hour before they were due out. She'd leave a note for Faith who wouldn't be in till midnight, and she would take a taxi. She made herself savoury toast at nine and had two cups of tea to fortify herself against the long drive.

She felt quite a conspirator, tripping along with her bag, the key clutched in her hand, having dismissed the taxi at the corner.

There it was, in exactly the same place as through all the meetings, and, to her relief, not directly under a street light. She peered in . . . yes, the tartan rug was there, tossed untidily on the back seat, the ends trailing on to the floor. She slid the key in.

Oh, bother, it was sticking again. These keys one had made as spares were never as good as the original. She ought to have taken it back to have it filed. But this was worse than ever. Oh, could Noel have forgotten to lock it? No, it was locked all right. Blast the thing! Wouldn't it! Now, patience, Julia, you've managed it before. She took the key out, slid it back, uttered another impatient sound, and at that moment a policeman appeared beside her.

"Having trouble with your lock?" he asked sympathetically.

"Yes . . . it's never been a very good fit. I just got it made last Monday. My brother's been down for this Young Farmers' special meeting and I'm going back with him. Oh, well, they'll be out in half an hour if they're up to time."

(But I must be under the rug by then . . . yet I mustn't appear too upset to this chap. He might think I was trying to convert the car.)

The policeman grinned. "Sure it's the right key? Let's have a look. Seems okay. Goes in easily enough but just won't quite turn. I wonder if you're thrusting it in too far."

9

He inserted it again, drew it back, fiddled round, was rewarded with a click. "There you are!" He leaned across the wheel, unsnecked the passenger door from the inside, went round with her, opened the door and put her in.

"Thanks a lot," said Julia gratefully. "You certainly appeared at the right moment." She got in.

He smiled, said it was a pleasure, and went on his way.

Julia looked after him reflectively. How long before he came back? And when he did, would he think it peculiar that she wasn't still sitting in the car. And if he thought that, might he become suspicious? Or would he just forget about it? But she dared not sit here too long. She must be under the rug and concealed before the men emerged from that meeting.

He came back almost immediately. Evidently his beat ended at the next corner. Julia's mercurial spirits rose immediately. That would mean he wouldn't be back again for ages. She thought of something. It would be stuffy under that rug, even in August, and it was a long way. Better get some air into the car now. She wound the window down, which was a pity, because the policeman took it as an invitation and came across. He leaned his elbows on the glass and chattered till Julia could have screamed. She thought he'd never go.

He asked her where her brother was farming, how many sheep he ran, how many cattle, talked of Common Market complications for New Zealand, asked how long she had lived in Wellington. He told her he came from Stewart Island and was shocked to know she had never been there.

"Next stop South Pole," he said. "It's the most beautiful and remote place in the world . . . you know what its Maori name means, don't you? Rakiura . . . the Island of the Glowing Skies. You'll never see such sunsets as down there . . . the sun rises from the sea and sets below the sea."

He dwelt at length on the bush-clad shores, the peaceful bays, the wealth of rare bird-life, the mutton-birding season, the iniquity of so many New Zealanders who had never set foot upon its matchless shores . . . the utter peace. Peace! Julia felt more like murder. She found her hands were damp, clenched together in her lap.

Just when she was in complete despair, facing up to the fact that he'd still be here when Noel came out and she would be scolded and ignominiously returned home, he saw a commotion on the far side of the street and took himself off.

As soon as he was obviously busy, Julie got out, hastily pulled the rug off the back seat, arranged it so that two-thirds of it draped over the floor between the seats and got in, hoping no one was interested in her, but they were too busy watching the fracas, so she locked the doors, slid under the rug and thanked her lucky stars. Her conscience instantly smote her, and, being Julia, she popped her head up to make sure the policeman didn't need help, and thankfully submerged again.

She pulled the soft leather shopping bag under her head to make some sort of pillow and rolled a cardigan she'd not been able to squeeze in between her waist and the hard floor. There was only a rubber mat on it, no carpet. Never mind, it would be worth it. She left her head poking out of the rug for the time being and would withdraw it as soon as she heard Noel.

Mercifully the meeting broke up soon

and by taking a quick peep she could see the men streaming out. Then, hidden again, she could hear Noel's voice, slightly muffled.

He sounded quite cheery, so perhaps the fellowship of the meeting had taken his mind off his loss. He was chatting away to someone at the bonnet of his car. Julia kept herself well under. Once they were under way he wouldn't stop till he reached his farm, Omairangi.

There was a conversation she could not follow, then his voice, slightly louder, "Well, nice meeting you. Sorry it had to be on the last night. See you next year unless you're up our way and would like to call in. Always a spare bed going as long as you don't mind bachelor cooking."

Julia grinned to herself. If this anonymous voice came to Omairangi he'd find a female cook installed.

The voice offered a return invitation, then added: "I mean that. It's easy enough. Just drive your car on the *Aranui* or the *Aramoana* and you're over Cook Strait in no time. Cheerio."

She heard and felt her brother get in, drop a folder of papers on the seat beside

him, insert his ignition key, start up. Ah . . .
lovely! They were on the move and she was
undiscovered. No setbacks now till she was
at the farm.

She poked a cautious nose through the
fringe of the rug and quietly breathed in a
little fresher air. He'd never hear her with
the engine running. She thought of something. What if she sneezed? That, she
realised, would be more than an unfortunate giveaway. What would it do to a driver
on the Rimutakas? For the first time a
feathering of apprehension ran along her
pulses. Then she took her imagination in
hand with stern determination. You could
repress a sneeze very effectively by putting
a forceful finger on your upper lip.

Through the fringe all she could see —
and that only by moving her head to an
uncomfortable position — were sodium and
neon lights as they flashed by. Julia
turned her head sideways for more comfort
and began to plan how she would do up the
farmhouse. There would be plenty for her
to do outside and in, at lambing-time. She
gave herself up to blissful imaginings.

They would be skirting the harbour now,
on the Hutt road, going through the Hutt

valley on their way to the East Coast. There must be a lot of traffic because Noel was just crawling. But it was hard to tell, huddled on the floor. Muddling to one's sense of direction too, because he seemed to have turned right. Oh, perhaps he had swung out to pass another vehicle and she hadn't felt him cross back.

Good gracious, now he was stopping. Don't be silly, Julia, he'll just be slowing for some obstruction or very slow-moving traffic. But he did stop. Oh dear. How maddening if she were discovered before they'd left the city. Surely he didn't suspect someone was in the car. But she heard him walking away. The sound of voices reached her indistinctly. Then one, a stranger's, was slightly raised. "You're the last. Straight on now."

How peculiar. Couldn't be a road-block because there had been no search of the car. At the thought Julia's blood froze. Just imagine if some prisoner had escaped and there *were* road-blocks! Would they believe her story? For the first time Julia had misgivings. If they did get searched it would take some explaining. They'd think she wasn't Noel's sister at all. They wouldn't believe him, they'd think he was abducting someone. Julia took a pull on herself. She was letting her imagination run riot. This was ridiculous. There could be half a dozen reasons why Noel had stopped.

Ah, he was getting back in. He drove off extremely slowly. Must have been something wrong on the road . . . but what? And why had that man said Noel would be the last? It wasn't terribly late . . . in fact the theatre traffic ought to be starting, and anyway, the Hutt road was always busy.

He positively crawled, came to another stop . . . she could hear shouted instructions. They seemed to turn a little, then back. How mysterious. But she didn't dare risk a peep.

Noel got out and she heard his footsteps retreating. How very odd . . . that didn't sound like a tarseal road. More like a bridge, like planking. Roadworks, no doubt. Perhaps some subsidence. Must have happened suddenly for men to be working on it at this time. She just hoped it didn't take long. She felt cramped and there were still a hundred miles to go. She'd like to be moving again. She supposed Noel was watching the gang.

It was very light through the fringe. They must have powerful searchlights on the job. But from this angle she couldn't see a thing and dared not risk raising herself. Imagine if one of the Ministry of Works men saw a head bob up and said to Noel, "Hey, mate, you've got company."

The next ten minutes seemed an hour. It must have been some terrific earth-moving machinery to make all these creakings and groanings. The engines of the machines sounded strained as they revved up, she thought. Half the road must have caved in to warrant all this.

There were a few final clashes and clangs, then movement.

Movement! But Noel hadn't got back in the car! Could men be pushing it? Very cautiously Julia raised herself on an elbow and peered out and up. Her range of vision was limited, but what she saw mystified her completely. They were in some sort of building. It . . . it looked like a gigantic warehouse. But what on earth would Noel be doing in a warehouse at half-past ten at night? Was it a garage? There were certainly a number of vehicles standing round. Was something wrong with the car?

And the car *wasn't* moving. Yet she still felt this odd sensation of gliding forward.

She twisted herself at a breakneck angle and saw two enormous pantechnicons belonging to moving firms and several vans.

Then a ship's hooter sounded, so this must be a garage or store near the wharves, it sounded so loudly.

Then it hit her, hit her with a shock that made her feel sick. She wasn't *near* the harbour. She was *on* the harbour! She was on either the *Aramoana* or the *Aranui*, one of the drive-on, drive-off ferries, and she wasn't in *Noel's* car at all. She was in the car of some unknown man, heading out towards the Heads, to Cook Strait and, finally, to Picton in the Marlborough Sounds of the South Island!

It was almost too much of a catastrophe to admit into her reeling consciousness even when the first impact had passed. She wanted to yell: "It can't be. It's a nightmare. It's got to be . . . I'll wake up soon."

But it wasn't a nightmare, and she was hideously awake. She would be discovered and there'd be the very hell of a scandal. She'd be classed as either a stowaway who couldn't afford the fare, or one of the girls who frequented the Wellington wharves and sneaked on board because of illicit relationships with crew members!

This time she had really done it! But — but who could have thought a simple thing like hiding in a brother's car could have turned out like this? That darned key . . . it had turned, with difficulty, after that policeman had fiddled round. The keys must be very alike. What absolutely foul luck. And of course there just had to be a similar tartan rug on the back seat. If there had been more light she might have tumbled to it. But what, oh, what was she going to do now?

Most likely the owner of the car would be up on deck, watching the myriad lights of the hills of Wellington recede. She raked her mind for all she knew about these inter-island ferries. Even in daytime you could get a cabin for an extra dollar or two if it was cold or you suffered from seasickness.

Seasickness! Julia had no idea whatso-ever if she were the seasick type. How ghastly. It didn't bear thinking about. Even when she had gone to the States with her mother, she had flown because her mother's illness had been urgent. Apart from the odd launch trip on Auckland or Wellington harbours, she'd not been on a ship, and Cook Strait *could* be one of the worst crossings in the world, with seas swirling in from the Tasman on the west and the Pacific on the east.

Well, seasickness was the least of her worries. The most dread thought of all was when and where — and how and by whom — she would be discovered. They would take some convincing that it was little more than a prank, and a prank with the best intentions in the world.

Julia, in a sort of frozen clarity of mind, began reasoning out the reactions of her discoverers and her chances of convincing them. Well, for a start, she had enough money in her purse to prove she was not destitute and therefore had not needed to stow away. And she could tell them she had no need to come to the South Island.

They might or might not believe she had opened the car with her brother's key. Oh, that was a point. She still had it. And they could contact that policeman. But how would that help? Well, it might. Then she thought of something. Faith would back her up. Faith would have the note — if she hadn't tossed it into the embers of the fire. They had still been red when Julia left. She had put the guard in front. But Faith could endorse her story, even if the letter no longer existed.

But it was going to take a hideous amount of time. It would be most unpleasant. And she had a feeling there could be a horrible amount of publicity. There were always reporters round policestations and a story like this was unusual enough to get press coverage that would be nation-wide! Julia clapped her hands over her mouth to stifle an involuntary groan.

Panic and a feeling of being trapped surged over her. She shook herself free of that, impatient for feeling like screaming. A lot of good that would do. Think, think! There were one or two things she could do . . . the main thing was to choose the one that would give least publicity.

The most important was how to get off the ship, undiscovered if possible. At present there were men walking round here. Some, she thought, might be the drivers of the big lorries. Presently they would go up top. A few were crew, but by and by they might leave too.

There were usually a lot of passengers who had not brought cars with them. This was a very popular crossing. The other way — Wellington to Lyttelton — which took you halfway down the Island, was an all-night one and everybody slept in cabins, but she knew from friends who'd recently done this trip that many stayed on deck the whole time, just over three hours.

If she could get out of this car and, without being challenged, get up to the promenade deck and mingle with everyone, she might be able to walk off unnoticed at two in the morning. It would be horrible having to walk round an unknown town for hours till daylight, but it would be nothing to the disgrace of being discovered, hiding in the bottom of a stranger's car!

Yes, it could be a solution, feasible only if every crew member left this lower deck. How many decks would there be? She did know, vaguely, that most of the cars were driven on up a ramp, so she must be on a higher deck. This was the railway wagon deck, so naturally was on a level with the rails on the wharf. Perhaps they always put the last of the cars on this deck too.

Well, she supposed plenty of women drivers brought their cars over, and occasionally some would be parked below, so if only she got out of here, her presence on the companionways leading up might not be questioned. There should be a number of women on board seeing it was still school holiday time.

This reasoning was making her feel better. Panic slowly subsided. If only those men would stop yelling out to each other and go away she'd have a chance! If only she'd thought to provide herself with some fruit she wouldn't feel so thirsty! Julia swallowed and tried to pretend she was drinking.

Suddenly one of the seamen called out, "Oh, hullo, Jock, didn't see you come on board. How are you?"

A reply, then the seaman again. "Are you going straight on down south when you take her off at two, or are you coming back on board to sleep till daylight?"

"No, I'm going on. I'll have breakfast at Kaikoura."

"M'm. I believe there's quite a crowd stopping on this time. It wouldn't do me.

Once I'd taken my car off I'd want to be on my way. Ten to one you'd not go back to sleep anyway."

The man Jock slammed a car door, said, "Well, that's it. Bill gave me permission to get my pipe. Be seeing you at two."

Permission. That meant drivers were not allowed back down to their cars once the ship had sailed, without specially requesting it. So she dared not get out now and try to get up to the passenger deck. Well, that information had put her in the picture. It sounded as if all vehicles must be driven ashore at two. To leave the decks free for oncoming cars, she supposed. Now, how would this affect her?

If she were lucky, the driver of this one would take it ashore and return to a cabin for some sleep. If her luck held and she were not discovered, she could unlock the car from the inside, slip unnoticed out of the car-park, and prowl the streets of Picton till the first trip back to the North Island.

Finally it remained her last chance. There seemed to be some activity around her all night. Perhaps this was the best way, anyway, to go ashore with the car, for with no experience of South Island travel, Julia had no idea whether or not you had to show a disembarking check. Naturally when you boarded you'd have to surrender a ticket. Oh, how awful to be so dumb about travel within your own country and yet to have been to America! No wonder that policeman had been a bit scathing.

It was a ghastly night, even though Cook Strait must have been like a mill-pond. Julia was cramped. She developed itchiness in the middle of her shoulder-blades. Her ankle-bones got sore on the floor and she just didn't dare shift round too much. Occasionally she peered out hopefully, but her angle of vision was never complete and the ship made so many noises as it forged ahead, you couldn't tell if men were working near or not. She did slide the window down a fraction for more air and the sound of water as the ship sailed on sent her nearly distracted, she was so thirsty.

One thing she had realised. The driver of this car was almost certainly the one Noel had bidden good-bye. It seemed he had just met him that night, so it wasn't likely

Noel had confided in him that he had lost his fiancée in May, but at least he might believe she was Noel's sister if she said her name if discovery came. It was Julia's only ray of comfort.

She found herself praying he would get back on the ship. That would solve all her problems. She could tackle the question of getting back to Wellington all right, even if the first trip over in the morning was booked out.

If this man was a farmer, he'd probably live out of Picton. If it was near he might drive straight home. If he lived well down the South Island, he'd probably come back on board to get some sleep before hours of driving. It would take most of the day, for instance, to get to Christchurch, say five or six hours. But then in that case he'd have probably taken the Lyttelton ferry. Julia suddenly found she had to concentrate on not falling asleep. It was ghastly. She wished her watch had a luminous face. If only, if only she knew the time . . .

It was just before zero hour that Julia began to consider that she might reveal her plight to the driver of the car, but a few minutes of imagining his reaction, his annoyance and embarrassment in being involved in such an escapade held her to her original resolve . . . to try, if possible, to make a getaway undetected by anyone. It would be just wonderful if she could manage it. Only Faith would ever know because Julia would swear her to secrecy. Noel must never know — he'd think his madcap sister had really gone over the odds this time.

Suddenly there was more noise and a change in the ship's motion and direction. They must be coming into Picton and the crew were preparing for the disembarkation of the vehicles.

Julia broke out into a cold sweat, her heart raced, her ears strained to catch every sound that might tell her what was happening. Movement ceased, activity increased, car doors were opened and closed. This one must have been last on . . . it would be first off . . . the car door opened!

He wasted no time. There were the small noises of a key sliding into the ignition slot, the self-starter springing the engine to life, the changing of gears and movement . . . good, they were nearly off, at least that much was accomplished without discovery. If only she got away from the ship, even if then he found her, there would be only one person to see and know.

In a moment she might actually be in the car-park. He might return to the ship for the rest of the night, and she would be free . . . she could tell they were off the ship and crossing the yards. She was willing him to turn and stop.

He kept going!

There was a turn to the right, she thought, a bumpy surface . . . some winding about, a swing to the left . . . how odd, if he were heading south, she'd expect him to keep right and go straight on . . . that much she knew from maps.

Well, it hadn't come off, her last desperate chance. She'd have to wait till his first stop, and it could be daylight by then. If he were going south it could be Kaikoura for breakfast like that other man. She dared not do anything now. It could put a man off the road . . . her mind flinched from what she would have to do. When it was light and he pulled up for his meal he was bound to discover her. There was just a faint hope that he'd be hungry enough to stride in and not notice that the rug had fallen on the floor and that something was under it. Still, luck might hold with her yet, seeing it had so far. At least now she was beyond the risk of publicity. Or was she? Imagine if the driver refused to believe her and brought the police into it!

But he didn't turn right again. Muddled and all as she was, she had enough sense of direction to realise that they seemed to be going round the bay, then uphill slightly, heading east. Oh, how ghastly if he had a farm in some remote Sound, one of those indented into this fretted coastline. She tried to remember all she had heard about some of the almost inaccessible Sounds. If he'd been stopping at Blenheim or Kaikoura on the main road, and she had managed to get away unnoticed, she could simply board a Road Services bus and go back to Picton to catch the next ferry. But he might be going somewhere not served by buses. God send this farm wasn't too far away and that if she made her escape, she could walk back.

The road, she thought, was skirting a bay. The driver had his window down and a tang of bush was mingled with a tang of salt water . . . he changed gear and began to climb . . . to dip, to climb, to dip again, to swing round corners that made her brace her heels and toes and hands. Her whole body was one big ache, her tongue felt stuck to the roof of her mouth. Under cover of more gear-changing, she raised herself a little and peered upwards. She could see nothing but a dark blur of bush-clad hills and a starry sky. The moon was obscured by clouds, which was just as well. She was on the wrong side to see any water, but as sure as God made little apples, they were winding round the myriad waterways of the Sounds to the east. But where? To some solitary bay? Some farmhouse where she would be in full view if she tried to get away?

It seemed endless, the swinging and the climbing and the dipping. Then they didn't dip any more but seemed to be on a steady pull and bearing right . . . were they going into some remote valley, or crossing a saddle? Were they getting away from the labyrinth of the waterways? A gear change, a gentle downgrade, then a sudden exclamation from the man in front and a hurried jamming-on of brakes. Julia's heart jolted up, lurched against her side, steadied. Was she discovered?

He leapt out but did not wrench open her door. She heard his footsteps retreating. She raised herself up and peered strainingly out. On her right a hill reared up. On her left glimmered a sheet of water that looked like a huge harbour. Behind her she saw shapes of far hills against a lighter sky and above the darker waters of the Sounds. She had been right. This was a saddle for sure. She could see the man's figure. He was moving very slowly . . . oh, much too slowly. He was far too near for her to open the door. It would sound like a trap going off in the stillness of this hour. He stopped. He was near a corner. He seemed to be examining something, peering down at the road, and up at the cutting. What a very narrow road it seemed to be there. The hill came right down and reduced the road to what looked at this distance to be scarcely wide enough for one vehicle. Oh, if only he would go round that corner! She'd be out of this car like a lintie and would scuttle into the scrub until he'd driven on.

Then, however dark or rough or eerie the road, she'd walk back to Picton. He was still near enough for her to hear him make a disgusted exclamation . . . he appeared to be examining the ground again. Then he turned and began to walk back.

At that moment something . . . *something* leapt in the door he'd left open, sprang on to the back of the front seat, eyes gleaming like emerald torches, and came down on top of the rug and Julia!

How she stifled the scream that rose in her, she hardly knew, but she kept her hand pressed to her mouth. The animal gave a faint mew, padded round, decided this was a fine place for sleeping, soft and warm, and settled down, somewhere about Julia's waist and hip.

Oh, merciful heavens, if it wasn't bad enough being trapped in this stupid situation, miles from anywhere, with a strange man, without adding a wild cat to it. Or was it wild? Wouldn't one of the untamed ones have taken off, spitting and screeching?

He got into the car and spoke to himself as he did so, nearly scaring seven bells out of Julia. "Well, that's it! Daren't risk a darned thing till morning. They must have had torrential rain."

He reversed the car, then ran it on a wide lookout sort of place. She was holding her breath. He was going to doss down in the car. Would he think he'd be more comfy in the back seat away from the wheel? Or even if he stayed in the front would he try to fish the rug up? Would he put the light on to do that?

His hand came over the back, feeling on to the seat for the rug that was now pulled right over Julia. He encountered only leather, evidently, and said, "Funny . . . could've sworn it was there. Oh, this will do."

(Must have had one on the front seat beside him, perhaps a smaller one. She hoped he'd find it warm enough and not institute a search.)

He settled back against the far side away from the wheel and from his almost instant heavy breathing, must have been dead-beat and had gone to sleep immedi-ately.

By this time Julia felt like taking great gulps of air, but had to control her breath-ing. How ghastly if she herself fell asleep, moved, grunted . . . anything that might wake him up. Just imagine, though, if this cat started to purr! He'd switch the light on.

But having survived this far, she was banking on her luck holding further. He might drive into his garage, and as it would be so early, his family might not come rushing out to meet him. He might decide to tiptoe in not to wake them and to unpack the car later. And she would slip out. But what a way back it was going to be. His farm must be down in this harbour below. But she'd give it a try. She wasn't going to turn down her last chance.

Just when she felt she couldn't lie a moment longer without moving, or shifting this whopping great cat off her, streaks of light appeared in the east, directly facing the windscreen, and the man stirred, grunted, must have opened his eyes, said, "Oh, of course," realising where he was, and stretched.

It disturbed the cat. It sprang clean into the front seat, landing squarely on him. He yelped, as well he might, said, "Where in the name of thunder did you come from? Oh, I left the door open when I got out to look at the landslip. You don't look wild . . . I think I'd better take you home or you will go wild — and do damage. Well, here goes." He got out, with strict instructions to the cat to stay put.

The sun was absolutely popping up this morning. Oh, if only it had stayed a bit darker and he'd gone a bit further, Julia might have fled. If they were going to be stuck here by a cliff-fall, she'd just have to reveal herself.

After a careful inspection he got in, commended the cat for settling down, stroked it, said, "Now, keep settled, mate, and we'll be home in half an hour and there are barns and mice galore for you."

Julia dared not look, as she realised, to her extreme terror, that they were going round that extremely narrow strip of road. The driver edged it round, stopping several times, backing twice, then they were on their way, coasting down. It was maddening not being able to see. When the descent was finished she thought the road ran by the shore, over level ground, then climbed and dipped a few times.

He slowed, made a sharp short turn, downhill, leading down a drive, she guessed, a sick feeling in the pit of her stomach, and without opening any doors, drove into a great barn.

He got out quickly, said, "Stay there, puss. I'll get the kids to butter your paws so you don't stray."

Oh, how truly marvellous! Thanks to the cat he was walking away, not even taking his cases from the back, those wretched cases that had deceived Julia into thinking it was Noel's Holden. Then she heard him say, "Why, Miriam, I hardly thought you'd be up to welcome me home!"

A short silence . . . Miriam was getting kissed, she thought, then a cool, youngish voice said rather tartly. "Up? I've scarcely been in bed. Luke made a beast of himself at Watson's party and was sick all night. At five I decided it wasn't worth going back to bed, so I showered and stayed up. The others are still asleep. But you're early, aren't you, if you slept on the boat?"

"I didn't. I decided to come home and just sneak into Ben's *whare* seeing he's away, but got stopped by a slip just below the saddle. It was cloudy, so I couldn't see what the road was like on the edge or beyond, so I dossed down on the front seat and when daylight came found it could be negotiated with care. But we'll go in right away. I'll come back for — " he broke off, said, "No, don't open the car yet, Miriam, I've got — "

He was too late, she had wrenched it open. Here it came . . . discovery! Julia, trembling under the rug, realised it was the back door, not hers — Miriam's voice said, "I want that case of grapefruit. We've eaten the last from the fridge. I just hope you got nice ones. I — " Then there was a wild shriek from her as the cat made a leap from the back of the front seat clean over Julia and out of the back door.

The man burst into roars of laughter. "I tried to stop you. It must have got in the car when I was examining the slip. I found it this morning. Some unfeeling person must have dumped it."

Miriam said, oh, so clearly, "Are they under here — " and yanked the rug off and shrieked again. As well she might. But it was a different shriek . . . shock, yes, but angry shock!

Julia scrabbled madly at the back of the seat in an endeavour to hoist herself up, gave that up as hopeless, shuffled along the floor and slung her cramped, stiff legs out, made another clutch and rose up incredibly dishevelled, ungraceful, guilt written all over her, and essayed speech.

The man said, rushing towards the woman and the car, "What in hell is — "

But he got no further. The woman called Miriam was white to the lips. She swung round on him, said, between her teeth, "*So* . . . you didn't want me to open the car . . . no wonder! You spent the night out on the saddle . . . what a very convenient excuse that landslip made . . . or is there one at all? How dumb do you think I am? What were you going to do with her, Adam? Smuggle her into Ben's *whare*, where I never go? Or into one of the shearers' cottages? I'd never have believed it of you!"

2

JULIA at last managed to get some words out. She shook the woman by the arm. "You don't havè to believe *anything*. There isn't anything *to* believe. It's not true. He doesn't know I'm there . . . I mean *didn't* know I was there till you yanked that rug off. I mean I stowed away . . . in the wrong car. I've been trying to get away all night. Oh, you *must* listen!"

Miriam's laughter was brittle and sceptical. "You aren't going to tell me a tale like that. That you stowed away and were undiscovered till you got here . . . that you got on to the ferry, were there all the time . . . getting off it . . . driving here . . . and while he slept at the top of the saddle!"

The man was still staring and he had a face like a thundercloud, a black-a-vised, heavy-browed man in his thirties.

Then he said in a tone of utter bewilderment, "Miriam, don't be so daft. I've never seen this tousled wreck in my life. She *is* a stowaway. I mean she *must* be.

One of those girls who hang round wharves at all seaports, I suppose. I guess she stowed on board some time yesterday, and perhaps nearly got caught and got into my car on the railway deck . . . is that it ?"

He glared at Julia.

Julia realised that all the conclusions she had dreaded were being leapt at and put into words, but before she could answer for herself the woman said, and her voice was icy, "Never seen her before ? Tell *that* to the marines . . . I was in Blenheim two days ago and saw that *Evening Post* photograph, the one of the reception . . . and you're standing right next to this — this girl!"

Adam took one contemptuous look at Julia, who visibly shrank before it, and barked: "Don't be ridiculous! I saw that photo, and haven't a clue who that girl is, either . . . the photographer took it unawares. I hardly exchanged more than a grin with that girl over his mistake . . . but it's certainly not this — this scruffy urchin. *That* girl! was really something! Long hair, all piled up on top of her head. Even if I only saw her for about sixty seconds I knew that much. *She* was glam. Well, you could see that for yourself in the photo. But look at this one . . . she's practically eton-cropped!"

Miriam's voice was charged with disbelief. "Don't ask me to believe that! She'd be wearing a switch, of course. But you *know* that, and you *know her* — you know her very well — and this is all a put-up job. You didn't dream I'd be up at this hour."

Julia was staring at Adam with reluctant and horrified recognition. She'd seen the photo too and had laughed over it with Faith. "That photographer was right off beam. This chap and I had just turned towards each other — almost collided — and this candid camera got us. I wonder who he was? Quite the hero type."

And now she knew who he was and he didn't look like a hero at all. He looked murderous.

She said, and her voice was filled with despair, "It *was* me! It *was* you! Oh, what a mess . . . the most ill-chance."

"Ill-chance!" Miriam positively snorted. "If that's all you two can think up you must be mad."

Adam seized Miriam and his grip must

41

have hurt. "I expect to be believed by my fiancée," he bellowed. "Now just listen to me. It does seem as if it must be this girl — though it's hard to believe — but before you go on bawling me out, I want an explanation from *her* and *you* are going to listen."

The words hissed out between Miriam's teeth. "I can't very well help hearing when you're holding me here by brute force and shouting like a madman . . . but I'm not believing whatever ridiculous tale you've cooked up between you, oh, no. I thought it was strange for you to go to that conference at such a busy time."

His eyes flashed. "It was an emergency meeting to meet a special situation — and, damn it, *you* persuaded me to go. They only threw in that boring social reception at night to impress the Australian visitors who came at such short notice. Now, just listen to *her*. Come on, *you*!" and he turned to Julia.

Julia felt a wave of sickness go over her, but pulled herself together.

Her voice was staccato. Her sentences and phrases were so jerky she knew they sounded artificial.

"I'm a typist in Wellington. My brother has a farm on the Wairarapa. He was engaged to be married and his fiancée died last May. I feel he's breaking his heart and needs a woman in the house. But he refused to take me, even though I'd left my job, so I hid in his car — as I thought — and I thought that when my brother found I was up at Omairangi, he'd give in and let me stay."

Adam said in a tone of utmost doubt, "It's pretty weak . . . why wouldn't a brother leap at the chance of a house-keeper?"

Julia hesitated, which was a pity, because Miriam noted the pause. The trouble was, it made her sound goody-goody. She said uncertainly, "He thought I'd made too many sacrifices for the family already. Thought I'd be burying myself in the country."

The man's voice was hatefully sarcastic. "I hand it to you, you're a quick thinker."

Miriam's voice matched his. "I think you're *both* quick thinkers. You're playing your parts very well. But one thing you can't explain . . . you were daft enough to bring your pet cat with you."

Julia sparked up, a fiery glint in her eye. "I never saw that cat in my life till it leapt in when Ad — when this man here — went to look at the landslip. I didn't know what was happening. I raised myself up and peered out and hoped he'd go far enough for me to unsneck the door quietly and walk back to Picton — but he came back too soon . . . and he'd left the door open and that wretched cat leapt in on top of me."

Miriam's lip curled. "Made a slip there, didn't you? Nearly called him Adam! You just don't get pet cats way up on top of the saddle, and a wild one wouldn't have stayed inside — and if you were stupid enough to get into the wrong car, why on earth didn't you get out before you got on the ship?"

"Because I didn't know I was on a ship. We went on the bottom deck — as I now know — the railway truck one. If only he'd gone up the ramp, I'd have realised. After this man left the car I peeped up and thought I was in a warehouse. I was completely bamboozled, couldn't think why Noel was calling at a warehouse — then I thought it must be a garage — then

— " she gulped — "it moved. The ship."

The blue eyes surveying her were like chips of glacier ice. "And why didn't you get out there and then? Come on, I'm sure your imagination — or Adam's — can supply a quite likely story to answer that."

Julia spread her hands out in a helpless gesture. "Because of the publicity, the embarrassment. They'd have thought just what this man thinks — that I was a girl from the wharves area, wanting to get to the South Island. I might have been arrested. At best it could still have meant a night in a cell till they could check my story. All I hoped for was for the driver to get back on the boat till daylight. I'd have slipped out of the car, wandered round Picton and taken the next ferry back. I — " she faltered. It was no good, they just didn't believe her. And the girl disbelieved the two of them. She added lamely: "And I only called him Adam because you did." She thought of something. Turning to the man, she said, intending to tell him she was Noel's sister, "Look, I think you kn— " but she got no further.

The cat reappeared. It stuck its head round the corner of the barn, gave a horrible yowl, a lost, lonely sort of yowl, took an appraising look round, marched forward, sat back on its haunches, surveyed them all consideringly, then walked straight across to Julia and began rubbing itself against her legs. She recoiled as if stung. Its action looked like sheer recognition. She loved cats, but this one was making a liar of her.

This time Miriam's voice held a sneering triumph. "And she says it's not her cat!"

There was a long and horrible silence.

Then all at once it was as if Miriam had completely forgotten her presence. She said slowly and deliberately to her fiancée. "It's too much, on top of everything else. I think you proposed to me solely because you think I'm so suitable . . . but you're not above amusing yourself on the side. It all adds up to incompatibility. I don't think I could stand the sort of life you'll expect me to live here. It's too much of a clan relationship, a self-contained community.

"For all the difference that road has made to your lives, you might just as well still be isolated . . . still dependent upon the sea for access to the rest of the world just as you were for well over a century. There's

46

all this space, yet you won't sacrifice one tree of that orchard to make room for the sort of house I want . . . away from all these grandparents and hangers-on! It's perfectly ridiculous . . . you're the older son, yet Daniel has the modern house and you have the old, inconvenient one. Nobody in their right senses would preserve that ancient cottage tacked on to the homestead. I can see how it would be — your grandparents are getting older and older . . . they would gradually infiltrate the house till it would simply become a home for the aged. It's cluttered now. Just cluttered! All these mouldering relics of the past — one that was hardly a cultured past. It just wouldn't work . . . I want landscape windows and stone-flagged patios and walls where you can see the pattern of the wallpaper, not covered with Victoriana and hideous old portraits.

"Nor do I want my home for ever overrun with broods of relations . . . I don't think any of them ever takes a holiday anywhere else. And I want a husband I can trust, not be deceived in. Neither do I want a softy like you who takes on responsibility after responsibility, who takes his brother's children while his brother and their mother go gadding, who won't stop his grandfather interfering. And as for trying to fob me off with far-fetched tales of stowaways and not knowing the girl you posed for a photograph with . . . ah, pah! I'm leaving! I'm leaving *now*. And I wish you joy of the situation you're facing. Your grandmother can't come out of hospital tomorrow without me to nurse her — and I'll tell you something. Not only Luke was sick last night — I have strong suspicions Susanna's coming down with measles! Now you've got to manage on your own, Adam Dare, you might realise your foolishness!" She went to flee, but was caught and held.

He said between his teeth, "Just you wait till *I* tell *you* a few things! I believe you think you can bring me to heel over this . . . that I'd turn my brother out of his house, or build you another by spoiling our view. I tell you I'm not taking on any mortgages at the moment, and I've no capital to build without. Besides which I couldn't bear to live anywhere else but in Captain Ephraim's house. At first you professed to adore it . . . you oohed and aahed enough — told Granny you adored the Bay! Ever since you came to house-keep you've been working up to this — and I've been fair sick of the nasty digs. Time you did lose your temper, we're getting the truth now. I'm going to tell you a few home-truths too . . . I'm going to start by — " but he got no further. Julia just flew across the floor and seized his arm.

"Don't say it!" she shrieked. "Whatever happens don't go on slanging each other. You've both lost your tempers, that's all! You'll say things in the heat of this moment that will be very hard to forgive, things you can't take back. I don't think either of you mean what you say. Oh, dear, and it's all my fault too . . . you owe it to me to do nothing foolish. Think of the remorse you're burdening me with . . . get me out of here . . . get me back to Picton. She'll soon realise that every word I've uttered is true. I mean it's too ridiculous for words — it was only the first shock of seeing me, I suppose. I mean what man would bring a girl back here when his fiancée was installed in the house? If it hadn't been for that stupid photographer

49

she'd never have thought a thing about it. Oh, if only I hadn't acted on impulse. But stop blazing at each other. Stop it this very moment!"

He shook off her hand. "You keep out of this. Just mind your own business. You started it, yes, but it's all been simmering underneath. If Miriam goes now she's not coming back. I don't want a wife who's discontented to start with. *I'm as I am*. This place is part of me. Why, my great-great-grandfather was the first whaler in this bay. Some of that house is made from pit-sawn timbers which he sawed himself. Its associations are priceless. Granny and Granddad are *never* going to be moved from that cottage. I am *not* going to cut down Camilla's sycamore tree. Miriam, if you can't take me as I am and Tupuna as it is, then go now, as you threaten."

Julia, tears in her eyes, flew across to Miriam. "He doesn't mean it — about letting you go. He's only furious at being put into a position like this — at not being believed — but you *must* believe him, and believe me too. Oh, why did I ever try to stow away in Noel's car? And why did that key fit? If only it had refused to turn — "

50

But she might as well have saved her breath. She didn't think they had heard a word she said.

The two of them blazed away, Miriam's once cool, cutting voice pouring out hot words now. Julia found herself rocking on her feet with the intensity of it all. If only they would pause long enough to enable her to get control of the conversation again, she felt she might have convinced Miriam, but her instant suspicion of Adam on discovering Julia seemed to have ignited a conflagration threatened for weeks, and smouldering till now, and they had quite lost sight of the original cause of the quarrel.

Suddenly Miriam turned, walked out of the barn, head held high, and disappeared round the corner. For once in her life Julia couldn't think of a thing to say. Adam was standing staring after Miriam, his hands clenched at his sides, his face unreadable.

Then they heard it, the sound of a car roaring to life, being backed out. With one accord they made for the barn entrance. Miriam, in a Mini, came out on to the drive from another open shed. She leaned through the window, said derisively, "Bad habit leaving keys in a car, as you told me the other week. But I'm glad it's a vice with me. Because I'm not even staying to pack my things. I'll go straight to my aunt's, and when that Blenheim jeweller has finished cleaning your ring, I'll return it to you. I hope you find her a good cook, Adam," and she set the car at the uphill drive at a pace that would do it no good.

Adam Dare turned and looked at Julia, his hands on his hips, his whole attitude threatening. The vials of his wrath were about to fall upon her.

Julia had never been so appalled in her whole life. The enormity of the thing she had triggered off was absolutely crushing her.

When he spoke his mouth was a thin, hard line, his words issuing from between his teeth in a sort of iron control.

"Have you anything to say? Anything you *can* say? If so, please say it slowly and distinctly so I can take it in — though I can't imagine what it will be! Have you anything to say at all?"

All of a sudden all the humiliation and

embarrassment left Julia. And oddly, fury filled the vacuum.

"Right," she said. "I'll say it loud and clear! And even though you can't imagine what it will be, you'll realise there is only *one* thing a girl *could* say — *could* ask — after being cooped up since half-past nine last night on the floor of a car, and that is: *where is it?*"

When he looked at her completely uncomprehendingly, she heaved an exasperated sigh, said, "Well, here it comes, louder and clearer still . . . *where is the nearest toilet?* And I hope to heaven it's outside . . . I couldn't stand meeting any more of your charming kith and kin at this moment, believe me!" and she glared at him like a cross baby.

His face cracked and he burst into the most reluctant chuckle she had ever heard.

"Suffering catfish, what an anti-climax!" He pointed, shakingly, past the car-sheds. "There's one in that building over there . . . first door on the left. Then report back here and I'll take you to Picton."

She came back to him, reluctantly, for it was going to be the most embarrassing ride of her life, her leaden feet only just carrying her along. The sun was amazingly hot for this time of year, she thought, and bright, dazzling her eyes so she couldn't see properly. She felt weak. Horribly weak. She must pull herself together. She'd tidy herself up on the way and try to look as respectable as possible to get her ticket. So many people took day trips over to Wellington, her lack of luggage wouldn't be remarked upon.

Oh dear, her legs did feel funny . . . just as if they were stuffed with cotton-wool. Must have been the cramped position of the last nine hours or so. And he was still standing in that threatening pose, looking as if he'd like to take her apart. No wonder. But she wouldn't look too browbeaten. She lifted her chin defiantly and the next moment felt the blood leave her head.

She put out a hand gropingly, but couldn't find anything to hold on to. She said, her voice coming from a long distance, it seemed, "I've — I've never fainted in my life — but I think I — " and she keeled over at his feet.

When she came round she was lying on some straw in the barn, had a wet handkerchief pressed to her forehead and was conscious that someone was entreating her to come round.

As Adam's face swam hazily into her vision she said, "Oh, you poor man," and caught at the handkerchief, put it to her lips and sucked thirstily on it. He got to his feet, rushed away and came back with an old enamel cup full of the most delectable water, cold and clear, that Julia had ever supped.

He had his arm under her head, assisting her. She said weakly, "Oh, thank you. That was wonderful."

He had a puzzled, not angry, frown between his brows now.

"I'm starting to believe you. Would you begin all over again if you feel up to it? But explain one thing. I locked my doors, I always do. How did you get into my car?"

She said ruefully, "I tried to tell you when your fiancée was here, but you were both too busy yelling at each other to take notice. The key fitted — not perfectly, but a policeman came along and helped me and he pulled it back a little and it opened. Truly! I wish now he hadn't. Then I might have clicked that it wasn't Noel's

55

car. I've got the key in my pocket. You can try it. I do wish she — Miriam — was here still. I could probably convince her too now. I think that although we didn't really meet the night that ill-fated photograph was taken, you must have met my brother last night — Noel Merrill. You said good-night to him at your car. I thought it was Noel's. Was his parked in front of yours? I wish now I'd got out of the car on the boat and faced the music . . . risked being caught. At least then the trouble would have been only mine, it wouldn't have upset your life and Mir — "

He made an impatient gesture. "Forget that. Finish your yarn. What had you intended doing?"

"I hoped right to the last I'd get out unseen and start back to Picton — that was after you drove straight off the boat. I thought you might have gone back on board. But you drove and drove — and when you got out at the top of the hill I hoped to sneak out — but you didn't go far enough."

"You'd have dropped in your tracks the first mile, the state you're in. It sounds the most addle-pated adventure I've ever heard of. But it looks as if I'm stuck with you for the next few hours. You'll have to have something to eat or you'll pass out on me again." He groaned. "That means I've got to explain you to the family. To my grandfather and the kids."

Julia clutched his arm. "No, don't do that, I admit I'm feeling groggy. But just bring me a glass of milk and a piece of bread and butter out here and I'll be fit enough to be taken back to Picton."

His exasperation was natural. "I've got to go in and explain Miriam's sudden departure. Oh, it's going to be marvellous! And I'll have to see how Luke is and above everything else I'll have to report that slip. That sort of thing has high priority over any embarrassment *you* may feel, believe me."

"Yes," said Julia meekly. "I can see that. But before we go in to face the music, let me say one thing. I'm quite sure Miriam will realise when she cools off that I'm what I said I was, an unwilling stowaway."

"Leave that alone, will you! There's more to it than just discovering *you*. Miriam's been spoiling for this for a long time. If you hadn't triggered it off, something else would have, so keep out of it. You merely supplied her with a righteous excuse. I'll most like have you out of here in an hour, providing Luke's sickness *was* too much party and not a symptom of appendicitis. Oh, probably not, but the way things keep happening, I feel apprehensive. My single worker is in hospital with an abscessed ear, and Granny fell and broke her leg. You'll just have to face the family's reaction. Do you feel able to stand upright now? It's not far to the house — and all downhill."

Julia wished it had been a dozen times as far. What a fool she was going to look! She said, with an attempt at dignity, "I don't need your arm, thank you, now I've had the water. I'm not given to swooning."

He said grimly, "I'd rather help you than have to revive you again," so she suffered the arm. She didn't dare ask could she get her comb out of the bag in the car and she must look as if she'd been pulled through a gorsebush backwards. Her clothes were hideously creased and her face would be dirty and shiny. Oh, well. . . .

They came out into the sunlight and

Julia was surprised into immobility with the impact of the beauty spread before her, so that Adam Dare's stride carried him on a pace and his arm was jerked from under her elbow. He swung round impatiently to see what on earth ailed her now.

For a magic moment all the humiliation of the last twenty minutes sloughed off her. She brought her hands together in front of her, her lips parted in amazement as her eyes went slowly from side to side, drinking it in. The sun in the east shone goldenly on the most lovely contours she had ever seen . . . high, rounded hills across the still harbour, shutting it in from the storms of Cook Strait, and running out to far reefs that were crumbling into waters so blue they dazzled your eyes.

Away to the south she looked to other misty lavender headlands, with a coastline between them and this, where rivers like silver threads ran out to sea. Some peaks had a glint of snow on them and Cook Strait melted into the infinity of the Pacific. Northward to the head of the harbour were lush, bush-covered hills dropping down to innumerable bays. The scar of a new road, very steep, gashed one of them. She looked down at the utter peace of this bay with its symmetrical curve, with white and scarlet launches riding at anchor, then, closer at hand, to the left, was the brand-new house that Miriam had envied, a low-eaved building, delightful in itself, but below, set in a garden of great age, a wide, spreading farmhouse with no particular shape or design, built merely to fit the slope of the hillside and probably added to as the need arose, through generations of Dares.

The man watched her, his impatience seemingly gone for the moment. She came back to awareness of him, said, lifting her eyes to his, still enchanted beneath its spell, "I've never in my life seen anything more beautiful. Where is it? Where am I? Is it one of the Sounds?"

"No . . . don't you know? This is Port Underwood, one of the earliest whaling stations, inhabited before colonisation . . . one of the safest harbours in New Zealand and quite — to me — the most beautiful. Until 1957 it could be reached only by the sea, or by bridle-track over the hills."

Julia made a gesture that embraced the

bay beneath them, "And this bay . . . this gem of a bay . . . what is it called?"

"Tupuna Bay. More properly Whanga-tupuna. The Bay of the Ancestors, or the Bay of the Grandparents."

That jerked her back to reality. The Bay of the Grandparents. Yes, there below them, tacked on to the house, was a little old cottage where this man's grandparents lived . . . where the grandmother was due to return from hospital and who couldn't now, because she, Julia, thoughtless and irresponsible, had set herself against her brother's decree and had thereby broken an engagement and involved other people in endless complications.

The man came back to awareness too. He said roughly, as if impatient with himself for giving her time to stand and drool over the scenery, "Come on, let's get it over."

The track narrowed and a chastened Julia followed at his heels. If only the next hour were over and she was away. She found herself praying that Luke's miseries of the night were due only to over-eating. Imagine if this child too were rushed to hospital!

That was settled immediately. They stepped on to a low verandah running right round the corner of the house. Adam Dare pushed open a door into a huge kitchen. He halted so abruptly Julia cannoned into him. Here was a small boy of about nine, sitting at the table with an enormous bowl of cornflakes in front of him, piled high with tinned peaches and sugar and cream and he was wiring in.

Adam Dare said: "Luke! What the hell do you think you're doing?"

Luke looked up, blobs of cream all round his mouth, gazed at his uncle with an angelic expression and said simply, "Having something to eat."

Adam Dare's voice almost squeaked. "But you were sick all night!"

Luke's tongue darted out, removed most of the cream, and he said in the most matter-of-fact tone, "I'll say I was. That's why I'm having all this. Uncle Adam, you ought to have been here . . . I was sick three times. And how! I don't reckon anyone has ever been as sick as me! I was — "

"That will be quite enough," said his uncle hastily. "We're not interested in the sordid details. And you're not finishing that! I'll make you some bread-and-milk in a moment." He removed the dish.

Luke suddenly became aware of the odd figure hovering unhappily in the doorway. "Good gosh," he said, "who's that, and where's she come from ?"

His uncle turned and looked at the doorway too. He scratched the lobe of one ear. "Well . . . er . . . that's a very good question. She came from Wellington, on the *Aramoana* in my car. But what her name is I don't know — oh, perhaps I do. Her surname, anyway. If she's telling me the truth, her name could be Merrill."

Luke gazed at her, big brown eyes full of astonishment, as well they might be. Then he swallowed and looked at his uncle. "I don't know what you mean. If you don't know her name and you think she tells lies what did you bring her here for ?"

His uncle looked grim. "I didn't know she was there. She was a stowaway."

Luke's mouth fell open. Even to a nine-year-old it was a tall story. There was a stir in the far doorway and there stood a tall, erect figure, spare and very handsome,

63

with silver hair and eyes that were as dark as Adam Dare's. Humiliation and shame washed over Julia.

Adam saw her flinch, turned and grabbed her arm, forced her to a chair. "You'd better sit down. I don't think I can cope with any more faints this morning."

That flicked Julia on the raw. Her chin jerked up. "I told you I wasn't in the habit of swooning. That's the first time in twenty-four years! And so would *you* have fainted, I guarantee, if you'd been cooped up in that beastly car all night without food and drink and then got involved in an appalling row the minute you were discovered! And before you start on the horrible explanations, you'd better ring the AA about that slip in case of accidents. You said that was the first thing you'd do."

"Slip?" asked the old man.

"Yes . . . just below the saddle. I didn't dare drive over it in the middle of the night, so I slept on the top."

The old man's eyes widened, then travelled to Julia's face. Then he said, "Where in all this is your Miriam? Hasn't she heard your arrival?"

Adam's face went like flint. "She has. Long ago. Before the swoon, in fact. *She* was the one who discovered this — this — discovered *this* in my car, under the rug between the seats. She chose *not* to believe I didn't know she was there and she's gone, to her aunt's in Blenheim."

Grandpa Dare boggled, said, "For land's sakes!" and grabbed a chair himself.

Nothing more was said till Adam Dare got through to the AA man in Picton. It seemed the longest five minutes of Julia's life. Old Mr. Dare stared pointedly at his feet. Luke propped his chin on his hands and stared fixedly at Julia. She squirmed outwardly and inwardly. Then Luke thought of something. He took a surreptitious look at his uncle, quietly slid the bowl back towards him, and, working at great speed, demolished the rest of the cornflakes.

Adam turned from the phone, said to his grandfather, "That must have been a terrific rainfall last night. They've had word that the road the other way is blocked in two places — right down near Rarangi. They'll put up signs at the Picton end of this one, though with care anyone will get round. And certainly Miriam would in the Mini."

A heavy silence descended. They all looked at Julia, who felt like a prisoner at the bar and quite unnerved. Into the silence came the clatter of footsteps. Dumbly Julia watched as the two girls, older than Luke, erupted into the kitchen and stopped dead.

Adam said sarcastically, "Well, now the whole family is assembled I'll come out with the story. No interruptions and no subsequent comments. Especially about Miriam."

Julia said weakly. "Don't you think *I'd* better explain it?"

His jaw set. "No. They can have my version. I feel yours would be heavily embroidered."

Julia got to her feet. "You don't seem capable of believing the truth. I can assure you every word I told you was true and that I'm quite incapable at the moment of thinking up any story that wouldn't sound completely fantastic to account for my being in your car."

His eyes were dark slits, his brows twitched together. "What makes you think your original version isn't fantastic?"

Julia made a helpless gesture, then said, glaring, "Well, it's the only one I've got, so you can damned well do what you like with it!"

Luke burst into a guffaw. His uncle's resultant look made the boy clap his hands over his mouth.

Adam Dare made a gesture as helpless as Julia's. He ran his hand through his hair. "I'm only glad I'm not telling it to the police. When I think of what she *could* have involved me in! Now look, you kids have got to know, but if you let out as much as one whisper to anyone, I'll tan the hides off you! I want her out of here and forgotten as soon as that's physically possible."

Julia said, still glaring, "That goes for me too!"

At that moment a large black-and-white cat, with a lordly manner, strolled in, looked about him, and sprang into Julia's lap.

She pushed it down, said despairingly and ineffectively, "Get out, you!"

One of the girls said, "Where did *that* cat come from?"

Adam waved his hands in exasperation.

"Look, I'm trying to tell you what happened. That cat's another complication. It was a stowaway too."

"*Too?*" Four voices said in unison.

Adam made a sound between a groan and a roar. "I'm trying to tell you. Will you all shut up!"

Silence descended.

He said, "The start of it was routine. I had my car . . . my *locked* car . . . parked outside the halt, came out, got into it, drove off. I had to go on the railway deck. I was last on, so we sailed immediately. Although I'd told you all I'd sleep on board, so not to disturb Miriam, I decided, in view of the fact that we're short-handed, to come home. Meant to take a nap in the bunk-house.

"At the saddle, I came upon the slip. Not right across, but as I didn't know how far it extended round the corner, I thought I'd doss down in the front seat and nego-tiate the rest of the road in daylight. I'd left the car door open while I examined the slip, and a wretched cat must have got in. I didn't know. It nearly scared seven bells out of me when at daybreak it sprang from the back on to me."

Julia saw out of the tail of her eye, Luke's hand come to cover his mouth again.

"I brought it with me. We can always do with an extra mouser, and I hate them going wild. When I got here I slid out of the car very carefully, and Miriam arrived. She'd not gone back to sleep after Luke was sick for the last time." He darted a look at Luke, saw the empty bowl, but only tightened his lips. "Before I could stop her, Miriam wrenched open the back door — she was looking for the grapefruit — the cat flew out, then she twitched off the rug and found *her*!"

His family weren't as sympathetic as they should have been — with one accord the two girls in the doorway and Luke at the table collapsed into shrieks of mirth!

Then, their first burst over, they became aware that their uncle was furious and that he was looking at them with the most threatening look they had probably ever had from him. One of the girls, with smooth brown plaits, gulped, said, "Sorry, Uncle Adam, but it — it sounded so funny. I mean . . . like something in a television comedy."

He said, still glaring, "It wasn't comedy, believe me. Miriam has gone. In her car. She's broken our engagement."

There was utter silence. Julia couldn't fathom the looks on the girls' faces. They didn't look stunned. They looked . . . well, unnaturally controlled. Unchildlike. Then she made up her mind it would be because they were realising the enormity of what this unwelcome stranger in their midst had done.

Grandpa Dare gave a hurrumping sound and said: "She'll be back. Common sense will take over. It's an odd happening, but there must be an explanation, only she'd be too mad to take it in. Too bad you let her get away without getting your stowaway to explain why she was there. Why were you, anyway?" He turned to Julia.

But Adam Dare wouldn't let her answer. He said, the derision in his tone acting like a whiplash on Julia's already taut nerves, "She says her brother needed her as a housekeeper on his farm at Castlepoint, that he wouldn't allow her to give up her job and go to him. So she decided to stow away. She also says that the spare key she had to his car, fitted mine."

"It did," choked Julia. "How else could I have got in?"

His eyes glinted. "I'm inclined to think I must have only thought I locked it. It can happen. But there's something damned odd about it. Sure, the chap she says is her brother *was* parked directly in front of me, and it was an identical Holden, but she *must* have heard us talking . . . she must have known it wasn't her brother who got into the car, who drove off. And then I stopped so soon."

Julia choked again. "I thought it was an obstruction on the road. You can't see a thing except occasionally electric lights when you're crouching on the floor of a car, peering out through the fringes of a rug — " the girls were threatened with the giggles again but managed to subdue them — "and you got on that boat so quickly and it moved out . . . I was just terrified. I thought I'd be taken for one of those girls who hang around the wharves if I got out and was spotted. The crew seemed to be coming and going all night . . . then I hoped against hope you'd go back on board and I could have got out and you'd have been none the wiser. I tell you my one thought was to get out of my predicament myself without involving the driver of the car. But you just drove and drove and drove and I didn't know where I was, and I was flummoxed when you stopped on the saddle. *You* knew what was happening, *I* didn't. And you were an unknown quantity. I thought you might have heard me breathing and were going to investigate . . . and I was alone among hills and sounds with a completely strange man. You could have been anybody."

"Like a sex maniac," nodded the plaited girl, her voice full of sympathy.

Her uncle said: "Susanna!" and she subsided like a pricked balloon.

"Exactly," said Julia, eyes flashing now. "After all, *you* don't know what it's like to be a girl! It's the sort of thing your mother warns you about from kindergarten days on. It *was* a silly, irresponsible sort of thing to do, I admit that now, but how could I ever have dreamed it would turn out like this? With the best intentions in the world, I was, after all, only stowing away in my brother's car!"

Adam Dare said surlily, "Well, I don't hold with stowaways, anyway!"

His grandfather said softly, "Oho, don't you now? What an amazing thing for a Dare to say! If it hadn't been for our own famous stowaway, none of us would ever have seen Tupuna Bay. *And* it was practically the same circumstances. Except that at least *our* stowaway got on the right ship! So what's so hard to believe? If a Georgian lass could do it, why not a twentieth-century Elizabethan? If my grandmother Camilla hadn't stowed away in the 1820s, the Dares, presumably, would still be fishing round Cape Cod."

This time it was Adam Dare who had nothing to say. Julia couldn't fathom it and now wasn't the time to ask, but at least a vestige of belief was beginning to dawn upon that angry face.

Luke said, "When are we going to have breakfast?"

"Oh, lord!" said his uncle savagely, "as if *you* needed any! Well, we'll save the rest of the inquiry till we've eaten. Whatever she's done and however much she's to blame, Miss Merrill is probably famished. Esther and Susanna can cook the breakfast." He thought of something, pointed a finger at Susanna. "Have you got measles, or haven't you? Because if you have, you'd better scuttle back to bed right now. After all, it would be the last straw if our — er — visitor caught them and couldn't leave!"

Grandpa Dare rose. "That's the most inhospitable thing that's been said at Tupuna in five generations. Susanna, take Miss Merrill to the bathroom so she can wash and brush up. And what's this about measles?"

Susanna said hastily, "Oh, we thought late last night I was getting measles. There was some at end of term at school, you know. Only it turned out I'd — er — sort of come into contact with my hairbrush."

Adam stared. "Come into contact? You twins carry loyalty too far. Esther, the truth now . . . did you hit your sister with the hairbrush?"

Esther was indignant and turned her pert, freckled nose upwards. "I did not! She — she accidently lay on it. And all the little red prickles looked like a rash."

Adam looked disbelieving, something he appeared to be good at. "I can't think of one reason why you should take a hair-brush to bed. It's not exactly a Teddy-bear, you know."

74

Grandpa Dare suddenly assumed authority. "Now, Adam, you've had enough of trying to solve mysteries . . . no need to go into the whys and wherefores of that. And you're not in a believing sort of mood. Let's eat . . . I'm fair clemmed. Esther, make the porridge — the quick sort. And when Susanna's shown Miss Merrill the bathroom, she can start cooking the bacon."

In a daze Julia followed Susanna into a large bathroom. Susanna preserved an unnaturally solemn face, trying to behave, Julia guessed, as if she were an ordinary guest.

She ran hot water into a basin, opened a cupboard and drew out faintly warm towels and a clean face-cloth and said, "Look, this is a spare comb and in that cabinet there's some nice talcum powder. I guess you feel pretty sticky and scruffy."

"I certainly do," said Julia with feeling, realising something . . . that kids enjoyed this sort of thing. They were always in scrapes themselves, so loved seeing grown-ups in hot water. "I'm terribly sorry I've caused all this rumpus. I can't believe it, yet it's happened. If there's anything I can do to set matters right between your uncle's fiancée and himself, believe me, I will."

A peculiar look crossed Susanna's face, instantly repressed. In fact Julia thought she must have imagined it. Susanna said smoothly, "Oh, not to worry. It's not as if they're exactly twin souls. Uncle Adam will take you down to Picton and you can get back home and forget about this, and Miriam will have to come back for her clothes and by that time she'll be sorry."

"Oh, thank you," said poor Julia. "Don't let me hold you up. I mean, you wouldn't wonder if your poor uncle is a bit testy. I'll come out too and help, soon as I'm respectable enough."

She picked all the fluff off her Black Watch tartan trews and combed and tugged at her tousled hair, washed thoroughly, then applied the powder and lipstick, probably Miriam's, that Susanna had thoughtfully provided, not spurning the latter on the grounds of hygiene. Anybody could browbeat you when your face was innocent of make-up. You felt naked, exposed.

Then, bracing herself, she went back to the kitchen. Adam turned down her offer to help. The porridge was made and so, to Luke's disgust, was his bread-and-milk. And a pan of bacon-and-eggs wafted delectable savours. Best of all, Grandpa Dare was filling a huge teapot.

Luke said, looking up with loathing from his bowl, "Which grace are we having this morning, Grandpa? I don't feel like saying any for this."

His uncle grunted. "I feel much the same. I'm not in a 'Thank you for the world so sweet' mood this morning, believe me, *nor* for offering up thanks for the blessings of the night!"

It was dreadful, because he said it entirely without humour, and Julia realised with horror that she wasn't going to be able to subdue a giggle. She made a manful effort, but it was no use, it spilled over. The three children promptly joined in, and were followed a second later by Grandpa Dare's mellow chuckle. Adam glared at them madly, then he too succumbed. How thankful Julia was. Some of the tension went out of her.

Adam Dare said in a much more approachable tone, "It shows what a lovely nature I've got, that I *can* laugh at a time like this! But I'm afraid, Miss Merrill,

77

that I just can't look upon you as a blessing."

Julia said firmly. "I can hardly expect you to. But at least laughing makes me feel hungry. I didn't know how I was going to choke food down in an atmosphere like this. But would anyone mind if I began to pour that tea? The very thought is like nectar."

She poured one cup, then Esther took over. "I'll pour the rest, you start drinking. Gosh, what an awful night you must have spent."

She drank thirstily, then Grandpa Dare said firmly, "It seems heathenish to start without offering thanks for food . . . I'll just say Robbie Burns' grace. It's short and to the point and not flowery."

They all bowed their heads while he said: " 'Some hae meat, and canna eat, and some wad eat that want it; but we hae meat, and we can eat, and sae the Lord be thankit.' "

The porridge was filling, the bacon-and-eggs delicious, the toast crisp and buttery, the marmalade the sort she liked best, pale golden jelly with wafer-like shreds of grapefruit in it. At last she was satisfied.

How humiliating to think that the consumption of food could so raise one's spirits.

She said, "Thank you. Now, may I be allowed to wash up before you take me back, though I realise you'll want me out of here before your fiancée comes back."

"My ex-fiancée, you mean," said Adam Dare, his lips a thin line.

Julia waved a hand, "Oh, by now she'll realise it couldn't have been anything but a ghastly mistake. It just got her off-balance, that's all. The moment she's cooled down she'll be back. I don't think she'd get any further than Picton before common sense set in."

He grinned mirthlessly. "In circumstances like these, it will take Miriam at least three days to get over it."

Julia gazed at him incredulously.

At that moment Susanna said triumphantly: "Got it! I knew I'd seen you somewhere before . . . you were in that photo with Uncle Adam . . . but then why did he say he didn't know you?"

Julia felt hot, betraying blood suffused her face.

Even Grandpa Dare looked startled.

Adam said savagely, "It's the foulest luck. There was one of those roving camera blokes there — snapping groups and giving out tickets. Miss Merrill and I hadn't even met, but I'd just turned away from my group. She went to put her glass on a table, and the photographer thought we were together and snapped us. We both laughed. I said, 'We don't want a ticket for that — we aren't together — ' and thought no more about it. He must have been a free-lancer for the papers too. I didn't even recognise her again. That girl had long hair, all piled up. I thought Miriam had gone mad when she flung that accusation at me. It's one of those ridiculously simple mistakes, yet frightfully suspicious."

"In fact," said Grandpa Dare, "as simple, yet as incredible as Miss Merrill's car-key fitting your lock! Bring a bit of logic to bear upon it, Adam. Miss Merrill won't feel half so bad then. You've done some daft things yourself in your time . . . like running away from boarding-school when you were so homesick and putting the lot of us into a frenzy by getting lost on the bridle-path."

Adam flung out a protesting hand. "I did *not* get lost. I was only held up because I sprained my ankle. Miss Merrill, I'll take that offer about the dishes. I'm a man short, so I'd like to go round the sheep before I take you to Picton. If you would wash, Luke could dry. Yes, Luke, if you're well enough to mop up all that fruit and cornflakes, you're well enough to dry dishes. The girls could make the beds. Grandpa, would you see to the fowls and the turkeys?"

Out he went and the girls said, "We'll help with the dishes. We'd like to talk to you."

Julia said firmly, "I'm in enough trouble now — off you go and make those beds. I might get into more hot water for encouraging you to flout authority." They recognised her tone as final and departed.

"Suffering catfish," said Luke, "we aren't half having fun this morning. Funny, you know, I thought these holidays would be dull till lambing started, but you'd never believe the things that have happened. Susanna fell off Ruddy Jack's Point because she was sure she'd found Captain Ephraim's cutlass down in the kelp . . .

but it was only a treacle-tin top . . . but it wasn't really deep — " Luke's tone was regretful — "but Uncle Adam walloped her good and proper after he fished her out. Then Ben was carted off to hospital with an abscess in his ear — do you know he was delirious and kept calling out for some girl we'd never even heard of! Gee, I'm looking forward to him getting home, I'll tease him like mad about his Sally. Then Gran fell and broke her leg and now that Miriam's gone off in a huff. I'd sure have liked to have seen her face when she discovered you."

"It wasn't a bit amusing," said Julia, whisking plates out of the soapy water on to the draining rack.

"Well, I dunno, not to you, I expect, but I'd have loved to have seen her lose her temper and — well, I dunno, what I mean really, but you see she never does. I don't like people who don't lose their tempers, they seem sort of queer."

"I think what you mean, Luke," said a voice behind them — Esther's, "that they don't seem human."

Julia swung round to see both girls. "Perhaps you'd each get a tea-towel. Luke is talking faster than he's drying." That might get them off the subject of Miriam. The Dare children had clear voices with a real carrying quality. What if Adam came in to find them discussing his beloved? She was in enough trouble now.

Susanna opened a cupboard, took out two more tea-towels. "You're not the only one to wish you'd seen it, Luke. Miss Merrill, did she really fly off the handle?"

Julia said, "I think you know, all of you, that I can't discuss it. I'm sympathetic about you wanting to know. I would if I were you, but honestly, it's just not done. I've caused enough bother without adding to it, and in any case, imagine if your uncle caught us at it. Men hate stramashings like this. Women can take them in their stride."

"What's stramashing?" asked Luke.

"I think you could tell from the way I used it."

"Yes, but I've never heard it before. It's a good one."

"Well, it's a Scots word. My grandmother was Scots. She used lovely words nobody else did."

"Like what?" asked Susanna.

Julia was grateful for the diversion. It might keep them off Miriam.

She searched her brain. "Well, when she was mad with us she used to threaten to skelp us. When she loved us dearly, say at bedtime story-time, she'd call us her cushie-doos, meaning turtle-doves, or sometimes her lambies. When she couldn't understand a thing, she'd say she couldn't thole it. She used canna instead of can't, and when I get excited myself — or upset — I sometimes use that word. With Gran it was always tapsalteerie instead of topsy-turvy, and I used to think the loveliest one of all was if we came to some eerie place, she would shiver and say it was a wanchancy spot. Oh, I do miss Gran."

The eyes of the children grew serious, instantly. The two girls said as one, "Like us." Esther added, "It would be just terrible if anything happened to Granny. She's always been here. And she knows every inch of Port Underwood. We can't remember ever being without her."

"Was she born here?"

"Oh, no, I didn't mean that. I mean that as far as our lives are concerned she's always been here. Granny is an American.

Grandpa went there to look up the Dares and fell in love."

Julia felt a touch of magic feather her pulses. How odd. She hadn't expected to know anything save humiliation this day, but here it was . . . the bare bones of true romance. The girls saw the light that sprang into the hazel eyes and continued.

"Grandpa said when he heard her name was Lydia that it was foreordained . . . you know, it tied in with the family tradition of Biblical names."

Julia said, "Oh, yes, Lydia of Thyatira, the seller of purple." She was completely fascinated. "Look, tell me more. I'll be here such a short time and — " she grinned — "I have a feeling your uncle will certainly not ask me to call again — why is there this tradition? It sounds like one of Joseph Lincoln's books to me."

A voice joined in, Grandpa Dare's. "Now, here's a remarkable thing. How many girls of your age have read Joseph Lincoln? He belongs to another era."

Julia gave a last wipe at the bench, shook out the dish-cloth, hung it over the taps to air, turned round and sat on the corner of the table. "Mr. Dare, I was brought up a good deal with my grandmother. She had all Joseph Lincoln's books. They absolutely fascinated me. Even in the midst of all the hoo-ha this morning, I recognised some of your expressions . . . when you said you were fair clemmed, for instance. And you said something about if your grandmother Camilla hadn't stowed away the Dares would still be fishing off Cape Cod. Where does Cape Cod come into it? I hadn't expected American-descended pioneers here, only English ones."

"They were American and Australian," said Grandpa Dare, "though since then there've been Scots, English and New Zealand brides here. Would you like to hear tell of how Camilla Dare came here?"

"Would I not? But there's so little time. Mr. Dare will be taking me to Picton as soon as he's gone round the sheep."

"Well, we'll just hope there's plenty to delay him. We like a new audience. But the kitchen's not the place to tell it . . . come. We'll go into the First Parlour."

Parlour! Not lounge, or sitting-room, but the parlour. More Cape Cod?

Yes, this was the right place for storytelling. She looked round her, the others

86

watching her. Here were the portraits Miriam had been scathing about. But she had been wrong. They were far from hideous. The faces that looked out of them were strong faces and had a serenity that matched the beautiful bay outside. Yes, it was cluttered with Victoriana, but what a feeling of belonging, a room like this could give you . . . a sense of roots put down, of lastingness . . .

Grandpa Dare waved her to an American rocker. They all sat down except Luke, who stood by his great-grandfather's chair and leaned on the arm.

Susanna said wistfully, "I expect you'd better tell it, Grandpa."

The network of laughter-lines at the corners of the old man's eyes creased more deeply. "No, I'd like you two girls to tell it. It's good for you, fixes it in your memory. I've always thought we should be able, just as your Maori playmates can, to recite our genealogy. Not that we could go back as far as the first canoes — we only know about five generations — but you can start with Camilla. Take it in turns."

Esther's dark eyes were starry. "It's a real-life love-story. It began with Camilla

Mannering, who lived in Sydney, and was the toast of the town. For her beauty, and her voice. She was born in Regency days. Just imagine! That's her picture over there. When Susanna has her hair done that way, with curls over her shoulders, she's very like her.

"She was brought up, and her brother too, by an aunt and uncle after their parents were killed when their carriage horses bolted. Her brother was mad keen on the sea and was gone for months at a time and she missed him horribly." She nodded at Susanna, who took it up.

"From one voyage he came back very excited. He'd been to New Zealand and had great tales of off-shore whaling to be told. They were thick around the coasts there. He'd visited the whaling station at Kakapo Bay here where the Guards were — where families of Guards still live — and decided to take up land there, in another bay, called Whangatupuna.

"Camilla wanted to go with him, but he wouldn't hear of it. She wanted to keep house for him. He said he'd not take a young girl into that sort of atmosphere. You'd never believe it now, but Port

Underwood then was thick with whaling vessels, and it was called 'the sink of the Pacific' — had a reputation similar to Russell in the Bay of Islands. Not that all the whalers were like that, oh no. They were from all over the world, some from America, from Nantucket and Martha's Vineyard and other places. Cape Cod men, descended from the Pilgrim Fathers, still Puritan in their outlook. Some of them anchored on the east side of the harbour in Cutter's Bay to avoid the chances of their crews mixing with the more rumbustious types. Rumbustious was right . . . there were women there and too much rum . . .

"Camilla hated the thought of her brother there, alone, with no home comforts, so when the ship that was to take him to Port Underwood called in at Sydney, she left a note for her uncle and aunt and stowed away. She was only sixteen. When she was discovered her brother was furious. So was the captain of the ship, one Ephraim Dare, from Cape Cod. They encountered terrible weather, were nearly wrecked in Cook Strait, and young Camilla proved herself an excellent adventurer, helping with cooking and nursing.

"Ephraim Dare was a stern man, tough as captains of such vessels had to be, but by the time they reached the haven of Port Underwood. Camilla had completely disarmed him." Susanna nodded to the portrait that flanked Camilla's. "That's Ephraim, Esther is very like him."

It was startlingly true. Without the beard, and with a turned-up nose instead of an aquiline one, Esther was Captain Ephraim in feminine form.

Esther said, "But the captain had to take his ship home, even though now he wanted nothing more than to set up a shore whaling-station of his own. It was nearly two years before he came back to Whangatupuna, on someone else's ship, and married Camilla."

"They were tough days, Camilla and Ephraim had a large family, but they didn't rear them all, but they themselves lived to a great age and Grandpa here, their grandson, can remember them. Camilla never lost beauty, even in age, and was still able to wear her wedding-gown at her golden wedding. And Ephraim remained a giant of a man, not stooped at all.

"The off-shore whales were killed out —

whalers go further out these days — and gradually the Bay came back to its old tranquillity. Until just over a decade ago, its only access was by sea or bridle-track, so life here has never been very easy till now. Even when Uncle Adam and Dad and Aunt Rebecca were born, our own grandma — their mother — had to go in to Blenheim weeks before, by launch, over the Wairau bar, to have her babies. Life is easy now. We have a road." That last sentence was like a song of praise.

Susanna came in again. "So it's from the Cape Cod ancestors that the Biblical names come — oh, and from some other places, because it was after the owner of one of the sailing ships, a Sydney merchant, that Port Underwood itself was named in 1826. He was a Josiah Underwood." She paused and looking across at her great-grandfather, said, "Have we done it okay, Grandpa, as you've taught us?"

He smiled . . . oh, what a handsome man he was, and very like his famous ancestor, "You've done very well. I've never heard it told better." He said to Julia, "It's important for children not only to be able to tell the story of their ancestors, but also to be able to tell it in language that suits the day and the age."

Esther said, "There are many other stories . . . it's a great place for adventures. What a pity you won't be here long enough to hear them all."

The strangest feeling swept over Julia. She felt almost desolated. How perfectly ridiculous to feel as if her whole life would be impoverished because she couldn't stay to hear those stories. She was an embarrassment to the heir to Whangatupuna, and the sooner he was rid of her the better.

Susanna said, "The one I love the best is of Grandpa. He went to America to look up his relations and find out about his forebears and found a girl who lived next door to his cousin . . . Lydia, the seller of purple, and married her."

"Aye," said Nathaniel Dare, smiling reminiscently, "I knew it was meant to be, the moment I heard her name and saw her. She was wearing a white dress with a golden sash, and frills. And she carried a parasol."

Esther said reflectively, "That was probably what sort of hypnotised Uncle Adam into falling for Miriam — the name. What a washout! *She's* no ancestor-worshipper."

Nathaniel said very quickly, "Esther, that'll be enough of that. People are always wondering what other people see in the ones they fall in love with. Adam didn't choose his wife-to-be with a view to pleasing his twin nieces. And it'd be the divil's own job to try, at that. You'd never think anyone good enough for Adam. And another thing . . . you two didn't give her much of a chance. It's not the easiest house to manage and she's a perfectionist. She's used to the most modern of households. And that business about the hair-brush . . . ye young varmints!"

Julia looked startled. Nathaniel continued: "They knew fine well she was nervous of infectious diseases. I heard them earlier saying they wished she'd go before my wife came home because she and Lydia are — are not exactly kindred spirits. They made up their minds to get rid of her and look after her themselves, which is less than intelligent because in no time they'll be back at school in Picton, and the lambing will be in full swing and their great-grandmother will need a lot of attention for a very long time. It's not like young bones mending."

Susanna and Esther looked most abashed. "Gosh, Grandpa, you won't tell Uncle Adam, will you? I mean, if he thought I got Esther to whack me on the chest with that brush to raise the rash, he'd wallop me for sure."

Her great-grandfather had a twinkle in his eye. "I'm pretty sure Adam suspects. He's no simpleton. I remember him, the same one, painting spots on at the end of one holiday. Your idea was a long way better'n his, but you ought not to have done it."

Esther jerked her pert nose up. "You're no better yourself, Grandpa," she said scathingly. "We noticed your capers. . . ." She fixed Grandpa Dare with a shrewd look.

To Julia's surprise he looked hastily away, said, "I can't think what you're talking about — and anyway, we've spent long enough in here. You'd better get some dusting done."

"Oh, no, you don't, Grandpa darling," said Susanna, "you were just priceless. Cunning too, not doing it in front of Adam.

94

Miriam didn't twig that. Really, those Cape Cod sayings! You've kept some, I know, but you just peppered your conversation with them. She winced every time you said: "Wal, I swan!" That was when she started talking about our lack of culture."

Grandpa Dare had the grace to look ashamed. "Well, I'll make a bargain with you," he said. "If you keep quiet about me, I'll keep quiet about the measles."

They all jumped when Adam's voice sounded from the doorway.

"Wal, I swan!" it said. "I just hope you're satisfied with what you accomplished. Evidently Miss Merrill's appearance was only the last straw. I'd no idea Miriam had been having such a time with you all."

Luke was the only one who managed speech. He said, with great relish, and a callous disregard of his uncle's lacerated feelings, "How long've you been there, Uncle Adam?"

"From about paragraph one," he was told sarcastically. "From how like Camilla Susanna is. I didn't interrupt because I thought you kids were telling it rather well. I didn't expect you to analyse my own love life, though, or to spill it out to the cuckoo-in-the-nest."

Grandpa Dare recovered himself. "That's not Miss Merrill's fault. You ought to know that once the Dare family gets into full spate there's no stopping them."

Adam said, "I've not finished. But what I want is some coffee — then in about an hour I'll get Miss Merrill back over the saddle."

No one enjoyed their coffee. The atmosphere was hardly relaxing.

3

WHEN he had gone out again Julia said to Esther, "Look, I'm feeling so responsible. I must try to set things right. What's the name of Miriam's aunt in Blenheim? And what's Miriam's surname?"

"Chillingham for both. But it's no go, Miss Merrill. She'll still be sulking."

Julia said gently, "She just may not be. You see you — or Luke was it? — said she never lost her temper, just sulked if things went wrong. Well, who knows, now she's lost it, she may have got it out of her system, so there's no need for sulks. Her aunt, too, may have told her she was foolish to fly off like that. Miriam may now be ready to listen to reason."

Esther's chin set itself in stubborn lines. Very, very like Captain Ephraim! "Her aunt thinks she's throwing herself away on Uncle Adam. Thinks she could do far better for herself!"

"Well, evidently Miriam didn't think

that way, so she must genuinely care for Adam."

She didn't convince Esther. "I think she was using Adam. She was impatient with him . . . and you just can't push him round. We know."

Julia said crisply, "Where's the telephone book? This is something I must try." Conscious that Susanna and Esther were practically breathing down her neck, she got the number. The aunt answered the phone and went away to get her in response to Julia's non-committal: "May I speak to Miriam, please?" She hoped it sounded like a friend.

She found her heart thudding at her side when Miriam's voice said,

"Yes?"

"Miss Chillingham, my name is Julia Merrill. I've rung up to apologise for the shocking upset I caused you this morning. I'm afraid I acted very carelessly, but quite unknowingly, when I got into the wrong car. But I'd like to ask you to — " got no further. The receiver was clashed down at the other end. Julia was left with the handpiece in her hand, staring at it in great dismay.

The twins started to say they'd told her so, but changed their minds when they saw she was really distressed, that there were tears in her eyes. They moved to her, as one, gently removed the phone from her fingers, replaced it, rang off, and, taking an arm each, guided her away.

Susanna said, "Please don't be upset. That's just Miriam. I think it was an act of Providence, your getting in the wrong car."

Julia's eyes widened. "Providence? What — "

Esther giggled, "She means you've saved Uncle Adam from a fate worse than death!"

The tears were checked, Julia broke down into giggles. Then she pulled herself together and said, "Girls, it just isn't funny!"

"Neither would it be funny," said Esther stubbornly, "to be married to someone like Miriam. She'd somehow winkle Uncle Adam out of here . . . he'd be out on the Wairau, breaking his heart for the Bay of the Ancestors. Oh, we know he would. And what's more, we think Granny knew what she was doing when she was taken to hospital and advised Adam to get Miriam to housekeep."

"What do you mean? That she'd show up as a bad housekeeper? But that doesn't mean a thing. Lots of girls don't know much till they get married, and they just love keeping house."

The girls doubled up. "Just the opposite. She was a demon housekeeper. She was a domestic science teacher and works to precision. At least she would if she could, but Tupuna just can't be run that way. It's too full of old things. She'd like to make a clean sweep, have a kitchen like a diet clinic. Just as well we're rid of her before the lambing starts, this place is going to be full of motherless lambs any moment."

Julia said very seriously, putting an arm round each of them, "Girls, you've had your bit of fun out of this — and I expect you're missing your parents horribly — but you'll have to drop your hostility. It's entirely between Adam and Miriam. She may be a completely different person when she has him to herself. They'll both have to make concessions. Let time take care of this. If Miriam comes back, don't twit her with the fact that she rushed away. I don't think that engagement is broken. And thanks for telling me Camilla's story. I don't feel quite so bad now. I'll never know the end of Adam and Miriam's story, but I hope it will be happy. He'll take me to Picton and I daresay he'll continue on to Blenheim. Once she knows I'm crossing Cook Strait, she'll come back to look after your Granny.

"Now look, a hungry man is easily upset. Can I help you prepare lunch before he comes back — then, if he should come back straightaway from Picton, at least there'll be a meal ready. What's in the fridge?"

There was a leg of hogget, plenty of pumpkin and parsnips. The girls switched on the stove and began peeling potatoes while Julia knifed dripping over the leg. Once it was in the stove and sizzling, she began peeling apples and stewing them. "Perhaps you could make a custard with them — I suppose you know how? Good."

At that moment two things happened. Adam came in. The phone rang. He answered it.

They heard him say, "Good lord . . . how long before they get it open? M'm. Yes, I suppose it will take that long. What about the other road? Longer? Why? Oh, the Port-Picton takes preference. Well, once we didn't have a road at all, I daresay we can get through three or four days. Thanks for letting us know. We'll contact the other families. You'll be busy enough."

He turned round and surveyed them grimly. "We're stuck with you, Miss Merrili. The slip has now completely blocked the road. It's even fallen away below it. That freak storm last night has caused slips all over the province and they can't get on to the lesser ones on the White's Bay road till later. Looks as if we were lucky we got round this morning." All of a sudden he looked horrified. "My God! Miriam! She was on it after us." He made a dive for the phone. "I'll ring — "

Julia said quickly, "No . . . she's all right. She got to her aunt's safe and sound."

He swung round. "How do you know?"

Julia said in a small voice, "I asked the girls where she was and I — I rang to apologise. She was there all right."

She didn't like the look on his face. He said, "And what sort of a reception did you get, may I ask?"

The blood rushed to Julia's cheeks. "She — she — I didn't get very far. She hung up."

He drew in a deep breath for control. "She'll be madder than mad now all right. She'll wonder why I didn't rush you back to Picton the moment she left. Now she *will* think there's something fishy about it. And I've realised while going round the sheep, time isn't going to make her cool off. She's going to think it extremely suspicious that your story coincides so much with Camilla's story. Stowing away to assist a brother! You and I know there was nothing in it, that I had no idea you were there, but I feel in my bones she's going to think you knew about Camilla and invented your story on the spur of the moment."

There was a stunned silence. Even the girls couldn't think of anything to say. Then Adam did. "You'd better ring your brother. There doesn't seem to be any damage to telephones, but you never know. Poles could still be undermined with seepage. He ought to know where you are."

Julia started to the phone, then stopped. "What now?" he asked irritably.

She swallowed. "He — I — I'd rather not. He doesn't know anything about this. I'd — I'd sooner he didn't know. I mean if it had been only a prank — with myself the only sufferer — it wouldn't matter. But — well, you and he met and he'd be furious and embarrassed to think his sister had caused a broken engagement. Not that I think it's that really . . . it's only a rift."

His lips tightened. "I've told you to leave that alone. That's up to me. Is your reason for not ringing your brother a true one, or don't you want to explain in front of me? How do I know otherwise that you'll give him a true version?"

Julia's hazel eyes flashed green. "You're the most doubting person I've ever met! And I won't ring my brother. I'll have to ring Faith, though, my flat-mate. I left her a note. She'll be at business now, but I can well imagine that she'll be ringing the farm tonight to find out how I fared in the back of Noel's car. I can ring her at work, and I want you to stand right there listening in, so you don't think I'm trying to get her to back up a phoney story, do you hear?"

"Suits me fine," he said, "go ahead."

"And," she added, eyes still shooting sparks. "I'll find out how much the call is and pay you. Perhaps when you see the dollars in my purse in the car, you'll at least stop thinking I didn't have the money for my fare across. That's what most stowaways do it for, isn't it? — because they're on their beam ends!"

She got through speedily. Faith said, "Oh, hullo . . . I was going to ring you tonight. How was the trip to Omairangi?"

Julia was holding the receiver a little distance from her ear so, as she had motioned Adam to stand close, he could hear every word.

Before Julia could start in on her explanations Faith added, laughing, "Tell me, whatever did Noel say? Were you discovered or did you lie doggo all the way? I'd love to have seen his face when you revealed yourself?"

Julia's eyes, triumphant in expression, swivelled round to meet Adam's.

She said "Faith, it's a long story — I can't very well tell you the lot in working hours, but I made the most ghastly mistake. Got in the wrong car." Faith's squeal could be heard right across the kitchen.

She said, alarm in her tones, "Julia, where are you? Tell me immediately? Are you all right? Oh, goodness, anything could have happened. When did you — I mean you must have got out — but where — and — ?"

"This is going to give you a shock. I'm actually in the South Island. This chap — he knows Noel, by the way, so you're not to worry — his car was parked behind Noel's. The key fitted and I got in unsuspectingly. But he drove straight on to the ferry. First I thought it was a roadblock, but we were on and the ship sailed before I realised where I was and what had happened." More squeals.

"It was all in the dark and I was terrified I'd be taken for a real stowaway, so I lay doggo and hoped at journey's end I'd be able to get away unnoticed. But I didn't manage it. Only I can't get back. This chap was going to run me back to Picton, only he had to go round his sheep first, and now there's been a landslip and we can't get out."

"Can't get out . . . are you in a valley? Only one way out?"

"Well, practically. I'm — hold your breath — at Tupuna Bay, Port Underwood. The road to Picton is completely blocked and there are two slips on that access road through Rarangi that they made for the power to go to the North Island from the South, across Cook Strait. You'd know about it at the time, I think. It's very steep and prone to slips, and a freak local storm early last night caused so much damage in Marlborough that this road — with only a few families affected — isn't top priority. But I'm all right. They're very nice people — " she hastily looked away from Adam, who was practically facing her now, leaning with an elbow on the wall — "and I can help with the children and the housework. I'll give you the name and the telephone number, but listen, Faith, you're to tell nobody. I want no publicity. The gossip papers would love an item like this. *Don't* laugh . . . some bits of it weren't funny at all!

"Keep my mail for me. I'll get back in a few days. If Noel rings don't tell him. I'd rather tell him myself. Just say I was so peeved with him that I wouldn't ask for my job back and decided to take a holiday in the Queen Charlotte Sounds. He knows I was planning to take one some time. And I must let you go. Yes, I've plenty of money. Here's the number, in case you want it . . . and mum's the word. Bye-bye, Faith."

She hung up and she and Adam looked at each other.

He didn't say anything. Probably he couldn't. The fact that this conversation had proved she'd been speaking the truth, plus the unpalatable knowledge earlier that due to the road damage he could not push this cuckoo out of the nest, was too much for him. He turned on his heel and went to march out.

Julia's voice halted him. "Mr. Dare, the least you can do is to apologise for having doubted my word."

He swung round. "Yes. Therefore I apologise. But I still think you must be the scattiest female it's ever been my misfortune to meet."

Susanna began to speak indignantly, but Julia waved her down.

"He's quite entitled to think that," she said.

Adam's eyes glinted. Her acquiescence seemed to annoy him, not placate. "How extremely magnanimous of you," and he slammed the door.

"Land sakes!" said Susanna, "I'd never be able to pronounce mag — whatever it is — even if I wasn't madder'n a swarm of bees. Oh, well, no one could say it's been a dull morning. I like things happening."

Julia didn't laugh with them this time. "That's not a kind thing to say when a man's engagement could be broken over those happenings."

Esther gazed at her with anxiety. "*Could* be broken . . . you don't really think they'll make it up, do you?"

Julia's gaze wiped the mischief off both faces. "I sincerely hope they will. Miriam is bound to come to the conclusion soon that it must have been just as I said, that Adam would never have brought a girl here. Imagine her saying he was going to smuggle her into one of the cottages!"

Susanna nodded. "That was clean daft,

but it was the photograph that did it, of course."

Julia looked unhappy. "Oh, yes, I'd forgotten it. It is here, I suppose?"

"Yes, in Miriam's bedroom, carefully cut out. I think she was going to ask Adam who you were." Esther flashed out of the room.

She came back with it and they all bent over it on the table. Julia said miserably, "Nobody looking at that would dream we'd been strangers till that moment. A thousand curses on that photographer! And when we'd told him we weren't together, why did he use it?"

"Because it's a really glamorous photo," said Susanna practically, "and how could he guess there'd be such a rumpus because of it?"

It was . . . a couple sharing a moment of spontaneous laughter over a mistake. Nothing posed or self-conscious about it. Adam's eyes, resting on Julia were alight. If you wanted to read anything into it, you could easily imagine it a moment of tenderness. Any fiancée would know a pang of jealousy over it. Julia groaned.

Esther said, "That's a beaut hair-do . . .

must be a very good switch. You look a million dollars, not like — " she stopped, reddened.

Julia giggled. "Not like I do at the moment. I love a hair-do like that for special occasions, but can't stand the amount of time you've got to put into looking after long hair. I like an urchin cut and riding round paddocks with the wind tossing my hair back from my cars and being able to just run a comb through it in the mornings. But oh, how I wish that photographer had had a dud film. Without this, Miriam would have been much less suspicious. Well, I can't do a thing about it, but I'll always have a burden of regret. I'll just try to pull my weight in the household till they get the slip cleared. Oh, if only the road wasn't blocked and I could get away!"

The twins spoke as one. "We aren't sorry. We think you're fun."

Fun . . . it wasn't fun to be the cuckoo-in-the-nest.

Lunch was not a comfortable meal. Adam's taciturnity had an effect upon even the twins and it was left to Grandpa Dare and

Luke to carry on conversation with Julia who couldn't manage, anyway, to reply in much more than monosyllables. And Esther hadn't stirred the gravy at the right time and it was lumpy. Adam pointedly arranged all his lumps on the rim of his plate and Julia felt responsible.

When he was safely outside again and the dishes were washed, Julia said, "Would you girls come out with me to that barn where your uncle put the car and I'll get my weekend bag off the floor. Well, just a shopping bag really. I used it for a pillow and I left my cardigan there. I'd rolled it between my waist and the floor."

Outside the door Julia stopped dead, once more almost stunned by the shining beauty of the bay in the early afternoon sunlight. The twins watched her, smiling.

Julia stepped off the low verandah, cluttered with pot-plants, shells, small tables, and rough chairs, on to a sort of open courtyard formed on huge smooth flattish boulders set in the ground.

She looked down on them and Esther said, "There were no asphalt or concrete paths in Camilla's day, so she got the men to bring them up from the foreshore, one by one. All our paths are like that. Not for the new house — ours — of course, but all the ones in the family house."

They were charming, with herbs and tiny flowers springing from between each one, and they meandered as no concrete path could ever have meandered . . . they ran between rustic pergolas, formed of rough-barked *manuka* saplings, and under symmetrically curved and bleached white arches that were huge whale-bones. They wandered under fruit-trees whose buds were just opening; they ran, lavender-bordered, to a little round summerhouse, fashioned from wood from the bush and covered with native clematis just beginning to uncurl its white, fragile stars, because spring came early to Port Underwood.

Susanna said, "Captain Ephraim built that for Camilla . . . she used to do her darning there, looking out over the whaling activities. I think that sometimes, when he was out, she'd forget the darning and just sit and watch for his ship putting into harbour."

On the hillsides surrounding the bay were lush pastures where ewes, heavy in lamb, were grazing, and nearer the house the sound of contented cackling announced that the hens were doing their duty. Ducks waddled through the orchard, geese took a single line file to some pond out of sight, small streams sang and gurgled on their way to the sea. What a prodigality of bloom and perfume there was . . . forget-me-nots dotting the corners with blue, great glowing clumps of yellow alyssum sprawling over rocks, smaller tufts of purple and white alyssum peeping out, snowdrops ringing dainty bells, aubretia in great purple and lilac pools, huge pendant lemons of a giant variety, crowding their trees, the scent of orange-blossom to stir the pulses. Even now, in early spring, there was a mildness in the air that made one realise that the top of the South Island was further north than the southernmost tip of the North Island.

Fuchsias abounded in every variety and the girls stopped Julia beside a huge camellia, waxen-white with a faint blush of pink on the frilly outer petals.

"Camilla planted these camellias . . . some bushes aren't as old as others, but all are grown from her first trees. Captain Ephraim said she must have her namesakes in her garden; and there, across the shell path, on that trellis, is one of her roses. When they bloom it looks lovely, one of those old-fashioned creamy clusters. We keep striking new cuttings, so Camilla's roses will always be here. Grandpa says there was so much that was rough and terrifying and crude in the life here, but Camilla, just as Betty Guard of Kakapo Bay did, created an oasis of peace and beauty up here on the hillside, away from the bawdy jokes of the whaling station, in which to rear her family."

Julia was fascinated by the way the girls dropped into the phraseology of an earlier day when they recounted these tales handed down through the generations.

In the barn they retrieved Julia's things and returned to the house. They took her into a bedroom that looked out on to the quarter-deck verandah and down to the bay. It had fluffy white lambskins on the old-fashioned linoleum on the floor and a double iron bedstead with a white knitted quilt upon it, a washstand with a yellowed bedroom set patterned in full-blown roses and a quaint bureau in dark red wood with a patina of hand-polishing that more than compensated for its chipped edges. A crocheted doyley set adorned the top of it and a black wooden hairbrush with what proved to be whalebone bristles. An American rocker covered with a crocheted wool rug stood in the window, asking to be sat in.

Esther fingered the mirror-stand on the bureau, tilting it so it would be the right height for Julia. "It belonged to Captain Ephraim's mother. We thought you'd prefer this to Miriam's room. Adam put *her* in the sunroom that was added on just two years ago."

Julia said crisply, taking out her make-up and renewing it, "Now we must work. I mustn't be a drone. I'm here only on sufferance, so I'd better pull my weight. And girls, I don't want to answer that phone. If Miriam rings and finds me still here she might hang straight up again, because she may not know the road is now closed completely and she'd expect Adam to have me out of here long since. So if she does ring, for goodness' sake get in first and say: "What do you think? We're

completely cut off by road now." I want no hanky-panky about it either, do you hear?"
"Yes," said the twins meekly.

The afternoon flew by, Julia made scones for afternoon tea at half past three, and though they earned no comment from Adam, she noticed, with inner satisfaction, that he disposed of an incredible number. They had almost finished when a huge fluffy cat walked in, surveyed his domain with great aplomb, and proceeded to walk round the centre table to the hearthrug. Then he stopped in outraged surprise. A sleek black cat, with a white front, was sitting right in front of the fire washing himself. The incoming cat fluffed himself out to a huge ginger ball, arched his back, spat and sprang.

The usurper lifted one elegant white paw and with beautiful timing swiped him clean across the face. The fluffy one turned a complete somersault and sprawled, springing back swiftly and coming this time slowly and menacingly to the attack, green eyes gleaming balefully. The black cat regarded him contemptuously and turned an indifferent back, continuing his interrupted toilet. The tension went out of the ginger one, and, deflated, he sat back on his haunches and surveyed that insulting back. Then he walked round face to face and stared into the intruder's eyes. The black one stared back unwinkingly, then slowly they leaned forward till their noses touched, sniffing. Then the fluffy one sat down beside him, also back to the company, and began his own toilet.

"Suffering snakes," said Grandpa Dare, "I've never seen Esau do that before. He won't allow one of the barn cats inside. He's always been the cock of the north. Can you beat that?"

Julia exploded. "Esau . . . the hairy one . . . oh, how apt!"

The twins burst into speech. "Jacob . . . we'll call that one Jacob." Esther added: "He's so smooth."

Julia giggled, "Not only that, but he's a master tactician, just like the Biblical Jacob. And, unlike me, he doesn't know he's a cuckoo-in-the-nest."

Grandpa Dare cleared his throat. "Well, the animals have shown us they can settle their differences, let's do the same."

Adam pushed his chair back, "Let's

waste no more time, I want more of those lambing ewes nearer the house."

The girls put her in the picture as far as the whole estate was concerned. Their father, the younger brother, had married at twenty, the girl he'd admired from pre-school days. Adam, now, his mother had ruefully decided was destined to be a bachelor, then he fell for Miriam very suddenly.

Julia said hurriedly, "Now, girls, that subject is taboo. We don't want to be caught out talking about it again. Tell me about the rest of you. What about Daniel and Adam's parents, where are they? And did they have just two boys?"

"No, Aunt Rebecca is married and living away up the North Island. Her husband is a lighthouse-keeper. But Nanna and Grandy are in Britain, having a tour. They're building a super house right in Picton. It's going to be good, because instead of boarding with people during school term, we'll just live with them. Then suddenly Mum and Dad had a chance of a trip that didn't cost them a penny. Mum is what she calls a compulsive competition enterer! She can't resist them. She didn't win a thing for years, then she got really good at the slogans, and won three in a row. We got a motor-mower, a cake-mixer, and this trip.

"This trip was a first prize. Mum had hoped for second or third, a dishwasher or a deep-freeze, but she got a trip to Hong Kong — oh, lots of other places too, Bangkok, Singapore, the Philippines. She refused to go, with Dad's parents away, but Adam made them take it, said it was the chance of a lifetime and that it would give Granny a lift to think she could still cope, and he was darned sure she could, and he had a jolly good single worker in Ben. So after a frightful lot of persuading — she always thinks we'll have accidents or fatal illnesses if she as much as leaves us for a weekend — they went. So when Granny broke her leg, Adam sent for Miriam. It's all right, I'm not saying any more than that about her."

Julia said, fascinated, "Did Adam pick his hired man because he was called Benjamin?"

"No. His name is really Alphonse. Just imagine! Alphonse Benson! But nobody

has ever dared call him that. Just Ben."
Susanna laughed and added: "Poor Mum
is the odd man out. Says she ought to be
Naomi or Elizabeth or Mary. But she's got
a French name, Antoinette. Oh, are you
making bacon-and-egg pies for tea? That
ought to melt Adam. He loves them. The
way to a man's heart! Oh, please, Julia, can
we call you Julia? We just can't keep on
calling you Miss Merrill when you've done
such gloriously mad things. All right,
Julia, we'll shut up."

Adam Dare wasn't as taciturn at the
evening meal. Certainly he talked only to
Grandpa Dare and the children, but at
least he did talk, and so far forgot himself
and his grumpiness to say: "Ah . . . very
good," after a second helping of pie.

He said, pushing back his chair,
"Grandpa, I think we should ring the
hospital and tell Granny I'm sorry she
can't come home tomorrow as the road's
blocked. She'll take it without whining. I
won't say a thing about the rumpus here —
can't anyway, since the message will have
to be relayed to her. When the road is
cleared we'll decide what to do after I get
Miss Merrill back. I don't think we dare

bring her here with no woman to nurse her."

Julia saw Grandpa Dare look swiftly out of the window, swallow, then say in a philosophical tone, "Oh, aye. She'll take it on the chin, she was used to being away weeks at a time when she had the little 'uns."

Julia knew an almost unbearable stab of pain. It was all due to her that Lydia couldn't come home to the place she loved. She and Nathaniel were so old they must hate every moment spent apart. Everything within her wanted to say, "I'll stay to nurse her," but she dared not. Every moment she spent beneath this roof postponed the making-up of Adam and Miriam. Well, perhaps that would come about quite soon and Lydia could come home.

Adam talked to the Sister and turned from the phone to see Julia make a dive at Luke to save him tumbling off his chair, fast asleep.

She picked him up, said gently, "His disturbed night is catching up on him. Where's his bedroom? Then I'd better leave him to you, I'm sure he'd hate to come to to find a strange woman undressing him."

"I'll take him," said Adam.

She shook her head. "It will disturb him more. He's not too heavy. I'll put him on his bed and you can take over."

To her surprise, he allowed her. She had a fair idea he liked his own way. But perhaps the chink in his armour was his undoubted affection for his brother's children.

He led the way past a bedroom obviously his to a little jutting-out porch with a stretcher bed in it close to the push-out windows. "It's a bit crowded, but I thought Luke'd better have his own things about him so he'd not miss his mother and father too much." He strode over Hornby railway lines, blocks, Meccano parts, a set of electric racing cars and a half-finished jigsaw.

He whipped back the tartan rug, twin to the one that had so disastrously covered Julia last night, then the rest of the clothes, and said, "Put him right there between the sheets. He's so flat out I reckon I'll leave his shirt on, just take his trousers off and slip his pyjama pants on. It'd be a shame to wake him. I'm so thankful it was gluttony

123

and not appendicitis. Antoinette would have felt so guilty and upset. Not that I'd have let on. She's such a brick. She's a grand housekeeper and a Trojan in the paddocks. But of course *she* was born and brought up in Port Underwood." Which, of course, brought their minds back to Miriam.

Julia went out of the room quickly. She was just about dropping on her feet herself, but nobody had even noticed that! Yet all of *them* had had *some* sleep last night!

They did the dishes and Grandpa Dare had the living-room fire red to its heart and a game of Scrabble set out on the tapestry cloth on the ancient dining-table. Jacob and Esau were contented black and ginger balls on the rag mat.

"There's very little on TV after the news, so I thought we might have a go. Do you play, Julia?"

She saw Adam Dare look very sharply at his grandfather. The astute old man caught the look. He said, "The girls are doing it and that's one of the privileges of being old. She suits that name. It's womanly. Now *you* wouldn't dare, without asking permission."

Julia almost giggled at the look on his grandson's face. As if he wanted to, or cared what name she bore! And as for womanly . . . in creased trousers and dark skivvy!

Julia said, "Playing Scrabble is almost a vice with me, though I hardly ever win. I get so side-tracked seeing if I can get out unusual words, I forget to reckon up alternate scores."

The twins chuckled. Esther said, "Grandpa's like that, but he nearly always wins, just the same, because he's lived so much longer than us. The longer you live the more you read and the more words you know. But tell you what . . . let Susanna and me play together, that evens it up a bit. We'll be one over otherwise."

Adam said, "Who said I was going to play? I thought I'd catch up on some reading. I've got a lot of *Life* and *Time* magazines not opened yet."

The girls were flattering and cunningly persuasive, vowing that it was no fun without their uncle.

They listened to the news, saw some shots of damage in Marlborough, then played. Julia had the most unreal feeling and wondered what on earth Noel would think if he could but see her. In this more friendly atmosphere, with both cats purring resonantly, and firelight dancing in the old pannelling, the events of last night and this morning seemed but a dream.

Yet in about three days at the outside she would be gone from sight and sound of this. Once the road was open she had no doubt Miriam and Adam would make up their differences. And though she hated the thought of never seeing Susanna and Luke and Esther and Grandpa Dare again, she'd have to let them go out of her life. How odd to feel this about them . . . and odder still to so regret that she would never see Lydia, not from Thyatira, but from Cape Cod . . . oh, how ridiculous could one get?

The games finished in gales of laughter because the two girls managed to get all their seven letters out, making, to even Adam's amusement, "stowaway".

"What a coincidence," he said.

Old Nathaniel's voice was dry. "Pity Miriam hadn't been here . . . she might then have believed in coincidences . . .

might have admitted a photographer could make a mistake."

Instantly embarrassment sat heavily on Julia again. She said, "Look, I'm just about rocking on my feet. I had no sleep at all last night. I don't want anything more to eat. I'll just go to bed. Good-night, all."

They chorused good-night and Adam Dare added: "Have you everything for the night — oh, must have, I suppose, you had a bag, didn't you? Well, if you find there's anything you want, help yourself out of Miriam's room. It's next to yours."

"I've everything I need," said Julia quickly, and went away.

She knew she hadn't, for she always had a few things up at Noel's for the weekends she spent there, so she hadn't put any pyjamas in. The girls' would be too small for her and no doubt all Granny Dare's nightware would be at the hospital. She'd sleep in panties, with a blouse for a top.

But the room was cold. It had been open to the breezes of the bay all day and no one had thought to close the windows yet. The treacherous spring wind had a knife-like edge to it. Julia shivered. And she'd rather die than borrow anything from Miriam's things. Imagine if the road got cleared and Miriam arrived before Julia had time to launder anything!

Her eye fell on the bureau; there just might be something there. Even a pair of men's pyjamas would do. She pulled open a drawer . . . it was full of embroidered pillow-slips, belonging to another day, and they were redolent of . . . well, what was it ? . . . not lavender sachets, but something similar, slightly more pungent . . . ah, lemon verbena. The next drawer contained scoured sheep's wool, in tiny tufts. Someone here must spin from wool gathered from the barbed wire fences . . . the third contained, oh, joy, a nightgown.

Certainly it wasn't exactly a modern garment . . . but it was good and warm, in that it had a high collar and long sleeves and there was plenty of it. What was it made of ? It had been unbleached calico in its heyday, she thought, but had been bleached snowily from many washings and sea-wind dryings. Well, it was quaint, with its embroidered yoke and collar and the frilly cuffs to the long sleeves, but it would be warm.

Julia slid into it, laughed over her

reflection in the mirror and turned back the bedclothes and put a foot in. Oh, what a lovely surprise, the twins must have switched on an electric blanket. She turned it off, snapped out the bedside light and snuggled down. In two minutes she was fast asleep.

It must have been the early hours of the morning when she was wakened to the most blood-curdling shrieks, one after another, not abating. She was sure they were shrieks of terror, not pain. For a spine-chilling moment she felt rooted to the bed, then switched her lights on, leaping out, and she rushed, as continuing shrieks guided her. She was aware of others rushing.

She got into Luke's room a split second earlier than Adam, snapped the light on, instinctively finding the switch, then stared. Adam bumped into her.

Luke was sitting up in bed emitting yell after yell, seemingly unable to stop, his hands in front of his face as if fending off something they couldn't see . . . then the most eerie sound — a sort of hoot — and a scrabbling and a fluttering . . . and there in the corner of the room was an owl, with one wing outspread clumsily, trying to rise and flopping, weaving its head from side to side as if it were just recovering from a knockout blow.

It took the merest fraction of time to take it in, then Julia sprang at Luke, saying as she hurtled across the room, "It's all right, darling, it's all right. It's only a bird . . . it's all right, Julia's got you, oh, my lambie," and gathered him close, while glass fell off the bed on to the floor.

The next moment the girls were in the room, eyes staring. Adam, bending over Julia and Luke, whose shrieks were dying away in a sort of mixture of hiccups and sobs, said sharply, "Mind, girls, there's glass everywhere, stay put!"

Julia sat down on the bed, lifted Luke clean out on to her lap, murmuring, "There, there," and "Hush, hush," and uttering little soothing noises. Adam picked up a jersey of Luke's and made a swoop at the bird, still struggling dazedly beside the wardrobe. He picked it up, said to the girls, "Get a broom and shovel . . . it must have flown clean through the corner window over Luke's bed. We'll have to get the glass up before anyone gets badly gashed.

But put your slippers on first and bring mine and Miss Merrill's. Also bring Jonah's old cage out of the laundry. Then I can do something else beside holding this."

He looked completely bewildered. "I've never known such a thing happen at night. Occasionally a bird will dash at a window in daylight, mistaking its reflection for another bird, I think, but an owl . . ."

Julia, patting the subsiding Luke, said, "I wonder if the moon — such as it is — was reflected in the window and the owl thought there was space in front of it, not a building."

Adam looked at her with respect. "I think you're right . . . the moon is right opposite that window."

Susanna, in slippers, began clearing a swathe of shattered glass in a pathway to the bed, tossing Adam his slippers first. Esther appeared with a parrot cage dangling from one finger and Julia's shoes in her other hand. "I couldn't find any slippers."

"I didn't bring any. I always keep some at my brother's farm."

Susanna, walking along the cleared floor, went to slip them on Julia's feet, dangling over the bed edge. She stopped, "You've already cut your foot." They looked at the blood dripping from it. Julia said hastily, "Oh, I hadn't felt it. It can't be much. I'll stick a bit of plaster on it in a moment."

Adam said, "I'll look at it the moment I get this bird settled, poor thing. Luke, he got a bigger fright than you, I reckon, and he must have knocked himself out to boot."

"Not right away he didn't," said Luke, shuddering. "Oh, it was awful, Uncle Adam. It fluttered and scraped and clawed . . . all over my face. And it was *warm* . . ." his tone held reminiscent horror. "And I tried to shove it off and I could hear glass going everywhere and then it thudded to the floor. He thought of something. "Oh, do you think I broke its wing, then?"

Julia gave him a tender look, gathering him a little closer. Even now, just recovering, he was concerned for the bird.

Adam shook his head decidedly. "No, if his wing had been all right he'd have been able to have broken the fall, especially as *he* could see. No, he'd have been flying with wings outstretched and the force of the impact with the glass would break the wing. But we can mend it, after all, we've mended plenty of gulls' wings. There, old boy, you stay in there till I can attend to you. That's the ticket, Susanna, you're making a good job of that. Ess, hand me Luke's slippers — no, better not, they might have splinters of glass in them. Get me a pair of his socks, clean ones."

Luke looked down on himself. "Why am I in my shirt?"

"You fell asleep over your dinner, so I didn't fully undress you. But we'll change you now because I can see tiny bits of glass all over you. And I think I'll put you in my bed for the rest of the night. I think you want company after a shock like that. It would have scared seven bells out of anyone." He went to lift Luke.

Luke clutched Julia. "I'd rather stay with her."

Julia expected Adam to look huffed, but he only chuckled and said, "Okay, if she doesn't mind." Then, "Now, Miss Merrill, that foot. Sue, a bowl of water, not too hot, and Dettol, and Ess, you get the first-aid kit."

Julia said, "It's only a scratch, more nuisance value than anything. I'll do it myself."

He grinned, and the dark-a-vised face looked quite different. "I don't think Luke will let you go at the moment. You're the only womanly contact in a shocking world to him just now." Luke, surprisingly, did not scoff at this.

They inspected the foot. "It's deepish, but open enough. And I think it's bled so freely any splinters would have been washed out. We'll see better tomorrow. I'm afraid this will sting."

But it wasn't bad. He bandaged it efficiently and sent one girl off for a pair of his socks. He caught the look of surprise on Julia's face as he looked up. He said, "We were all coached in first-aid extremely young. This was so self-contained a community we had to be able to attend to most things. When I was a kid, only serious mishaps went down by launch, over the Wairau Bar, to Blenheim. We couldn't call a doctor, you know."

He stood up, then looked down on her and a smile lifted the corners of his lips. "Miss Merrill, what on earth is that prim garment you're wearing ?"

Both girls giggled. They were beginning to enjoy themselves after the scare.

Julia went scarlet. "I didn't bring any night things. Hiding under the rug the way I planned to, I knew I'd have no room."

Adam said quite mildly, "But I said to help yourself to Miriam's things."

She flushed again. "I — I didn't like to. Not when — "

He nodded as if he understood that.

She said, feeling guilty, "I was just going to bed in my — well, in what I had — but it was cold and I found this in the bureau."

Esther said, eyes sparkling, "It's Camilla's, isn't it, one of the hand-made ones ?"

Julia looked horrified. "Oh, no — good heavens, I might have ripped it. I mean if it's as old as that it might have just disintegrated. I could have ruined an heirloom."

"Not that," said Adam. "Things were made to last in those days. It's as tough as sailcloth. But tomorrow we'll give you one of Granny's. She didn't take them all with her, and she's a vain lass if ever there's one . . . wears the most modern stuff. But we won't disturb Grandpa seeing he's actually not wakened. But that wall between us and the cottage is pretty soundproof. It was built of stone hewn from the hillside."

Julia said, "But I'll take it off. I'd feel dreadful if anything happened to it. Perhaps, after all, I'll take one of Miriam's."

He shook his head, "No, I'm sure hers will be too flimsy. You might catch cold. Besides . . ." he stopped very suddenly.

Susanna said, "Besides, what?"

"Oh, never mind." There was that in his tone that shut the girls up.

Was he realising that Miriam would hate to think the girl who bust her engagement was wearing her nightgowns?

"I'll pull the bed away from the window in case of rain and shut the door. We'll fix it in the morning. Let's go out into the kitchen and make ourselves a hot drink. The range should still be on, I banked it up. Though I must splint this wing first, out there."

It was very interesting to watch. The girls assisted, with much advice from Luke, recovering now, but still on Julia's knee. Julia marvelled that a man with such large hands could be so gentle and accomplish such a fiddling task. The owl was less wobbly now and objected vigorously, but

136

it was going to have to be kept captive till its wing mended.

"We've never had a morepork before," said Esther with great satisfaction. Adam inserted a very low perch across the cage. "It could tumble off the high one, it's had concussion. It could get dizzy. I won't give it anything to eat, it's probably got a tummyful anyway, it would start hunting just after nightfall. I hope it's the one who lives in the giant macrocarpa. We can free it up there."

Susanna said practically, "I'm starving. Do you think we could heat up some soup and make toast?"

To Julia's surprise their uncle agreed. When he wasn't, as Susanna had said, 'madder'n a swarm of bees' he was evidently an indulgent uncle!

It was very sensible. It restored them and probably meant Luke would not now have nightmares, as would be likely after such a shattering experience. He dropped off on Julia's knee, exhaustedly, as soon as he had eaten. When she finished her own she said, rising, "I'll get him into my bed without disturbing him. No, Mr. Dare, don't take him."

"But you might open up that foot again."

"What odds? It's well bandaged."

He grinned, looking for a moment very like the mischievous Esther, and swooped, lifted them both, and strode off with them.

Julia dared not struggle. It would waken Luke, who'd had enough night terrors. Adam must be terrifically strong, just like that giant of a man, Captain Ephraim. The girls, giggling, darted on ahead and turned down the bedclothes. Earlier they had switched on the heat again.

He put his burden down carefully, said, "I hope he doesn't kick or talk in his sleep. That's why I thought I'd take him, but Luke turned me down."

Julia said apologetically, "Well, I expect he probably misses his mother and I'm the next best thing."

He grinned and there was a wicked glint in those almost black eyes. "Sure, you're much more like his mother . . . biologically!" and swept the squealing girls ahead of him, out of the room.

Julia found she was blushing again.

Well, at least he had a sense of humour . . . perhaps that would tide him over the next few days till Miriam came out of the sulks. Better by far, however, if that road hadn't been blocked and he could have got the cuckoo-in-the-nest safely back to the North Island. Miriam wasn't going to like her being here with Adam in this enforced isolation.

4

GRANDPA DARE was most amazed when he found an emotionally disturbed owl in old Jonah's cage the next morning. "What in tarnation is this?" he demanded.

Adam said solemnly, "No need to stress the Cape Cod utterances now, Grandpa, Miriam's not here, remember? And let me tell you I think you must be the world's best sleeper . . . that thing flew into Luke's bedroom window last night, showered glass all over the room, scrabbled at his face, and Luke just about screamed the place down . . . the noise outdid the witches' scene in *Macbeth*, believe me!"

He knelt down by the cage, put his hand in to examine the morepork and was rewarded by a vicious nip. "A worthy successor to Captain Ephraim's Jonah," said Grandpa. "Many's the piece he's had off me."

Julia, coming in, said, "Oh, do you remember the Captain's parrot?"

"Do I what? They live a terrific time, parrots. Even Adam's father can remember him. He was the greatest embarrassment of the family. He learned to talk on board whalers."

"Oh, I wish *I'd* been privileged to see him. Imagine what a link with the past that would have been." She had spoken without thinking and Adam, from the floor, looked up at her so sharply, she coloured.

But he just said, "I'll have to get this bird into the wash-house, I think, before Esau and Jake come in. They'd scare the living daylights out of him. And seeing he's a night bird, I'll put a dark blanket over him. He looks more perky this morning. Susanna, they eat mice and moths and beetles, don't they? Do you think he might take a bit of raw chopped-up meat? Get a bit of that topside steak out of the fridge and cut it up."

Suddenly Julia realised this wasn't really the place for a demon housewife called Miriam. She got a cloth to wipe up the bird-droppings. Miriam, from what the girls had said, belonged to that stratum of life where daily events ran on oiled wheels . . . she could see her as a business executive's wife, entertaining with superb skill and aplomb, and nary a pet in sight.

She felt a little sad. There would be friction always. And this peaceful bay wasn't meant for friction. The Bay of the Ancestors . . . would Miriam make old Nathaniel and his Lydia from Cape Cod so unhappy they would move into Picton, away from the harboured tranquillity of Port Underwood, with its twenty miles of azure waters bitten into the hills? She pulled herself up. It was nothing to do with her. And once they got the morepork out of here, she must get breakfast.

She wasn't as awkward as she might have been, fumbling round a strange kitchen. Things seemed to be where you'd expect them to be. They were in time-honoured places. Oh, how different it was from flat life, where storage had to be space-saving. What a plentitude of everything in the larder. It was modernised in the best way too, with glass-fronted shelves that ensured protection from flies and with large working benches in the kitchen. She noticed at the far end, where the fuel range was, a sort of slot on each wall. "What would they be for?" she asked Adam.

"Oh, we shut that end off when we get weak lambs in here. Most go in boxes with lamps, but there's almost always an overflow and this saved Mother having reviving lambs under her feet all the time. We built a collapsible barrier — hinged — like a baby's play-pen, and we slip one end in each of those slots. Means that when they perk up as they do so soon with warmth and food, and they skip madly about, they're confined here. As you'll know, lambs are never exactly — er — house-trained."

Julia said with feeling, "I know. How marvellous. I must get Noel to make me one of these."

His voice was dry. "Oh, so you do intend telling him of this escapade?"

"Yes, when it's safely over. He won't be pleased with me though, so I won't rush it. He can put up with unhygienic lambs in his kitchen this year, seeing he spurned my help."

The morning flew. The farm seemed to have a good workshop, and Grandpa Dare and Adam managed to cut a piece of glass and putty it into Luke's window-frame. Julia and the girls got every fragment of glass off blankets, floor and mats. They were late with midday dinner and Julia decided she'd better leave the washing till the next day. If she did that for them, and the ironing before she had to depart, it would be a great help.

The three children were not going back to school till a week come Monday, so she supposed the girls could manage to keep house till then. They went to school in Picton and came home for week-ends. But that would not solve the problem of Granny Dare.

When, after the evening meal, Adam went outside, Julia knew that the girls would be occupied for some time with the dishes, and Grandpa was busy helping Luke with a complicated Meccano model.

Julia slipped out after Adam into the cool spring twilight. The sunset was still staining the over-harbour hills and headlands with changing lights, rose and gold and burnt orange, but this side was in shadow because of the immense hills rising up beyond the road. Through the window she had noticed which way Adam had taken. She followed through the trees of the orchard, down the uneven rock steps, water-worn from the waves of the shore, and turned through some gnarled *ngaios* to come upon him rather more suddenly than she had expected. She stopped short, aware that she was going to intrude upon goodness knows what thoughts.

There was a beautifully curved arch of the gigantic whalebones here, over an equally white path of crushed sea-shells, and it framed a view of wind-ruffled waters with hills beyond dappled with gentle shadows. Peace. But there was that in Adam's pose that suggested in the way one hand leaned heavily on the whalebone, utter dejection!

He would be trying to think out how he could unsnarl the tangle of his life, the tangle Julia had unwittingly caused. It smote her with a physical pain. But she must leave him to it. How terrible it was, to want to comfort someone — anyone — and to face the fact you might only make the wound worse, because you had brought about the situation. But perhaps if he pondered long enough, he could make himself sink his pride and make an overture to the girl he loved.

She turned, with utmost stealth, to retreat, but the brittle shells beneath her feet betrayed her. He swung round, said brusquely. "Yes?"

She faltered, said, "I — I — came after you to — but it doesn't matter. I'll — "

He said impatiently, "Well, if you wanted to see me alone about something, what better time? So what's the matter with you?"

Oh, if only her colour wouldn't rise. "Oh, I don't know. . . . Mr. Dare, I'm so wretchedly sorry about having caused this break, and I — wanted to talk with you, and up there at the house, I knew exactly what I was going to say, I rehearsed it for ages . . . but now it's gone right out of my head and I'm just plumb scared!"

His face broke up into laughter lines. "You're catching it off Grandpa." He added to her puzzled look, "You just said you were plumb scared. What on earth are you scared about? I won't eat you! What is it?"

She felt a bit better. He was accepting now the fact that though she had been a bit rash, she hadn't meant to involve anyone else. She said in a rush: "I feel so awful about it all. Imagine what it must be like to know you're the cause of an estrangement between two people who love each other! I don't mind situations where I can do something to put it right, but I feel so helpless. Worst of all, I feel Grandpa Dare is fretting for his Lydia. It's through me she can't come home when the road is clear. But for me, Miriam would have been here, to keep house and to dress her. When a person has plaster on, it's so awkward. She — Granny Dare — will need another woman."

"So — ?" His eyes were very intent upon her.

"So I wondered if perhaps you'd cooled off enough to — oh, I feel so interfering . . . if you'd cooled off enough to — " she stopped.

"If I'd cooled off enough to — what?"

She said gratefully, "To make some step towards healing the breach. Then Granny Dare could come home."

His face was unreadable and his voice strange. "I can certainly see things in a different perspective now. In fact, that was why I came down here. I wanted to think the situation out."

Her face was eager, upraised to his, her chestnut hair ruffled in the off-sea breeze. "Then — then I've not worsened the situation by butting in like this. You — you're considering ringing Miriam up and — "

"I didn't say that," he said.

She looked dismayed. "Mr. Dare, I wonder if I could make you see it from the woman's angle?"

"You could try." Oh dear, that dry tone again. But she must continue.

"You see, you've been used to this . . . the life here. Because you were once used to greater isolation, you regard this now as very . . . civilised. To Miriam it may seem very remote . . . doesn't she come from Auckland, our largest city? She — she may have a — a clinical turn of mind, like everything methodically done. She sort of got plunged into an emergency here . . . three children, and elderly grandparents, and — well, it might have been just too different. She may have been very homesick, and — " she paused, how to put it?

"And . . . ?"

"And she may have thought she could

take the life here if she had a home like Daniel and Antoinette."

"*Could take it* . . . you make it sound like an endurance test!"

She rounded on him. "Mr. Dare, that's ridiculous . . . could *anyone* think such a thing of here? Why, this to me is . . ." she waved a hand that took in in a single gesture the sequestered peace of the deserted harbour, the distant glimpse of the Pacific curving down to the headlands of Kaikoura, the clouds that were turning to amethyst rimmed with fire, the whistling of mating thrushes in the quivering poplars, the bridal lace on the pear-tree boughs, the narcissi starring the grass at their feet, the snowy-fleeced sheep, the sweep of the smaller bay that was Whangatupuna.

"To me this is paradise . . . a small Eden, set in a southern sea. But you don't have to look at it from my standpoint . . . I'm trying to get you to look at it from *Miriam's*. Oh, but you're a very stubborn man! I expect it's Captain Ephraim in you! It's so different for men. They have a way of life, the way *they* want to live, and won't allow for the fact that it can be almost a revolution in a girl's life to marry someone and live where *he* wants to. Oh, I'm a believer in women following their men . . . my grandmother came thirteen thousand miles from Scotland to marry hers . . . but a woman can't adapt overnight. You ought to take it easy.

"I think Miriam's used to domestic science. She teaches it, I believe? She does? Then you've got to give her time to get used to a different routine . . . hers has been all method and orderliness. On farms, there's a different crisis every week, just about. She'd been here such a short time. And it was quite different from being married. When you're first married it's only a case of two people adjusting to each other. She had to fit in with your grandfather, pet though he is, and three high-spirited children who seemed to have taken her in dislike. You must make allowance for all this, Mr. Dare.

"I daresay she was tired, and the kids had needled her . . . and you'd probably been most unyielding over the house. And then when she found *me*, the girl you'd been photographed with, hiding under a rug in the back of your car . . . well, I ask you! It was just a spark to tinder. I'm sure she didn't mean all she said, any more than you meant all you said. See what I mean?"

The dark, hard-to-read eyes gazed down into the beseechingly earnest hazel eyes. Adam Dare said, "I see a very great deal I didn't see when I came down here to think this out. I've been very blind."

A light came into the hazel eyes. "Oh, I'm so glad . . . I don't think I could bear to go back to Wellington knowing I'd messed up your life for you . . . I mean knowing I'd messed up two people's lives."

"Had me — us — on your conscience, did you?"

"Of course."

He said, rather strangely, because how did it apply? " 'So conscience doth make cowards of us all.' "

But it hadn't been cowardly. She had been just terrified he'd tell her to get the hell out of it.

She said resentfully, "Why cowardly? It took a bit of grit to make me broach the subject to you."

He smiled, quite mirthlessly. "It wasn't your conscience I was thinking of, it was mine."

She let it go, she could not go on delving.

She looked past his shoulder, through the great curving bones and caught a gleam of white on a far headland. Eager to change the subject because she thought she ought to leave well alone now, she said, "Oh, what's that catching the light over there . . . at the end of that island in the harbour, or is it an island? It looks as if a causeway leads to it."

He motioned her to stand beneath the arch. He was so tall that when he leaned on it again, his arm was above her head. "It's a natural causeway at low tide. That island is Horahora Kakahu and that's a stone commemorating where sovereignty was proclaimed over the South Island. Don't you remember that from your history books? That it was proclaimed at Cloudy Bay? — that's the big stretch of water from the Wairau, away up to Port Underwood. The HMS *Herald* put in here on the 16th June, 1840, with the Treaty of Waitangi.

"The next day Major Bunbury got a number of chiefs to sign the treaty. A brother of the famous Te Rauparaha signed it, on condition his European son-in-law, Captain Joseph Thoms, signed it too, the only European signature. So that day the Major, Captain Nias, and a party of Marines landed on the *pa* on that island, hoisted the British flag and proclaimed Queen Victoria's sovereignty over the South Island and fired a salute of twenty-one guns.

"It was amazing that this never became a main seaport . . . of course when the Sounds were fully explored and opened up, Picton and Nelson were developed instead. But it's one of the best harbours in New Zealand."

Julia's eyes were adream . . . she could almost see HMS *Herald* under full sail, coming down that fair harbour, the numerous whaling vessels, Russian, Dutch, Portuguese, Scandinavian . . . and the fleet of Maori canoes. The singing and the joy of that moment.

She said, "But I'm glad it wasn't developed. I want it to remain like this, unspoiled, almost as it was in the earliest *pakeha* history here, for future generations. Tell me, are there many Maoris left here, or have they gone into the cities?"

He said, "Most of them have been gone a long time, save for the few here and there. There's a chap in the next bay — a relation of ours. That's his fishing-boat down there. Dan and I are not in it commercially. We just go out with Orewa when the mood takes us, it's in our blood, of course. And there are heaps of crays to be had. Granny, of course, calls them lobsters.

"The mass migration goes a long way back." He waved towards the head of the harbour, many miles north. "Ngakutu Bay lies there. There's another bay of that name on the Sounds — don't confuse it. But to this one came the Reverend Samuel Ironside, a Methodist missionary and his wife, a girl barely twenty-one."

Adam's voice took on a ring of pride. "Samuel was as strong as an ox, in his mid-twenties, and a lineal descendant of Edmund Ironside, last of the Saxon Kings. They were landed on the beach at Kakapo Bay among the cosmopolitan bunch of whalers, a rough and iniquitous lot for the most part. But from the start they recognised that Samuel Ironside was well named.

"He won the confidence of Maori and

pakeha whaler alike, almost immediately. The spread of the Gospel was almost unbelievable. He built missions and chapels all over the Port and all over the Sounds. He visited the most remote parts, marrying and baptising — his wife's curtain rings came in very handy — and at Ngakuta Bay, believe it or not, one hundred and fifty Maoris built a church capable of holding eight hundred. One young English carpenter from a whaling station was employed for the joinery, but the others did it for love. The Maori women grew crops and cooked the food while the men laboured. But the women dyed the reeds for the glorious decoration of the inside.

"At its unauguration service in 1842, the whalers came from far and near to be officially married to their Maori wives. The mouth of Port Underwood is a score of miles from the open sea, but many came from much further, from right round in remote bays and sounds, and it was said that the waters sparkled and gleamed, then darkened with so many canoes and whale boats. The Maori singing had to be heard to be believed and the harmony and happiness of the voices. Some of the canoes had come from even as far away as D'Ur-ville Island, through perilous seas . . . 'We will call this church *Ebenezer*,' Samuel said to his wife, '*Ebenezer* . . . hitherto hath the Lord helped us.'

"It seemed almost impossible that within a year so much work could be undone. Have you read much of Buick, the historian, Miss Merrill? He tells how one Sunday in the winter of 1843, Samuel saw a Maori paddling his canoe very swiftly up the bay, despite the drenching rain. He sent one of his mission boys to inquire. . . . But the boy, hearing the news, did not come back.

"After a very uneasy night, with a gale gusting, news began to trickle through of the massacre at Tuamarina. Twenty-two men, leading colonists of Nelson, had been killed in a conflict with Te Rauparaha and Te Rangihaeata in a dispute over the land. Ironside had written just shortly before this, warning the Englishmen not to take their armed surveying party to the Wairau, to attempt to arrest these chiefs. He had considered the chiefs had right on their side. Posterity agrees with this . . . so much so that nowadays it's not referred to as the massacre, but as the Wairau Incident.

"Ironside was a chained giant, fretting to go to Ocean Bay at the entrance to the Port, where some survivors had arrived, and to Robin Hood Bay next to it, where the two angry chiefs, who had also lost dear ones, had arrived. But in this violent southerly, beating up from the Pole, he could not launch his boat.

"At last the storm diminished and a crew of whalers took him down where he learned the details from the chiefs themselves. On his asking permission, they reluctantly agreed to allow him to travel down to bury the dead. They took their lives in their hands to cross Cloudy Bay and on over the Wairau Bar. He buried the bodies, as he reported, 'with tears we could hardly restrain'.

"Worn out and sad, he returned to Ngakuta and couldn't believe his eyes. Not a Maori was to be seen. But at his home he found his two Maori servants, the only ones left in the bay. As the news of the killing spread, a general migration of Te Rauparaha's people set in, northward, across Cook Strait, fearing reprisals.

"Not a trace of the great church, the first in the South Island, can be seen now, though a memorial has recently been erected. But Samuel's great gifts were not wasted. He too crossed Cook Strait. It has been said that but for him and for the Reverend Octavius Hadfield's intervention, Wellington itself might have been destroyed in the 'Hutt War' of 1846."

He turned to find tears in Julia's eyes. She looked embarrassed, then she said, "I'd learned of Tuamarina at school, of course, and of the death of Arthur Wakefield and his men, but I hadn't realised what a terrible misunderstanding it was, and what a tragedy too, for such a number of Maori people who had lived here so happily."

He said, abruptly returning to the present day, "I asked Grandad to put a nightgown of Granny's on your pillow and I got Susanna to hunt up some warm slippers for you. And — I quite understand your reluctance to wear Miriam's things under the circumstances — but tomorrow you might get the girls to take you over to the new house. I think you'd find Antoinette's things would fit you. No, she certainly wouldn't mind. She's not going to hear anything but good from the kids about *you*."

"I'm afraid so," admitted Julia. "It's not *their* lives I've upset."

He looked at her quickly. Their eyes met, clung, they both started to say something, changed their minds.

Adam said, swinging round, "Well, I suppose we should go in. History is fine, but one is also living history, right this very moment, and one has to go on with it."

For some reason Julia found it hard to reply to that. She wanted to hold time still.

They came up the shell path with the cool sweet wind blowing at their backs.

Adam said, as if there had been no pause, "But this will be only a fragment of time in *your* history, won't it, Julia? An escapade you'll only remember to tell your grandchildren as an instance of how their grandmother, too, was a tomboy."

She said, "I wonder. I read something in a magazine at the hairdresser's the other day. It said that no young woman ever imagines herself as a grandmother. As a mother, yes, but not as a grandmother. I thought it was true, then."

His heavy brows came down and he glanced at her sideways. "What do you mean . . . *then*?"

Julia stopped on the path, as if she needed a breather. A line appeared between her brows. "I don't know. I didn't even know I was going to say that." Her eyes swept the bay as though demanding of it the answer. And she got it. "I think it must be because of being here in the Bay of the Ancestors. One begins to wish that, as most Maoris can do, one could recite one's genealogy. I can go back, in names, only three generations. But you — all of you, even the children — because of Grandpa Dare's stories know your ancestors by name. Know them by personality and anecdote too, for about six generations. Not only the ones who lived here, but the ones in Cape Cod, and the Australian forebears who emigrated to Sydney from England. So that it seems a natural thing to think of one's descendants to come."

"You mean you can now think of yourself as a grandmother, despite that magazine item?"

"Yes. It must be the spell of that house. It's such a Topsy sort of house . . . it just growed! Nice to think of it like that. The back part first, I suppose . . . the lean-to, with a verandah and a bedroom sticking out at the side. Then adding a passage and a bedroom each side of it, as Ephraim's and Camilla's family grew. Then more length of passage, the First Parlour and another bedroom. You can see all the additions in that passage. It's like a family tree. Then, I suppose because it kept going downhill, the cottage on the side was tacked on. Why was it made so separate, Mr. Dare? It even has a lock and key!"

"It was when their son — the eldest one — went over to Wellington to sell some goods. He didn't like the whaling, you see. He was the one who first began to farm — Jonathan Dare. He met this girl there, Mary. And Camilla said that a daughter-in-law brave enough to forsake the gay life of Port Nicholson for love of a man shouldn't have to share a house with her mother-in-law. That she ought to have a kitchen of her own, where, if she fed her cooking failures into the pig-trough, no one else would know; where she could have a spirited fight once in a while, in private, with her husband, because fights in front of other people were apt to stay more serious than they needed to be. What Camilla said, according to tradition, was: '. . . they could become long days of lowering cloud instead of thunder and lightning, then sun.' "

"I like that," said Julia, "that means that Camilla and Ephraim had their spats . . . and made up. Often we hear the pioneer women so extolled they sound saint-like. It can be discouraging. I mean it makes one feel so inferior. Think of the conditions they coped with, the isolation, the terrors . . . they *must* have known terrors. But if you know they too lost their tempers once in a while, it makes them seem warm, and human and their qualities not so unattainable."

He chuckled. "Oh, they had their spats all right. Camilla was young and impulsive, never looked before she leapt, the stories say. Otherwise she'd never have stowed away. She always vowed that Captain Ephraim only just refrained from beating her when she was discovered. But she was what he needed . . . a staid conventional type would never have faced the life here . . . and enjoyed it. She was what he needed in other ways too. He was, to begin with, a dour man, very conservative, but they said she could twist him round her little finger."

A pause fell. Julia felt reluctant to go in because her time here, in this small Eden, was so short. Yes, that would be why, *must* be why, she felt like this. To find such beauty and to know, because of what had happened, you could never return. So naturally you wanted to drink your fill of its loveliness, to remember always. Well, the first Eden had been only an interlude too ... once that pair had sipped of knowledge, there had been no return. How ironic that the thing that had brought her to Whanga-tupuna, her madcap escapade, was what would keep her away. The angel with the fiery sword. Oh, if only she had come here some other way, so that she'd have had the right, like any other visitor, to drop in occasionally. Why, it was within the bounds of possibility that if Noel had decided to take Adam's invitation to visit him, he might have asked his sister to accompany him! But in a day or two this would be nothing but a memory.

Adam looked above her at another whale-bone arch held in the twining grip of a gnarled old wistaria, "Oh, it's certainly going to be an early spring. There are actually buds, very tight, but still buds."

Julia became very still, looking up at them, "I'll never see the wistaria drooping down, in bloom," she said.

At that moment a peal of the most delightful young laughter came from the open windows. They both looked up. "Oh, that's Phemy," said Adam. "Hark at her, nobody laughs just like that."

Julia said, "Did you say Phoebe?"

"No, Phemy. Short for Euphemia. She's Orewa Watson's daughter. There is always a daughter called Euphemia in their family. You see, Captain Ephraim saved the life of Orewa's great-great-grandmother, Hine Kuru. She was drowning — she'd been fishing from a canoe near his anchored ship and a line wrapped round her ankle. It was during an official visit from a Naval corvette and various brass hats were aboard, so Captain Ephraim was dressed for the occasion.

"When he saw Hine had not bobbed up, he sprang over the rail, divesting himself of his cutlass as he did so, flinging it back on board. But it struck something and fell into the harbour. It's always been a dream of each succeeding generation to find Captain Ephraim's cutlass. Hine was expecting a baby, which turned out a daughter, so Euphemia was the nearest thing in feminine form they could get to Ephraim. Let's go in and see what Phemy wants."

As they stepped on to the verandah, two figures came flying out.

"Uncle Adam, Phemy's come round with some groper and we'd like her to stay the night."

"You'll have to ask Miss Merrill. She's the one to do the extra cooking and washing."

Julia laughed, "Goodness, that makes me feel like some ancient family retainer who has to be humoured! Of course." How strange that he had even consulted her.

The girls shot off and appeared again with Phemy. The child, almost a woman, was outstandingly lovely. She had long black hair and a graceful carriage, a faintly olive skin, and her features were flawless.

She said, "You'd better make it right with Mum. She said I wasn't to ask to stay. She said it wasn't as if Aunt Toni was home, and that Miriam wasn't so used to coping with extra children. But the twins say she's not here. Why not? And — "

Adam's voice was dry, a little rasping. "Didn't they tell you why? Oh, I suppose they've not had time. Well, I'm sure you'll hear the whole story, richly embroidered, in bed tonight."

Susanna's voice had an unchildlike dignity. "We weren't going to say a word. Julia has already impressed it upon us that we mustn't gossip about what happened. But *now* we may have to!" She sounded every bit as derisive as Adam himself. Oh dear, thought Julia, here we are back to square one, and this last half-hour has been so pleasant.

To her surprise he burst out laughing. "Well, that's one on me! You are obviously growing up if you can manage to keep secrets. Or else Miss Merrill has cast some curious charm on you. Oh, well, Phemy is family, so off you go. Tell her the bare bones and no embroidery."

They turned as one, then Esther, with her puckish charm, looked over her shoulder and said, eyes dancing, "It doesn't *need* embroidering, Uncle darling!"

Julia and Adam were left looking at each

166

other and feeling unaccountably foolish.

Julia sought for something to say. Her eyes fell on the parcel of fish, just inside the kitchen. "I'd better clean that fish," she said weakly.

"That's no job for a woman, but in any case, Orewa would never send it over not cleaned."

They walked in together and unwrapped it Beautiful fleshy groper.

He turned and looked at her. "Miss Merrill, I think you're feeling what happened very deeply. Don't lose any sleep over it. I know I was madder than . . ."

He paused for some reason and Julia absentmindedly filled in for him, ". . . madder'n a swarm of bees."

He grinned. "Thank you very much. That describes it exactly . . . I take it one of the twins put it that way."

She gave a gasp of dismay. "Oh, I'm sorry. It's second nature to me to fill in the gaps. My boss relies on me to do it for him. It's rather funny the way he gets stuck. He snaps his fingers and I come in with it. I must try to break myself of the habit."

"Well, I *was* madder'n a swarm of bees to begin with, but I'll hand it to you, you've pitched in in great style with the work, and you must have felt plumb mortified about the whole thing. And I realise, from what you said down the path, that you'd do anything to put it right. You explained — very tolerantly and kindly — Miriam's reactions as being fairly natural, and you tried to mollify her yourself, but it was too soon. So — when you go — just forget the whole thing. It's rather beastly to have something on your conscience you can't do anything about."

Julia looked down and bit her lip. She had a horrible moment when she thought she might burst into tears. Never had she expected such thoughtfulness from the man who had called her the cuckoo-in-the-nest.

The girls came dancing back. "Uncle Adam, can we sleep in the double bed all together? It's fun."

"If you don't talk till all hours of the morning, or is that expecting too much?"

Esther said solemnly, "Well, we'd never keep a promise not to do that, but we won't disturb you half as much as if we were in separate beds calling out to each other."

"I suppose that's fair enough. Ring your

mother, Phemy, and tell her you're staying. And thank your father for the groper. Oh, better tell her Miriam's gone back to her aunt and that the sister of a friend of mine is keeping house. You can tell her the details later, and ask her to keep it to themselves. After all, family members have got to know."

He said to Julia crisply, dismissing the subject, "Would you like that groper cut into steaks? How do you like groper best? Fried? I suppose you've cooked it before?"

"Yes, but I'll do it whichever way you prefer. You mean for lunch tomorrow? My brother likes it best baked in the oven with a wee bit of milk, dotted with butter, and covered at the last with breadcrumbs with butter rubbed in, seasoning and a fine grating of cheese on top to brown it, but if — "

"Oh, we'll have it thataway. Sounds fine."

Julia thought of something. "Would you come out to the barn with me, Mr. Dare? I want to prove to you that with a bit of jiggling, that key does fit."

He looked surprised. "Oh, I believe you now. No need for that."

Julia felt a warmth at her heart. Good to be believed. But she said, "Just the same, I'll leave it with you when I go — Noel can get another one cut — so you can convince Miriam when you see her."

Adam didn't even reply, just went on cutting the fish steaks.

Well, it had been a more pleasant day and Julia didn't feel the weight of guilt so much. Also, it looked as if she didn't fall too far behind that paragon of cooks, Miriam Chillingham. Julia was suddenly aghast at the vehemence of her own thoughts. How perfectly ridiculous, she wasn't competing against Miss Chillingham.

By the day after tomorrow, probably, the slips would be cleared. Adam would take her into Picton, and she would sail for Wellington up the lovely, enchanting world of the sounds, and away from the South Island, leaving behind her for ever this small Eden.

Julia looked down on herself and decided she could no longer bear these clothes. Slacks were fine for working round in, especially here where you were in and out of the farmyard all day, feeding scraps to the hens and putting out tins of milk for the barn cats, but tonight she would wear some of the clothes the twins had brought across from their home.

She showered quickly, used skin perfume, slipped into a light-weight woollen frock that was something between green and brown and had a swinging green girdle in tasselled leather. She would take it in to the cleaners before leaving, and ask the girls to pick it up for their mother. She polished her tan brogues, and took pains with her hair, brushing it till it shone like a polished chestnut. There was a rope of green wooden beads to go with the belt. She twisted them once and let them hang loosely.

Old Nathaniel rose instantly when she came into the First Parlour, that small, cosy room with its beaded hassocks and tapestry chairs. "My dear, how nice you look. Thank you for doing us the compliment of changing for the evening. Lydia always does. It was one way, in the old days, when we had no road, of preserving some sort of style. Of breaking the monotony, really, so that life wasn't all work. And with Phemy here tonight we'll have some music. That dress is exactly the colour of the new beech leaves in the New Hampshire woods . . . with the sun shining through . . . golden and green."

Julia turned to see Adam in the doorway. His expression was unreadable. Was it turning the knife in the wound to find his grandfather and his nieces and nephew all liked her?

Phemy seated herself at the old piano that Captain Ephraim had brought from Sydney for his bride. It was kept beautifully tuned and had the most mellow tone, as if all the songs of all the ages had hallowed the keys. They sang all the songs Nathaniel Dare loved best: *"O, believe me if all those endearing young charms"* . . . *"O, who will o'er the downs so free?"* . . . *"The Last Rose of Summer"* . . . *"The Bluebells of Scotland"* . . . *"Robin Adair"* . . . and others of a similar vintage.

The air of sadness, a certain wistfulness, that sat upon Nathaniel just now, disappeared. He had been missing his Lydia. He was recapturing romance in these songs.

Adam said, finally, "Thanks, youngsters. Do you want the guitar out? Any pop music?"

172

Phemy shook her head, leaning back against Adam in an attitude of sheer affection. "No, not tonight. Grandpa only puts up with that because of us, don't you, sweetie?"

Nathaniel leaned forward and tweaked a lock of her hair. "I thought I'd disguised that very well. Well, you're good brats, all of you. Phemy, have you made up your mind yet whether or not you'll take further singing lessons?"

A slight shadow fell across the young face. "I don't know. Isn't it a good thing I don't have to decide till I'm through High School? I'd like it fine if it didn't mean being away from Port Underwood so much."

Nathaniel said, "It isn't easy. But don't forget, whichever way you decide, you'll find great compensations, so no looking back with regrets. I never heard that Camilla had any, yet even at sixteen she had great audiences in Sydney. You'd find a lot of creative satisfaction in a concert career, Phemy, though of course you'd miss this." He turned to Julia. "She's the only one who inherited Camilla's voice, and with it, too, of course, is blended the natural harmony of Maori singing. She has a superb gift."

Julia had realised that. This had been an enchanted hour. She said, eyes sparkling, "Oh, you mean she too is a descendant of Camilla's and Ephraim's?"

"Oh, yes, the first Euphemia married Camilla's third son. We're related by blood. Did you think the 'Uncle' and 'Grandpa' just courtesy titles? Of course it's more like cousins twice removed by now, but 'Uncle' and Grandpa' are easier."

Julia felt refreshed, not tired when she went to bed.

Her eyes met her mirrored eyes. She thought of the budding wistaria on the whalebones, of Adam standing beneath them. "He called me Julia," she thought. Then an awareness crept into the mirrored eyes. Something she wouldn't recognise. She turned hastily away. That was foolish, truly foolish.

How stupid *could* one get? This was nothing, *nothing* more than a reluctance to say good-bye to the most beautiful setting she had ever lived in, in a home where the harmony of gracious living had lasted for nearly a century and a half.

5

DESPITE the moments of real remorse that gnawed at Julia for having caused such trouble, happiness enveloped every hour, even the household chores were glamorised because she was treading historic ground . . . using dishes Camilla had used, seeing the same views out of the small-paned windows that Camilla had loved, even using her recipes. To read that delicate, well-formed handwriting gave Julia real delight.

How *could* one be so conscious of someone who had been dust so many decades? Yet wasn't this in itself the timelessness of a world that had known the Resurrection? Wasn't this the answer to those who feared that death might be finality? How could it be, when every spring Camilla's camellias bloomed so lavishly, thought Julia, bringing in a vaseful for the kitchen table? When every summer her roses would scent the air; when autumn would mean the gathering-in of her tawny-coated pears, and the pine-logs burning in the great open fire-places would spread their incense through the whole house to remind them that Camilla had got the Captain to plant them for posterity, to warm descendants yet unborn? When through the rooms sounded the mellow cadences of Phemy's voice that was Camilla's voice, and Phemy's elfin laughter that Nathaniel vowed was so like the mischievous chuckles of Camilla's great old age?

A lovely, lovely world. How wicked of Julia to wish it might be a week before the slip was cleared. She disciplined herself a dozen times a day to smother the unworthy thought.

She jumped guiltily when Adam turned from the phone to say: "Just had a report that it may be a day longer before they get the road clear. The men had to be diverted to something with higher priority, and they want to make a good job of this, and the ones near Rarangi."

Reprieve . . . one more golden day to be added to the others. Though, as it turned out, the reprieve day could scarcely be called golden. They woke to a howling southerly and the first of the lambs.

They were all out helping. Adam said, "Scrap meals today, Miss Merrill. I'm darned glad you aren't a novice at the lambing. Your brother must've been mad to turn you down. I guess you've often helped him?"

"Oh, yes and Robert too. My sister-in-law, Denise, was ill for months. They're up by Dannevirke. We all love Denise and we were lucky she came through. It's the oddest thing. Both Mum and Dad were city-born and bred and so were we, but both boys returned to the land — I *think* it was a return . . . something born in them."

Adam nodded. "But their farming will be a bit easier. On the flat — or almost flat — you can go for miles with ewes in trouble, in those latest sheep-hoisting type trucks."

"Yes, it's certainly harder here . . . but just look at those two girls dragging that trolley up the hill, and Phemy, with only Luke to help her. Can you spare me now? I'd better get away up with them, all the boxes with lambs must be full."

"I'll come up with you. I reckon Grandpa ought to have a break, but he doesn't like to be studied too much. A hot drink would be good."

He turned to call the old man, further down the hill. "Come on, you toughie, we're having a cuppa. Come on, Julia." He held out a hand to her, which she accepted gratefully. He grinned, "I can't possibly go on calling you Miss Merrill . . . we haven't time today, so make it Adam, would you?"

The kitchen was warm and steamy. They'd dropped their wet windcheaters on the verandah. Adam put the barricade up and they had lambs, in various stages of weakness, on sacks close to the stove that purred, a very welcome sight, and kept kettles singing.

They had hot coffee and the scones Phemy had made before going out with the others.

The kitchen floor was covered with mud and the dishes from breakfast, still unwashed, were stacked on the bench. Adam had decreed that. The girls had, as they said, "simply closed the beds up", and gone out too. Just as well Miriam wasn't here to see the mess! Certainly you had to have domestic method most of the time in farming life, but times like this, house-pride was out. The main thing was to save all the lambs possible, getting life back into them with warmth and milk.

They wasted no time in getting back to the paddocks, Julia had a huge soup-pot on the back of the stove and there was plenty of cold mutton and bread. Tupuna Homestead always kept bread in the deep-freeze. Tonight she would contrive some sort of dinner. No frills, just hot plain food. Perhaps she would just scrub the potatoes and bake them in their jackets. Every moment saved was precious.

Outside, the wind lashed their faces as they stepped off the verandah on to the beach-stones. There was ice in it now, sleety and horrible. Adam groaned. "All that marvellous weather, mild and balmy, came too soon."

The lambs that were born quickly and without complications and got a drink from their mothers immediately were all right in the main . . . but Julia resented the fact that they had not been born into a world of sunshine, with little warm zephyrs and smiling paddocks. Neverthe-less, this farm had plenty of shelter-belts and copsy clumps of trees, with sturdy hedges to the paddocks.

The sheep were so patient, mostly, seeming to sense you were trying to help them, but some, after their lambs were born, were just plain stupid, said Julia, with heat, trying to get a ewe to stand while her quite robust lamb tried to drink. "This one, confound her, has no more idea than — than a ballet-dancer — what her her primary responsibility is. Look at her . . . trotting off every time that poor little thing tries to nuzzle. Talk about instinct and Mother Nature . . . she hasn't got a shred!"

Adam came up, held the ewe forcibly till the lamb had had a good drink. "You make me laugh, Julia."

She laughed back. "Well, if you can laugh on a day like this, you've sure got what it takes to be a sheep-farmer. Oh, Adam, quick . . . that one's lambing over the edge of the creek!"

Incredible to think that in a few days these slimy, cold weak creatures would be fluffy white lambs, gambolling with pure delight in living. They would be on verdant pastures instead of these wind-lashed hillsides, with the trees bending agonisingly away from the force of the gale beating up the coast. The bay below was blotted out with a curtain of grey rain.

After a hurried lunch they drove round the road a little distance into a much more level paddock. Here the truck, with its contraption for lifting the weaker, rain-sodden ewes that needed attention at the farm, was of more use.

"Now, don't rush it," Adam cautioned the girls — Luke was working with Grandpa nearer the house — "and whatever happens, be sure you get the right raddle on mother and lamb. If I find a lamb without raddle on it, watch out! We've enough on our hands without trying to do any matching. As it is we've far too many orphans and too many ewes deprived of lambs. We're going to have a fine time getting them to foster."

It was the second load when Julia was dashing into the kitchen to scrub the potatoes when she heard Adam's voice raised. "Here's a lamb without raddle! I told you to be careful. This is a real go. Now sort through the ewes and find out which one is marked but hasn't a lamb to match."

Julia decided she'd better forget the potatoes. She came dashing out, prepared, if possible, to divert Adam's wrath from the girls, but heard him say, "Oh, it's all right, girls . . . you've been bricks . . . I'm madder'n a swarm of bees, but you've worked like Trojans, and this is the first slip-up."

They began sorting them out, then Julia gave a shout as they reached the last one. "We've got a lamb too many . . . these are all paired off." She gazed despairingly at the ewes. "One must have had the second of twins on the way up . . . without as much as a grunt. We were in the back with them. Now we really are in trouble. No way of telling which is whose! Adam, it's pretty weak and slimy. Should I bath this one?"

He nodded. "Okay. Practically speaking, it's hardly worth the trouble when we've got our hands more than full, but I suppose it would break your heart not to try?"

She nodded and disappeared with the lamb. Even after the hot bath it didn't appear to have much life. She put it in a box on a piece of sheepskin and scrubbed up thoroughly to do the potatoes. She took a plate of chops out of the fridge. She called out: "Don't disappear. I'll make you some tea."

Adam came in, saw what she was at with the big casserole, said, "Look, don't bother peeling carrots and onions . . . this is the moment to scatter tinned vegetables and dried onions round that meat, we aren't looking for anything Ritzy. And we can just have preserved fruit and ice-cream for a pudding. There's a storehouse past the wash-house door. Mum did a full lot from the orchard, just for times like these. Mum's like you, likes the outside work."

Julia, slicing fat off the chops at speed, said, "Then why is she going into town? I mean Grandpa and Granny Dare aren't."

"She's doing it because she believes in young couples being on their own, for one thing."

With a jerk, the thought of Miriam was back.

"And for another thing, even though we've a road into Picton now, and the kids can be home every weekend, Mum thinks it would be wonderful for them, if instead of boarding they could just live with her and Dad through the week. Antoinette is thrilled, of course. And Picton is not like a city, it's just a small town, poised on the inlet of the sounds, a happy tourist town, and Dad may even run sightseeing launches."

Grandpa Dare came in, after scraping mud off, and his eyes held sheer affection as they beheld Julia. "My, but we were lucky you happened along, pulling your weight both inside and out."

Adam and Julia turned away from each other self-consciously.

They sat down to huge slices of bread-and-cheese this time and some of Miriam's incomparable fruit-cake.

"What a marvellous cook she must be," said Julia, in a conciliatory gesture.

"Ay, she's all that," said Grandpa dryly, but Adam said, lifting his head, "I believe the wind's abating, and the rain too."

It had. When they emerged they didn't have to thrust against any force. The world was bedraggled, but already the bay was visible.

"Thank heaven for that," said Adam. "With a bit of luck we may get a good day tomorrow."

Fortunately before he even finished speaking, he had gone striding off, so didn't hear Susanna say: "With a bit more luck we might even get another slip."

Julia swung round on her. "Susanna, it's bad enough . . . don't make it any worse. Your grandfather is past being tactful. But *you* needn't rub it in. Miriam will have qualities that are apparent only to Adam. And he could be eating his heart out right now."

Susanna said, giggling, "What, *Adam*? I don't reckon he's given her a thought today, except perhaps to thank his lucky stars that you were here and not her!"

"That's just not within the bounds of possibility," snapped Julia. "Not the strongest and most efficient land-girl could make up to a man for the loss of his true love."

The girls collapsed with laughter. At that moment Adam, outside, yelled out, "Come on, come on! What's the hold-up? I want to go up to the far paddock again."

As they piled in Adam said suspiciously, "I didn't like the sound of all that. You're laughing at me. What's the joke?"

Phemy laid a hand on his sleeve. "You're

not the joke, Uncle. Julia is. Some of her ideas are just too quaint for words."

When they came back for the final time the weakest lamb was on its feet staggering round most uncertainly, its wool drying out. The kitchen was steamy and full of the sound of bleating, hungry lambs.

Adam said, "Well, I'm fair clemmed myself, but I'm not making all that much fuss about it. Listen to them!" He groaned. "And I suppose we're going to have to feed them before we have anything ourselves!"

Julia said, "Well, if you could eat dinner while all that clamour is going on, I couldn't, but I tell you what . . . let's all have a bowl of soup, then feed the lambs, then have the rest of the meal."

Grandpa Dare seconded that, the others all concurred, and they scrubbed up and mopped up their soup.

Julia said, "I'll fix that floor first before we start. Isn't it a pity they're not born house-trained?"

But they accomplished the feeding speedily, because of the condition of the lambs, due to the earlier use of the Lamb Reviver. This had been invented by a

Southland doctor, with a farmer son. It precluded any weak lamb from choking by drawing milk back into its lungs and had saved thousands of lives, not only in New Zealand. Once, the lamb had been revived by the mixture fed direct into its stomach by the tube, they were able to suck on the ordinary bottles. When it was done and the lambs in the heated boxes attended to and the more frisky ones put into the wash-house, Julia said, "Now, Adam, when Grandpa comes out of the bath, you have one and sit down and relax while I go on with the dinner, it's very nearly ready."

He looked at her. Amazing how that dark-a-vised face could gentle. "No, you're going in next. In the cottage bathroom. I'll go in as soon as the kids are finished with this one. I think one's under the shower and one's in the bath so they won't be long. I'll set the table while you're having yours. Then you can just dish out." He held up a hand as she went to demur. "No, Julia! It's a tradition of the Dares . . . if you can call it by so grand a term . . . if the women work outside, the men give them a hand when they come in."

Julia looked up at him. "That's a very good tradition. All right, I can hear Grandpa coming out now." She crimsoned to the roots of her hair. "I mean I can hear Mr. Dare. I'll be off, then." She seized a couple of towels from the cylinder cupboard and beat a hasty retreat.

Oh, the hot water was good! Julia lay back and revelled in it. There was a warmth about her heart. Even though she had caused such a disruption in the Dare household, they wouldn't — even Adam — remember her solely as the cuckoo-in-the-nest. They would give her credit for having pulled her weight.

It felt good to be clean again and dry and . . . even attractive. Julia slipped into a button-through green corduroy frock of Antoinette's. Antoinette must be a little bit slimmer than she was, so it fitted rather neatly, but was charming. There was a golden scarf to fill in the neckline, threaded through slots. Above it Julia's chestnut hair curled a little round her forehead and ears because all day the ends had been wet with rain and she had towelled it vigorously. Because she was deadly tired, her face was whiter than usual, and the pepper-pot freckles stood out more than ever across the bridge of her nose. But the hazel eyes had a sparkle in them that had never been there before.

She donned a nylon smock in primrose to protect the frock and went into the living-room. Adam had even put her vase of camellias in the centre of the table and had used a clean white cloth. Julia fingered it. "That's rather a good cloth for everyday use, isn't it?"

He nodded. "I expect it is, but I think it's good to use these things once in a while. It's only been used for parties till now. It came across with Camilla, but had been her mother's. It was convent-made in Ireland."

Julia looked at it with reverence, rolled the edge between her fingers, marvelled at the infinitesimal stitches. "I shall launder it with the utmost care," she said.

Soon they were all gathered, tubbed and in clothes no longer bedraggled.

Adam had set a huge tureen of Camilla's on the table and filled it with bottled pears from her trees, and he had whipped cream till it could stand by itself and set it in a green glass bowl with a fluted white glass edge, that was an heirloom, Julia was sure.

They were using the horn-handled knives that had been Captain Ephraim's, and ancient blue-and-white plates. Julia only hoped there would be no breakages.

They were so hungry they ate the jacket potatoes, skin and all, rich with butter, and nobody left a drop of gravy on their plates and all took two helpings of pears.

They did another round of feeding, got themselves some reading matter and gathered round the fire, ready to relax.

With the promptness of a stage-cue, the lights went out.

The grown-ups groaned, the children were delighted.

Adam said, "I can't understand why kids think this is fun! I'm all for the convenience of electricity. We've come to depend upon it so."

Esther said, as they groped round, "I expect it's just like I said to Julia, we like things happening."

Julia knew alarm. Their uncle was astute. She gave a warning kick in Esther's direction.

Adam said, "Ouch! Mind where you're going somebody." Then he added: "What does she mean? I mean *what* happenings?"

Julia said quickly, "Oh, they meant things like storms in the midst of lambing and so on . . . look, do find the candles, I've got a cake in that electric oven and I want to see if it's at the stage where I can safely transfer it to the fuel stove."

It created the necessary diversion. Adam said, "Cake? Gosh, you're a glutton for punishment, aren't you? When in the world did you find time to put it in?"

"While you were bathing. Oh, it's not the sort of cake that would win a prize at a show. I made it double and put it in a roasting-dish. It's just a plain old gingerbread, the sort you can make quickly. You just boil the milk and syrup and butter and soda and pour it with some beaten eggs into the flour and sugar."

"And ginger, I presume." There was a smile in Adam's voice. "I do hope, now that you've stimulated my salivary glands, you haven't forgotten the ginger."

Phemy said to Luke in answer to a query, "He means it sounds mouth-watering."

"Well, why didn't he say so? Julia, will we be able to have some for supper?"

"Goodness no, it mustn't be eaten till tomorrow. It will be too hot to eat."

Adam scraped a match and set it to the first of the candles. "We *will* have it for supper. It's a tradition of the Dares, always to eat the first of their gingerbread hot."

Esther sounded suspicious. "I never heard of that one before."

"Of course you didn't. I just started it myself this very moment. After all, traditions have to start somewhere. Ours don't all have to begin with Camilla or Ephraim. Anyway, don't you fancy hot gingerbread?"

Julia had the oven door open and a delectable odour issued forth.

"I should just say I do," said Esther.

Julia reflected that if Adam *was* breaking his heart, she had to hand it to him that he did not allow it to cast a cloud over the family circle. Or was it just that in his heart of hearts he knew it had been only a flare-up and would not last?

Fortunately the cake had been in the oven for almost its full time, and the transfer wouldn't do it much harm, but she warned them she was not to blame if it sank in the middle. "And you're only to have one piece each hot, because I made it to help out for snacks tomorrow. I get very tired of those tins of bought biscuits."

Adam said, "Oh, I should have told you. There's a separate small deep-freeze unit in the far store-room. Miriam spent two days stocking it up with all sorts of biscuits in bags, all professionally decorated like a cake-shop in town."

Oh, how foolish of Julia. She felt quite flat. Served her right . . . she'd felt almost proud of herself today . . . helping Adam. She knew she'd been as good as a man out in the paddocks, but Miriam had prepared against the lambing too . . . in the expert way in which she'd been trained. The family might feel she was not the wife for Adam because they were all tarred with the one brush . . . they were adventurous, like Camilla, and they liked the outside work, but Miriam had her points.

Besides, Adam might prefer a wife who would have everything ready when he came in, the table set, the silver winking back, a dinner that would please the eye as well as the palate, not just chops slapped into a casserole with tinned vegetables.

Julia could see it all . . . Miriam's cool perfection, the blonde hair smoothed back into groomed elegance, the faint perfume, the deeply blue eyes, the rose-tinted cheeks, not a freckled tomboy who had worked beside Adam all day, reeking of sheep, smeared with mucus, blood and manure . . . wet hair clinging to shiny cheeks, even torn slacks where she'd negotiated a fence with less than her usual skill. Oh, yes, for a man there would be compensations . . .

Adam said, "I just wish we knew how long this was going to last. If it's off all night we'll have to bring those lambs in from the boxes on the verandah. I hate to think what the kitchen would be like to-morrow morning. And they'll bleat half the night. Well, I might get some information out of the powers-that-be later, provided the phone's not out too."

At that moment it rang. He went across. His voice, even though surprised, instantly warmed. "Oh, hullo . . . this is marvellous. How wonderful to just hear your voice."

Julia felt as if someone had winded her. How stupid! This was what she had longed for . . . a making-up, the olive-branch.

He went on, "But how have you managed to get to the phone, Granny?"

Granny!

Julia had another queer feeling.

"On crutches? You old goer! I take it then that the infection that kept you in bed is gone? Good. Look, I'm terribly sorry the road's still blocked. This storm won't have improved it, either. But as soon as possible we'll get you home. No, we're fine. Yes, we've started lambing, but Phemy was here too and the girls all pitched in. You should just see the kitchen, it's full of bleating lambs. We only lost five, but unfortunately we did lose a few more ewes. Could have been worse. . . .

"Oh, she's managing fine. She filled up that little deep-freeze with stacks of cookies last week . . . yes, it's something to have a professional around. That sort of thing is right up Miriam's street. Don't worry about a thing, we're well catered for, believe me."

In the flickering candlelight, Julia saw the children's eyes grow round. They evidently regarded their uncle as a sort of George Washington, as one brought up in the Pilgrim Fathers tradition of truthfulness, and here he was, lying his head off, letting Granny think Miriam was at the helm. Well, it was understandable. He didn't want to worry her, neither would he feel capable of explaining there was another woman in the house, a stowaway at that, and that his engagement was broken, temporary though that state might be.

Adam talked on for a bit, then said, "Yes, I'll call Grandpa now. Just watch those crutches, Granny. I know you . . . you'll get over-confident. Just make haste slowly, as you're so fond of telling us. Bye-bye, darling."

He met his grandfather halfway across the room, seized his arm, said quite unnecessarily, "Let her go on thinking that Miriam is here and doing fine."

Nathaniel was sweet to his wife. Even the way he said Lydia gave Julia the instant impression of a man speaking to his true love. And he was very clever, answered all the questions as obliquely as possible. Yes, it had been a long day, but the storm was over. The forecast was good. They'd had a great meal, had been supplied with hot soup and fresh scones all day, and right this moment the spicy odour of ginger-bread was wafting through the door.

They all burst out laughing when he returned to his deep chair by the fire, the children having by now got over their initial shock.

Adam said, "Well, we can't play Scrabble tonight, or Monopoly. And if we want to read I'll have to fill those lamps. One isn't enough to read by. That's my fault, only Granny is the one who always sees they're refilled. I ran out of kerosene the other day and pinched the lot out of the other lamps. Grandpa give that fire a poke. Children, draw a bit closer. Grandpa will tell Julia about Betty Guard, the famous child-bride, who lived at Kakapo Bay. One of her grandsons lives there yet, and another grandson at Oyster Bay at the far end of their property. And great-great-grand-children. Betty is even more famous than our own Camilla . . . after all, Betty is in the New Zealand history books . . . Camilla was just an entry in Captain Ephraim's log-book."

Nathaniel stirred the fire to a blaze. The candles flickered and flared, dancing in shadow patterns on the children's intent faces. They had heard this story many times before, but still loved it, even when they shivered over the more gruey bits.

"Betty Parker was born in 1814 — the year before Waterloo! When she was thirteen, Captain Jackie Guard visited her parents' home in Sydney, Australia. Betty wasn't strong and Captain Jackie advocated a sea-voyage for her — in particular his next sealing trip to New Zealand. A month later Betty went aboard the *Waterloo* of which he was joint owner.

"In Cook Strait the ship struck a terrible storm and was being driven mercilessly towards the extreme tip of the South Island. When all seemed hopeless, they suddenly found themselves in calm water. They had been carried by some tidal current into the sheltered waters of Tory Channel leading into the Queen Charlotte Sounds. Betty was enchanted with Te Awaiti, which means the Little Channel, but she called it her Fair Haven. I'm afraid the whalers who came were too lazy to pronounce the Maori name properly and it became known locally as Tar White.

"Captain Guard was excited to find whales passing up the channel to their warmer winter quarters and lost no time in getting back to Port Jackson . . . Sydney harbour . . . to gather together a whaling crew and gear, returning to Te Awaiti to establish the first of many shore-whaling stations on the treacherous New Zealand coast. His son, John, born there was the first white child born in the South Island. Later he moved his family to Kakapo Bay in Port Underwood." Nathaniel twinkled at Julia. "Guess who was the mother?"

She was as starry-eyed as the children, lips parted a little, in eagerness. "You don't mean — but you do, don't you? That he returned and married Betty?"

"Aye, you've got it. Two years later, when she was fifteen. She had fallen in love with the young, black-bearded giant and she was an adventurous lass, gay and gallant, and she took on a life which must have been vastly different from her life in Sydney. She thought nothing of sailing to Sydney, with Captain Jackie, to have her babies baptised. In 1834, with her three-year-old son, John, and her daughter Louise, who was just a baby at the breast, their ship, the *Harriett*, was wrecked on the Taranaki Coast in the North Island.

"They all got ashore, but most tragically were set upon by a band of hostile Maoris and twelve of the crew, including Betty's own brother, were killed. Betty herself was tomahawked, but she was wearing an enormous tortoiseshell comb in her hair — you can see it in a showcase at Blenheim library some time — and it deflected the blow. The story goes that the chief's wife intervened as the next blow was descending, though the Government Encyclopaedia of New Zealand states it was through Matakatea's intervention that the rest of them were spared after the first hasty killings. Wiremu Kingi Matakatea was a high-born Taranaki war chief, who much later embraced Christianity.

"The Maoris agreed to hold them till a ransom was paid and Captain Jackie Guard was allowed to go to Port Nicholson — Wellington — to arrange ransom. This was accomplished and Captain Morris in the *Joseph Weller* agreed to take the ransom, but they were blown far off course and had to make for Port Jackson. Imagine that . . . imagine Guard's feelings . . . to be right across the Tasman, knowing his wife and children were prisoners! It roused great sympathy and aid in Sydney and the Governor dispatched the HMS *Alligator* to rescue them. Trouble ensued. The crew were handed over, but Betty and the children were being held in a distant *pa*, and the captain of the *Alligator* took a Maori as hostage. Betty and her children were finally handed over, but tempers were hot, with the crew members recalling the fate of their friends, and shots were fired on the Maoris on the beach. It was regarded by the authorities as a merciless retribution and it stirred up great protests and an inquiry. Some of the cannonballs used were dug out of the cliffs later, and are also displayed in Blenheim library.

"Betty was only twenty years old when this happened, and had survived six months' imprisonment, but had to live with the memory of having seen her young brother killed and eaten.

"But she came back to the beauty of Kakapo Bay. Little John, incredible as it may seem, lived on into the era of the motor-car and the aeroplane, dying at a great age in 1920.

"At Kakapo Bay Betty created a garden of great beauty, even as our Camilla created one for us here. I still see links with Sydney there, especially in spring when you can watch our honey-eating *tuis* flying down for nectar in the red *waratah* blooms. We'll take you to Kakapo some day. You'll see how Betty too brought culture and antiques to a remote outpost of the world, the first white woman to live in the South Island, with John the first white child born there. Emily and Helen Guard will show you Betty's beautiful china and glass, and her French prints. You must go into Blenheim, Julia, and see Captain Jackie's giant cutlass, his top-hat and flint-lock pistols.

"We often wonder if Captain Ephraim's cutlass could be as big. He too was a giant of a man. Though perhaps I was such a small boy he seemed gigantic. Perhaps we shall never find the sword. But we always hope."

"Days of romance!" said Julia, sighing.

Susanna said, "Not only in those days, Julia. Other Guard brides have come from over the sea. Helen Guard is a Scots-woman, one who, in her business life, had worked in London's West End. She too came to the Bay when there was no access except by sea or bridle-path, and not so long ago, in the sixties, Betty's great-grandson brought a bride from Sydney too. At least, she came here, seeking her Port Underwood connections . . . Elaine belongs to a distant branch of the family. And she married Edward Guard and stayed in the Bay."

Julia was enchanted. She had forgotten her weariness, the trouble she had caused, the fact that soon she must go from here, never to return. "And I'll be able to meet them . . . how wonderful . . . for once I've got enough romance to satisfy me."

The story-telling was over, the ginger-bread cut and eaten, spicy and warm, and a delicious languor was stealing over everybody. The children said good-night, kissed their great-grandfather and went off to bed.

Nathaniel said, looking after them, "Even the girls won't be talking till the wee sma's tonight . . . if you know what I mean. Nothing like good hard physical work and fresh air!"

Adam choked. "Fresh? It was fresh all

right, spleet-new from the South Pole where they manufacture the coldest winds in the world. We'll sleep the sleep of sheer exhaustion tonight."

Nathaniel said, "Well, I'll help you with the last round, then I'll away to my bed. Even the fact that Lydia isn't beside me tonight won't keep me awake. I sleep well enough once I get off, but oh, I do miss her reading out bits from her book. We've done it for more than fifty years."

Adam said, "Oh, Julia and I will do the rounds. You get away off, Grandpa. You stood up to it like a forty-year-old today. I hope I'm like you at your age."

Grandpa Dare began to demur, then suddenly accepted it. He came across, dropped an unexpected kiss upon Julia's cheek and went out of the door. Julia knew a rise of tears, blinked them back, put up an appreciative hand to her cheek and said, "Oh, isn't he a sweetie?"

Adam's voice was dry. "Well, to you he is. He can be cantankerous, especially if he doesn't like someone. But if he likes you then you're his friend for life."

Julia ignored what she knew was a reference to Miriam and said lightly enough, "Well, in my case it can't be for life, only for a few days. I'm just a temporary rift in the lute, and soon forgotten."

She didn't know what the ensuing silence meant. But she was glad Adam didn't murmur polite and insincere denials.

He said in a normal tone, finally, "I ought to be unselfish and tell you to get off too, you've had a gruelling day, but honestly, I just can't face all those lambs myself. Listen to them . . . getting perky, just when we're all in."

They fed the lambs by lamplight and stoked the range with wet slack so it would last till morning, put the old-fashioned iron guard round it, arranged dry sacks on the floor and turned to leave the kitchen, at which moment the lights sprang on.

"Thank goodness," said Adam. "I was scared the fault might have been local and they'd not have been able to repair it till the road gave them access. If it had lasted, the deep-freeze stuff would have gone off." Then, laughing at his own contrariness, "Though I admit candlelight has its charm."

As they said good-night in the passage,

Julia wondered if his philosophical behaviour would drop from him the moment he was alone, so she added, "Well, the lights are restored and no doubt the road will be too, soon, and — other things could start coming right, Mr. Dare. I expect that, like your grandfather, you're too tired to lie awake mulling things over, but once you get me off the property and back to the North Island, I'm sure Miriam will realise there was nothing to it."

His face immediately hardened. "Just a little ray of sunshine, aren't you? A sort of Pollyanna, always thinking you can set the world to rights. It will take more than you to sweeten this situation, believe me!" And he stalked off to his own room.

It was just as well that Julia too was tired to the point of exhaustion.

6

SHE decided next morning, as soon as she woke, that she'd better not try any more reconciliation. She only made him madder still. Perhaps Miriam wasn't the only one to sulk.

Except for broken and battered shrubs and the waifs in the kitchen there was little trace of yesterday's storm, because here rain drained into the bay from the steep hillsides.

There were one or two casualties from the coldness of the night and they had a heavy morning attending to the ewes still lambing, but nothing seemed as desolate as the day before when every step had been a battle with the elements.

Phemy's father and mother were attending to the sheep on that side of the hill, some their own, some belonging to the Dares, because they were not going out after fish.

It was still extremely hectic and Julia took as many short cuts as possible with

207

the meals. By night Adam had heard from someone in one of the other bays that work had started on the slips and they saw a few examples of damage in other parts of Marlborough, on TV.

Julia asked Adam how long they would take. He said a couple of days probably. She looked out of the window to the darkening landscape with never a glimmer of light to be seen from here. Further down the hillside you could see tiny lights far, far down the coast towards Kaikoura. She wanted to imprint upon her mind's eye every changing mood, every view, something to remember for ever. She wandered out to the quarterdeck verandah. . . .

How sad to find Eden and be banished from it for ever. She thought of something . . . she might never have seen it at all! How ghastly.

She thumped her fist on the verandah rail and said aloud, quite violently, "So I'm glad . . . glad in spite of all, even if I ought not to be!"

"Did you call out?" asked Adam, suddenly materialising beside her, in the cool spring dusk.

She jumped, accused quickly: "You

208

startled me . . . I might have fallen over the rail."

He laughed, said callously, "Well, you wouldn't have broken any bones. You'd have landed in Granny's wallflowers. Look at them, blooming already under the impression that it's summer, though they're a bit battered by yesterday. Trouble was, we had too mild a winter. Now everything could be nipped back. Anyway, I asked you what you said?"

"You didn't. You asked had I called out."

"Goodness, that's splitting hairs. What *did* you say?"

"I was talking to myself, so I shan't tell you."

He seized her and turned her to face him. "You're on the defensive. Why?"

She said calmly, "I don't suppose anyone wants their own private communings overheard. It makes one self-conscious."

"I suppose so. But sometimes it's only in our own thoughts that we're completely honest. I like to hear kids talking to themselves. I often used to listen-in on Luke when he was tiny. He'd be playing outside with his toy tractors and trucks and saying all manner of things. It somehow added up to happiness. And happiness is a good thing shared."

Julia felt a stab of nostalgia and she uttered a tiny sound, quite revealing, though she did not know it, of pain.

He looked at her sharply, "What's the matter? You're upset. Look, though I was as cross as nobody's business with you when you first appeared and that you may tie to, I'm now ready to admit that you must have gone through a most gruelling time . . . getting into the wrong car, realising you were in some remote area with a strange man . . . I expect you had all sorts of purely feminine fears . . . getting trounced by Miriam and myself, and involved in a most appalling row . . . and now cooped up here by landslips. Are you feeling a bit of reaction? Feeling strange . . . and lost?"

Strange? Oh, no, never strange. How could she when she had discovered more beauty than she had ever known? Lost? Oh no. Not with all these dear people around her . . . Nathaniel with his stories of the robust past, Susanna, Esther, Luke, Phemy, with her golden voice and elfin laughter, even the ones she'd never meet, like Antoinette, whose clothes she wore, and Lydia, the seller of fine purple . . . and Camilla and Ephraim. Was she homesick? Oh, how could she be when this had been a coming home! As if you'd found what you longed for all your life!

He said, "You've gone into a daydream. Come on . . . *were* you feeling lost?"

She gave a crooked smile. "In a way, yes. It's just that . . . well, I've not seen my father and mother for two years and those were the sort of things Dad used to say. Like happiness being a good thing shared. It took me back to his quoting someone, I don't know who — saying there's no duty so underrated as the duty of being happy. That happiness ought to rub off on other people. But that last bit was Dad, Stephen Merrill. I miss him horribly."

Adam said slowly, "Where is he? I sort of assumed you'd lost your parents when you spoke of going up to your brother."

"Mother and Dad are in Canada. Dad's a Trade Commissioner there. They'll be back some time next year and we'll be a family again."

His grasp on her arm was warm. It ought to have been comforting. It wasn't. It was disturbing.

He said, "You said: 'So I'm glad . . . glad in spite of all, even if I ought not to be!' What did you mean, Julia? Did you — "

She had to interrupt quickly. "Nothing that you would know anything about. After all, Adam Dare, I did have a life of my own before I got snarled up in your affairs. I-I-I was thinking back."

He smiled, mirthlessly. "You've been — rather a brick trying to patch up things here. Is it anything I could help with . . . advise on?"

She drew away from him as if he had put a finger on a sore spot. "No, no, you couldn't help. But thank you."

His tone was wry. "I don't blame you for not wanting advice from me . . . I've not managed my own affairs very well. That's what you mean, isn't it?"

"I rather think you're jumping to conclusions . . . there are other problems in life besides loving and falling in love."

She had to say it, because it was imperative that Adam Dare should never know why she had uttered that to herself. It had been a moment of revelation to Julia, a painful one.

He said, turning from her and putting both hands on the rail, "There's a difference, isn't there . . . between falling in love and loving ?"

There was a bleat behind them. They both swung round. Julia, grateful for the interruption, scooped up a small woolly body against her. Early this morning it hadn't had much life in it, but now it had had enough vigour to somehow get over the barricade. She said, laughing, "The multitudes await us. I think they're fair clemmed. We'd better stop blethering about love and go and feed them."

By the time that chore was done, the headlands and bays were folded in darkness and the children wanted to play dominoes. Nathaniel dozed in his chair. Julia had a sense of timelessness. Had Captain Ephraim ever dozed in his chair while Camilla played dominoes with her children, these same worn dominoes ? Those would be the nights when she was glad his ship was safely harboured, and the house, smaller then, would be shuttered against the winter storms. What stories had been told on those nights? Had Captain Ephraim, rousing, gathered them about him, talking of Cape Cod and early American days . . . had Camilla recounted tales of Sydney, the concerts she had sung for, the soirées and outings in the bush, the gaiety of the young colony? Had there been tales of bushrangers, of convicts, transported for, often, trifling offences? Did their spines chill deliciously?

That night Julia went to bed knowing that tomorrow would more than likely be the last full day she would spend at Whangatupuna. The next day she might be packing to leave. She set her alarm for a very early hour. She had a foolish whim to see the dawn come up. She had not yet seen a sunrise over Port Underwood. She wanted to imprint upon her memory every single aspect of life at the Bay of the Ancestors.

Odd how a place could take hold of you. Had it been that way with Camilla? Had she loved it as they said she had loved it, because of its own beauty, or simply because this was where Captain Ephraim wanted to live?

Suddenly Julia knew she had to face up to that moment of revelation on the quarterdeck verandah. She couldn't then, Adam had been there.

But she did now . . . it wasn't just the spell of this small Eden, the untouched, shining wonder of it . . . it was Adam himself. He was all she wanted in a man. This was why she had recoiled from the finality of promising Murray she would marry him . . . because there had been something lacking. They had so nearly drifted into that, and despite what her friends thought about Murray falling for Gillian, seeing in it a betrayal of herself, he had been right, had been courageous. He had found in Gillian what she, in turn, had found in Adam.

But in coming here she had caused the man she loved a great anguish. What was it the girls had said in one of those sessions when she just couldn't head them off? That Adam had never, till then, kept company with a girl . . . had been friendly with them all, nothing more. "Then," Susanna had said, "he was swept off his feet by Miriam. Honestly we'd never seen him like that before."

As she recalled it, jealousy struck at Julia for the first time in her life. Imagine having a man like Adam Dare feel like that about you? Didn't Miriam realise what a wonderful thing it was? Adam would bring all the riches of his heritage to his loving. His ancestors had all had strong natures, as the stories revealed . . . Elizabeth, the daughter-in-law of Camilla, disarming a drunken whaler who had knocked out Aaron, her husband, in a brawl on the foreshore, and had stood guard over his inert body, with the whaler's own knife, till help had arrived; Joshua, who had done without sleep for six days and nights once, when his wife, Constance, had tossed in the delirium of fever, who had brought her back, the story went, from the edge of the grave, by sheer will-power; Samuel, who had gone to Sydney to see his grandparents, Camilla's mother and father, and had saved *his* bride from a loveless marriage . . . Samuel who had sired Nathaniel. Oh yes, Adam would be a lover to stir a woman, if there was anything in her to stir!

But Miriam wanted to tame all that was inherited in Adam . . . wanted to have done with these relics of a glorious past. And yet, and yet, it was Miriam Adam loved. There might be a story in that too, because it was not ended yet. He was going to be unyielding in his stand. She *must* live in his home. He could not see it dropping into disuse, decaying, battered by storms and sun. Perhaps Miriam was just trying it on, to see if she could get her own way. But she might come to realise Adam was the type to be master in his own home, to decide his own destiny, a destiny that was inexorably entwined with this old, weather-beaten house.

Julia found she was lying with clenched fists, eyes open, tearless eyes, staring into the darkness. She felt so impotent; she longed to help. She tried to think of her father. Was this a time he would counsel waiting? "Time takes care of many things," he'd said once, "but it's hard to wait when you're young." But then again he had once said: "Though sometimes there's a tide to be taken at the full. This is where one must exercise judgment."

Above all, she wanted Adam to be happy. He must have been deeply hurt to have kept it up so long. The girls said that while Adam could lose his temper quickly, he apologised just as speedily. But this time he was in no mood to extend an olive-branch. Perhaps he had so idealised Miriam that nothing less than a return to that standard would satisfy him. Which meant that Miriam would have to admit she had been wrong, that she ought to have trusted him, believed him. But how to get Miriam to that state of mind?

This was all that concerned Julia. Between them, once reconciled, the two would have to compromise about the house. It had always been added to. Perhaps a couple of rooms that Miriam could furnish in modern style would satisfy her?

Julia decided that if she didn't get to sleep soon, she'd be in no trim for the dawn-watching, or the busy day ahead. Perhaps if she made herself a cup of tea, she might get drowsy. She got up, switched her light on silently, slipped into a turquoise dressing-gown of Antoinette's that matched the nightgown the girls had given her.

Antoinette had exquisite taste, that was evident. It had a ruched neckline that was a foam of lace ruffles and tiny loops of turquoise satin ribbon, and it flowed right from the shoulders to the hemline at the back, and in front the waist was caught with a tie from each side seam and knotted at the centre. The trailing hem was edged with the same ruffles. Julia must be an inch or so shorter than Antoinette.

She had begged the girls to get a plainer garment, she'd been scared something might happen to this.

The girls had giggled. Susanna said, "Mum just doesn't have plainer garments . . . oh, for outside she has utility things, but says just because we live at the back of beyond, it doesn't mean we have to be lacking in glamour. So she has ravishing undies."

She'd have to hold it up from the floor. Thank goodness you could boil an electric jug in the scullery. She wouldn't dare risk waking the lambs.

She went silently down the passage, turned a corner and stopped dead in astonishment. Light was streaming from Miriam's room. Yet it adjoined hers and she'd heard nothing. She pulled herself together. This was hardly the place for burglars. It would be those girls, possibly up to some hideous prank. She must get them back to bed without waking Adam.

She peered round the door and was met by the sight of Adam, still fully dressed, with all the drawers and wardrobe doors open, packing Miriam's clothes into two suit-cases he had upon the bed.

And at the very moment she peered in he crossed back with an armful of dresses on hangers and saw her before she could draw back. His scowl was instant proof that he'd wanted no witnesses to this.

Julia crimsoned. "Adam, I'm sorry. I — thought it might have been the girls, that something was wrong — I — "

He shrugged, throwing the things down. "I don't suppose I care. After all, you've been right in the centre of the donnybrook. And I'm not doing it by stealth, either. I just didn't want any comments from the kids. They're not exactly souls of tact. Besides, there's not much time during the day. The moment the mail-man gets through, I'm going to ask him, as a personal favour, to deliver these to Miriam's aunt."

Julia felt herself paling. "Oh, Adam, is that wise? It will add insult to injury. Oh, I don't mean *you* injured her. *I* did. But — look, you'll just have to meet each other halfway. I've been thinking. Perhaps you could compromise. There has to be give and take. I daresay every room that was added on here meant controversy, if I know men! How about suggesting to Miriam that she has a couple of rooms built on to furnish to her own taste? Say a sitting-room and a bedroom where a guest could stay? She could furnish it in modern style . . . startling colour schemes, if she wanted to, where it wouldn't clash with the old, faded, mellow tones of the rest of the house. Then she'd feel she was entertaining her friends in the sort of setting that suited her. I mean every girl has her own dreams of her own house."

He picked up the dresses, hauled the hangers out roughly, folded them anyhow and stuffed them into the cases, all without saying a word. He didn't have to, his very back registered offence.

She said in a small voice, "You think it's no business of mine?"

He swung round. "Well, is it?"

She lost her humility, jerked her chin up. "Yes, I think it is. *I* bust up the romance, so naturally I'm trying to conciliate!"

He said, his own chin upthrust, "You'll have no more success with me than you had with Miriam, except that I'm in a much worse position."

Julia was bewildered. "How? What — "

"*She* could slam a receiver down. *I* can't!"

"You've made your point," said Julia furiously, and turned to go.

She tripped over the trailing frills she had forgotten to lift! Flat on her face she sprawled. Her humiliation was complete.

He let her pick herself up.

He growled, "Anyway, you can't see the light from your room. What are you prowling about for?"

"Oh, just trying to sneak off with some of the heirloom silver! I certainly wasn't spying on you! I couldn't sleep and decided I'd make myself a cup of tea. But I'll just go back to bed now. You aren't worth lying awake worrying over!"

His brows twitched together. "Worrying? Over me? What do you mean?"

She said miserably, "What do you think I mean? I got myself horribly involved, caused a rift, in a household that's so sweet — apart from *you* — " she glared at him, "and Lydia can't come home, it's keeping her and Nathaniel apart. And if that wouldn't worry a girl, I don't know what would, though — " to her horror she hiccupped on what was almost a sob — "though why on earth I'm worrying about a great, unforgiving, unfeeling hulk of a man like you, I don't know!" and she flashed out of the room, holding her skirts high and almost running.

She flung off the gown, jumped into bed, and pulled the clothes over her head.

She couldn't believe it when ten minutes later there was a discreet tap on the door. It could only be Adam. She ignored it. He would think she was asleep and go away.

But he entered on the heels of his tap, switching on the light as he came, and he bore a small tray, with tea and biscuits on it.

Julia felt foolish as she emerged, ruffled, from under the blankets. She drew her knees up, tried to assume a dignity she did not feel and said: "Will you kindly leave my room at once!"

"I will very shortly," he said, moving the bedside lamp a little and putting his burden down.

Julia looked with loathing at the tea and said, "It would choke me!"

"It won't, you know. And I think you

might need something sweet to restore your loss of blood-sugar."

She said scathingly, "How can chocolate biscuits ease a guilty conscience?"

She looked up as she said it and caught him with one eyebrow up and one down, in a most whimsically rueful expression, and the next moment, to her annoyance, they were both laughing uncontrollably.

She said, sobering up, "But I don't *really* think it's funny. I don't *want* to laugh!"

He said, "Not to worry, Julia. Laughing is the best note of all for ending a fight on. When we were kids and Mum and Dad had a spat we always looked so hopefully for the first signs of Mum's mouth crumbling. She could never stay mad for long."

Julia said, "Then, if you admire that attitude, why don't you apply it to this quarrel? Yours and Miriam's. I feel you ought to be able to have a jolly good laugh over that awful moment when she snatched that rug off and found me. Then it would all be over."

He sighed. "Did anyone ever tell you that you are the most persistent and pig-headed girl in the world?"

"Yes, often. My brothers, and my boss and . . . but seriously, Adam — "

His eyes went so sombre he stopped her in mid-flow. The eyes met hers squarely. She could not look away from them. "Julia, you're so obsessed with your conscience that you haven't looked at this from all angles. Has it never occurred to you that by now Miriam *must* have realised I'd never have brought a girl here that way? So it means she just seized on that as an excuse — a dramatic excuse to break it off?"

Julia gasped, looked away uncertainly and surprised a strange look on Adam's face when she glanced back, a look of real anguish.

He said, turning away a little, "I didn't think you're even interested in that. You only want things restored so you need never have us on that troublesome conscience of yours. So that you won't feel twinges of remorse every time you think of Whangatupuna."

He went out of the room.

Thank goodness breakfasts were family affairs. A tête-à-tête would have been

225

unbearable. Not that Adam showed embarrassment. He was so ordinary, Julia felt she must have dreamed the whole thing. It was a pity he hadn't left the room just after their shared laughter, then she wouldn't have gone on to say what she had. Though in another way it was as well. She had been given a glimpse into Adam's real feelings. He wasn't just cross, and unforgiving, he was doubtful, and perhaps was giving Miriam the chance to think things over, and to be sure of her own feelings.

It was a glorious day with zephyrs that were spring-like and gentle so that all the lambs went outside. No doubt some would come in, later in the day, but in weather like this, perhaps fewer, and they could be accommodated on the verandah. Phemy stayed on and was a great help. She was just that much older than the others, and particularly good with Luke.

Phemy switched on the washing-machine and she and Julia hung the clothes out on the long lines near the orchard where they would blow in this clear, shining air and become scented with narcissi and flowering currant. They would be ironed and put away in cupboards redolent of verbena, since all generations since had adhered to Camilla's custom.

Today Julia had time to thaw steak out of the deep-freeze for a pie and tomorrow she would cook one of those large legs of wild pork, so that when the road was cleared and she was gone, they'd have something cooked to eat. She supposed they were fairly well used to fending for themselves, and till school reopened Phemy would be a great aid.

They joined the others outside at eleven. It was an uneventful day, yet it seemed to go by on remorseless feet . . . oh, if only one could slow the ticking of that big old clock! But Adam was very taciturn . . . or tired . . . or something. Perhaps putting into words his fears about Miriam's state of mind had depressed him?

But if there was something light and bright on TV it might cheer him up. She said, "What's on tonight?"

Adam replied, "Oh, I meant to tell you. I switched it on earlier. I think a valve's gone — no picture, no sound. We'll have to make do with radio."

"I hate to tell you," said Nathaniel, "but

that's gone bung too. And the batteries in the transistor are flat."

Luke said, "Gosh, they've not lasted long this time, have they? We're practically marooned. No radio, no TV, no papers. The rest of the world could be blown up and we wouldn't know."

Nathaniel said, "Back to the old days . . . now see how you like it."

They played Scrabble and Ludo, but somehow the games were flat. Everybody seemed dull tonight. Finally they all sat round the fire reading. Nathaniel fell asleep. Once he murmured quite audibly, "Lydia?" and his hand moved out as if seeking her. It gave Julia a pang.

She was quite glad next morning when Adam told her he could do without her help outside. You had to catch up with the household chores sooner or later, and anyway, perhaps she should stay away from him.

She defrosted the fridge and asked Adam at morning tea would he mind if she used up all the left-overs for lunch. "The fridge is just full of bits and pieces and it crowds it. There's not enough of anything to make an adequate dish for all, but if I warmed them up separately, it would save waste."

"Of course, of course, I told you we don't expect ritzy meals at lambing-time. Do what you like."

Just the same, she wanted to giggle when she called them in. She had contrived a curry out of the scrag-end of the leg of mutton for Adam and Nathaniel, had heated up the two chops left from the casserole for the twins, flaked the remains of the groper into a hard-boiled egg sauce for Phemy and Luke and was sitting down herself to a poached egg on toast.

Luke thought this was hilarious, like being able to pick from a menu, he said, and was pleased he was allowed what he'd fancied most. He was just starting to say grace, as commanded by his uncle, when the door swung open and in walked . . . Miriam!

It was a very effective entrance. All of them were struck dumb.

She stood there, leaning against the door jamb, surveying them with a sort of icy humour. She was dressed in a suit that was the last word in elegance. The blue and white checked skirt had a plain blue loose jacket with a long scarf collar tossed negligently over one shoulder.

Her complexion was flawless, delicately tinted, and the pearl bubbles at her ears set off the gold of her newly-set hair and the deeply shadowed blue of her eyes. A very womanly woman. One to stir the pulses.

She let her eyes roam round the table, at the conglomeration of dishes. Nobody had as much as picked up a fork. She said nothing and said it very eloquently.

She looked at Julia, then back to Adam, and said, "How odd. When you informed me you didn't even know your — er — stowaway — you said you'd have her back over the saddle and across the strait in no time. *But she's still here!*"

Julia flashed into speech. "So he would have, but the road's been closed. There were two lots of slips. As soon as it's open he's — " her voice trailed into silence as she realised it *must* now be open!

Miriam continued to look at her, smilingly, but not in a kindly way.

Julia, seeing Adam seemed incapable of speech, tried again.

"Don't you see, Miss Chillingham, we've just been too busy. Lambing . . . right through that storm. No one has let us know the road was open. No one has come through. We haven't heard a single car."

Miriam said coldly, "It was open before dark last night."

Julia's mouth fell open. She looked across at Adam. She expected him to say, "Oh, of all the luck, they must have slipped up on letting us know." But he didn't.

He said with a sort of devilishly provoking grin, "Oh, Julia is first-rate at lambing *and* at housekeeping. So when they let me know, I kept mum. Oh, sure they let me know, but Julia wasn't around when they rang. I didn't want her taking off hot-foot for Wellington. I packed your things last night and left a note in the mail-box to ask the mail-man to come down to see me. He'll be late, with so much mail banked up. I was going to get him to drop them in to you."

Julia got up agitatedly. "I knew nothing about this. I would never have consented. Adam, immediately after you've had your lunch you can take me over to Picton.

I can get that twenty to seven ferry. I'll be in Wellington by just after ten."

Adam said, "You'll do nothing of the kind. We can't do without a woman at the helm. You caused this, so you'll see it through. The girls go back to school next week, so even they won't be around and Granny is eating her heart out at not being able to come home. You came unasked, so you can jolly well stay. I'm not breaking into Dan and Antoinette's tour for anyone.

"I suppose you came for your clothes, Miriam. Right. Phemy, put our lunches in the oven. We'll get your cases right away. I presume that's all you came for?"

Miriam said, "Not quite all. I wanted to give you this."

She laid a small white box, a jeweller's box, in front of Adam's plate.

He rose, took it, pulled open the sideboard drawer and tossed it in among the teaspoons. "Thanks. Now we'll get your things."

Miriam said coolly, "Just a moment." She turned to Julia. "Did you mean that? Are you on the level? That you'd like to get the evening ferry across?"

"Yes. Definitely. Why?"

"Because in that case I'll take you." Her eyes dared Julia to refuse.

"Right. Thanks very much. That solves everything."

She went to cross the room. Luke burst into a roar of crying.

But Adam was in front of her in a flash. "You are *not* leaving, Julia. I *said* you weren't."

She looked at him firmly. "Of course I'm leaving. You can't keep me here by force."

She'd have liked to wipe that grin off his face with the back of her hand, but wouldn't give him that satisfaction.

He said, "Can't I? But that's exactly what I'm going to do. Like this." He seized her.

Julia swallowed, held herself very erect, said, "I find this ridiculous." She turned to Grandpa Dare, who hadn't uttered a word. "Mr. Dare, ask your grandson to release me, please?"

Nathaniel said crisply, "No. I want Lydia home. She's fretting. I knew the road was open too. Adam and I planned to see if the car ambulance would bring her over tomorrow — that's why we nicked

233

out the radio and TV valves, so no one else could hear the road was open. We thought once Lydia was here, your conscience wouldn't let you go."

Julia had never before been so furious she couldn't find words. While she was still trying, Adam said, "Girls, help Miriam out with her cases. Luke, stop making that abominable noise. Julia *isn't* going to leave us."

Julia stood there in that hurting, unyielding grip while the girls, silently, but with ill-concealed enjoyment, solemnly marched after Miriam with the cases. There was the sound of a car starting up and being driven away. The girls returned. Luke's tears dried up like magic and he started in on his fish.

Adam released Julia and said in a perfectly ordinary tone, "Well, let's finish our lunch."

Julia said, "Thank you, but I'm going to my room."

He said impatiently, "Don't be so ridiculous. I was going to *ask* you to stay. Miriam coming like that simply precipitated things. I'm not apologising for being so summary. Once I'd let Miriam take you away I couldn't have done a thing. Be reasonable, Julia!"

"Reasonable!"

"Yes. Your conscience was bothering you last night. You said you were responsible for the fact that Granny couldn't come home to convalesce, so I thought I'd give you the chance of getting square with your conscience by staying here and looking after her. That's logical enough, isn't it, even if you are in too much of a stinking temper to admit it!"

Julia said, slowly and distinctly, to prove she was in control of herself, "If that's a sample of masculine logic, it proves it's nothing but a myth."

His eyes narrowed. "Oh, I get it! You were just acting a part. You haven't got a conscience after all. You don't give a damn that Granny is eating her heart out, that the kids will have to cope with housework and meals and feeding lambs . . . you've had enough, haven't you? It's been a novelty till now. Once a job gets tough you cut and run. I daresay it was all eyewash about wanting to help your brother . . . you probably got tired of your office job and it offered you a grand opportunity of running

235

away and getting credit for a sacrifice. If the truth be known, when you nursed your mother, it would be because you were finding varsity study too hard!"

Julia stood there, hands clenched at her sides. She drew in a deep breath and said between her teeth, "Phemy, get my poached egg out of the oven. I'll stay here till your grandmother is skipping about like a spring lamb!"

"Hurrah!" said Luke. "May I leave the table, please?"

7

NOBODY could have called it a pleasant meal. Even the children were unnaturally quiet, except Luke, who lay on the mat and played with Esau and Jacob.

When they had done, Adam said, "Now, girls, it's up to you to do the dishes. I want to leave as soon as possible, so that Granny comes home while the sun is still shining. Phemy, would you ask your mother to drive over? I don't like the children being left on their own."

Julia was jerked into speech. "But I'll be here."

Adam surveyed her with a sardonic look. "I have got *some* savvy. You'd be off, walking to Picton, before I'd got a mile on my way. And once you were in the North Island, I couldn't do a thing, so you're coming with us. And back."

Julia said, "If you think I'd walk out, leaving these youngsters on a farm, then you — "

"I find you quite unpredictable, so I'm

taking no chances. Hine would love to come for the afternoon, anyway. And wild horses wouldn't keep Grandpa home now the road is open and he can see his Lydia. Only the fact that we got the news too late yesterday *and* the fact that he was afraid you'd take off right away kept him home last night."

Julia said, "But there should be fresh flowers in her room, and scones straight out of the oven — and you brought in those two lambs — I must clean up. And — "

"Granny mustn't be made to feel a guest in her own house. Every spring there are lambs in the kitchen, and Phemy will make the scones."

Julia turned mutinous. "Well, you can jolly well give me time to do some flowers," and she walked out of the room.

Her legs were trembling as she went down the steps from the verandah. Lydia's wallflowers were in bloom. She picked a few, broke off two or three sprays of the white, true spiraea blossom that her own mother always called meadowsweet, then she hurried to another corner, sheltered beautifully, where, beyond the oldest pear-tree, clusters of small sweet purple violets grew. No florist's violets, however large or long-stemmed, ever smelt as these did. So fitting for Lydia, the seller of rich purple.

She hurried in, arranged them quickly and took them into the cottage. Nathaniel was getting into his jacket. She put the small jar of violets beside their bed, and the wallflowers and meadowsweet on the old-fashioned fireplace. Nathaniel had set a fire ready for a match two days ago. It was piled with apple-logs and pine-cones. How cosy the two old people would be here tonight. She must bring in the brass hand-bell so Lydia could ring if she needed her.

As she stepped back from the fireplace, Nathaniel came to her, put his arms round her. "There, lassie, Adam's in the right of it. In the heat of the moment you'd have gone with that mischief-maker, but in a cooler one, you'd never have run out on Lydia." He patted her shoulder.

Julia had to blink tears away. She put her head down on his shoulder for a brief moment of comfort.

She said, "It — it just seemed to me that I'd be better out of it. The longer I stay, the more trouble it could cause. I just don't understand Adam."

Nathaniel chuckled. "I'm not sure I understand him myself. He's playing some deep-laid game of his own. But since I want Lydia home I'm with him all the way. Come on, now, love. It won't be for so very long. The others will be home in a month. And my Lydia will be spry by then, if I know her."

Julia raised her head. "You're so sweet, Mr. Dare. I'll do all I can for your Lydia. But what's really getting me is what on earth is she going to think? I mean, what a tale to greet a woman newly out of hospital with!"

Adam's voice supplied the answer. "I'm going to tell Granny that Miriam and I split up. The broken engagement won't upset or surprise her, but I don't want her to hear all about the shenanigan yet. Grandpa, have I your co-operation on this? I've just had a word with the children. Even young Luke could see it wouldn't be wise to burden her with such a story . . . a stowaway and a discovery, and Julia forced to remain here against her will. I don't want Granny to feel a problem now or ever. She wasn't very happy about things as she went away. Miriam made it very plain she wanted no ageing in-laws on her doorstep. I saw the look Granny cast round the Bay, as if she thought she might never again set eyes upon it. So I want her homecoming to be everything a homecoming should be."

Julia said, "We won't find it easy — after all that's happened — to act a part like that. And, as a point of interest, just what *do* you intend telling her?"

"I think it's a fine story, I'm proud of my inventive powers. A good novelist was lost in me. And being known as the soul of truth, I'm likely to be believed. It goes like this . . . Miriam and I, shortly after Granny went to hospital, and just before I went to Wellington, decided to part. Incompatibility. She won't be surprised at that.

"When up there I met a chap called Noel Merrill, who said his sister had just got back from nursing their brother's wife in Dannevirke, that she was a rattling good housekeeper, and a fine land-girl to boot. So she came over on the *Aramoana* with me — see how closely I stick to the truth, when possible — and has proved a real brick. She can bake and she can brew, as the song has it, but doesn't make a fetish of housework, puts first things first, especially motherless lambs. I reckon it's a corker."

He waited for comment and when he didn't get one, said, "Poor Julia . . . she knows a story like that is sheer genius but won't give the devil his due!"

Nathaniel said warningly, "Adam, don't press your luck too far . . . or goad Julia too much. You've got your own way about this . . . don't rub it in. And you know fine what Lydia is . . . shrewd as they come. You'd better not be flinging too many veiled comments about . . . you know what I mean, barbed thrusts under cover of light badinage. Now, let's be going. I wouldn't help Julia to flee from here because of Lydia, but I will not see her needled."

Julia said, "Thank you, Mr. Dare. Be warned, Adam. Personally, I'd prefer armed neutrality, but for your grand-mother's sake I think it must be un-conditional peace. It sounds to me as if she's had an uneasy mind for some time."

"Exactly," said Adam. "We're of one mind. That is just what I meant. A bee-yew-tiful story, calculated to make even the astute Lydia unsuspicious."

Hine Watson was coming down the drive as they piled into the station-wagon. She pulled up, came across, smiling, and said, "So Aunt Lydia's coming home tomorrow. How marvellous! Phemy says they've a lot to tell me, that Miriam is gone, but that you're not upset, Adam."

Julia held her breath. Not upset!

"She also said you had a marvellous person keeping house for you, and that everything is going to be all right."

"Dead right," said Adam. "Look . . . the marvellous person is sitting here, right behind Grandpa. Hine, this is Julia Merrill, Julia, Hine. The kids will tell you the whole thing. Don't think they're romancing — it's all absolutely true. Nobody could improve on it. Julia was a gift from the gods, even if I hardly thought so at the time. But as far as Granny is to know, she's just the sister of a friend of mine who stepped nobly into the breach left when Miriam fled."

After they drove off, Julia waxed sarcastic. "Would you mind telling me how you're going to explain to your grandmother why you allowed her to think Miriam was still at the helm?"

"Oh, easy. We didn't want her to worry about the children having to adapt to yet

243

another stranger, so we let it go till she could come home herself and see how beautifully you fitted into life at Whanga-tupuna."

"Well, she'll knock holes in that for a start. How are you going to explain the fact that I'm wearing Antoinette's clothes? These, for instance."

She had the satisfaction of hearing him give a winded grunt. Presently he rallied and said, "I'll think of something to explain that, before we get to Blenheim. After all, it's seventeen miles past Picton."

"That should certainly be long enough for an accomplished liar like you."

He lapsed into silence, whether to rack his brains or because he was offended she neither knew nor cared. She looked at Nathaniel, sitting beside his grandson, and saw to her annoyance that his shoulders were shaking in uncontrollable laughter. Really, these Dares! He was thinking of them as just quarrelsome children!

Despite her anger, she couldn't resist looking about her eagerly. Oh, what beauty she'd not been able to glimpse on that fateful drive over! They swept into Kakapo Bay where Betty Guard's descendants lived . . . there was another low, spreading house, just such a one as Tupuna, with a new one nearer the road. And above the road, as Grandpa told her, pointing, the cannon that was probably the true Blenkinsop one that had failed to diddle Te Rauparaha . . . good for Te Rauparaha, thought Julia . . . then the plaque marking the first whaling-station, and a big try-pot. And above that the row of graves. Captain Jackie Guard, his Betty, little John who had been captive for six months, but had lived well into the twentieth century, and Kuika, wife of a storekeeper, whose murder had gone foully unavenged till poetic justice had stepped in.

Grandpa Dare told Julia to look down to see the point where her murderer had been drowned, with a bag of sovereigns he had stolen from a ship across the harbour.

"Was it the weight of the sovereigns that drowned him?" asked Julia with relish.

Adam laughed. "We like to think so, especially Luke. It was a tragedy in more ways than one, for her murderer was known, though it could not be proved. The Maoris could not understand this facet of British justice, and as some Maoris had paid the death penalty for the murder of a European not long before, this led to a great deal of feeling."

They passed Oyster Bay, then came to Hakahaka and began to climb to the saddle.

"Here's where we spent the night," said Adam coarsely. As they crested it he drew to a stop and said exultantly, as if he owned the view, "Get out and look."

Julia got out because Nathaniel would be disappointed if she didn't, but as soon as she stepped out on to the green turf, patched with Spanish ling, and here and there gilded with gorse, every ill-feeling slipped away from her. There was no room for anything in her heart save an awareness of the fairness of this corner of God's earth. It was like beholding the world for the first time, in the dawn of creation.

Beyond and below shimmered the labyrinthine ways of the Queen Charlotte Sounds . . . hills sculptured aeons ago, by who knew what agency? . . . then clothed with all the lush, moist sweetness of the tangy evergreen New Zealand bush. It shimmered, it seemed as if the very air sang . . . bellbirds and *tuis*, fantails and *riroriros*. Two wild black goats broke cover, looked startled, and diving across the road, disappeared into the scrub below. Above the sounds sea-birds wheeled, their wings blindingly silver against the blue. The folds of the hills beyond the water seemed limitless. You could hardly see which were peninsulas and which islands.

Julia said to Nathaniel, "I can see a bit of blue away over there . . . is it a lake deep in those hills ?"

"No, that's a glimpse of the Kenepuru Sound. You'll have heard of the Portage — the famous Guest House between the sounds, where the Maoris used to transport their canoes over the hill to Kenepuru? Beyond that again is Pelorus Sound and Mahau Sound, and further out still count-less small islands and miniature sounds with, furthest of all, and largest, D'Urville Island, named by Jules Sebastian Cesar Dumont D'Urville who explored it in 1827.

"And back over here," he gestured towards the east, "is the Tory Channel into which Captain Guard's ship drifted in the storm when the thirteen-year-old Betty was on board. You would come through there, of course, the other night, under Adam's Rug." His eyes crinkled up with merriment at the thought of Julia, the unwilling stowaway.

As they got back into the car, Adam said, "Have you never been through in day-light?"

Julia said shortly, "Till I came the other night I'd never been through."

"You mean you know the South Island only by going down on the Lyttelton ferry to Christchurch? Why, you miss all that glorious coastal scenery round Kaikoura that way. It always seems a pity to me that some folk don't come via Picton and see the whole South Island."

Julia said calmly, "This is the first time I've ever been in the South Island at all."

Adam said, "What? And you're . . . what did you say?— Twenty-four? And, so help me, you took a trip to America! I heard you talking to Grandpa about it. That makes me slightly mad . . . people who go overseas but don't know the half of their own country!"

Julia said quietly, with no rancour, "I'd agree with that in the main. But it depends upon circumstances. We lived in Auckland when we were small. Dad had a very ordinary position in the Civil Service. He began to work up, but didn't have the sort of money for long enough, to take us for expensive holidays. He gave us the sort kids like best, seaside ones, not too much travelling.

"Then, just when we could have afforded it, and I was beginning to get itchy feet . . . a New Zealand itch, not an overseas one . . . Mum was ill. It took every penny we had to fly her to Boston where they performed what was almost a miracle. It wasn't a pleasure trip. I was the one who went with her. It was rather terrifying. I was only nineteen and alone and afraid, coldly afraid Mother wouldn't come through. I'll never forget the kindness of the Americans. They were strangers at first. We came back and all we wanted to do was to stay put. It was so wonderful to be home and to know that Mother was cured. I can still remember the wonder of the first day when Mother laughed again.

"It took us a long time to pick up financially. But lately I've been saving for a South Island holiday. It was to start from Picton, in February, and I was going to try to persuade Noel to come with me." She stopped, felt smug and self-righteous, so laughed lightly and added: "You remember I said a policeman assisted me to unlock your car? Well, he was from Stewart Island and he held forth at some length on the iniquitous behaviour of New Zealanders, North and South Islanders alike, who have never visited 'Third Island'. Perhaps if the South Island had retained its early tag of 'Middle Island' we'd be more aware of Stewart Island."

Adam's eyes met hers in the mirror. "I grovel, Julia. That was a pretty stupid remark of mine."

Grandpa Dare beamed on them both. The children had made it up!

Picton was a gem, lying in the folds of its valleys with bright houses and motels on the hillsides and the gracious curves of the shore . . . launches bobbing on a full tide and the memorial arch framing the blue of the bay and the symmetrical backdrop of Mabel Island. Phoenix palms fringed the shore and shaven turf ran right to the edge of the bathing beach. An overseas ship was loading salt from Grassmere and the *Aramoana* was filling up with cars and passengers.

Julia expected them to drive straight through and turn south, but Adam turned into the main street and stopped right outside a draper's shop.

Grandpa Dare said, "What do you want in here, Adam?"

His tone was nonchalant. "Some things for Julia. I'm glad she mentioned it. Granny would think it very odd that she's wearing Antoinette's things, especially that frock she's got on at the moment. That sort of mustard colour is rather striking and Granny would recognise it immediately. You look as if you're a stock size, Julia. Very fortunate."

She said quickly, "Oh, can't we think up something else? You can't possibly do a thing like that. I — I could say my luggage went astray, that — "

He shook his head. "It's no go. I've worked out all possibilities and not one of them would deceive our Gran. In you come."

Nathaniel chuckled openly. "You're hoist with your own petard, my dear. Better just submit. He can afford it."

Julia said in a venomous whisper as they entered the shop, "I'll repay you for every

251

single thing. I won't take as much as —
as — " she choked.

"As a pair of pantie-hose," he suggested
urbanely. "It's hopeless to protest, you
know. I'll buy you what I dashed well
please. The labourer is worthy of his hire
and all that . . . and you've had none and
worked like a Trojan. I'll put you on to
wages when we get back, too."

Julia caught at one objection as at a
straw. "The girls will give you away.
They'll squeal at new clothes. Girls always
do."

"True. Thank you for mentioning it. I
shall ring them from the Post Office to
warn them. They're enjoying all this
immensely, you know."

Julia said, "You great big horrible
beastly — "

"Watch it," he warned, "a saleswoman is
bearing down upon us and it's a small
town, I want no gossip."

She recognised Adam immediately, said,
"Oh, hullo, Mr. Dare, how's your grandmother?"

"She's fine. Dashing about on crutches,
we hear. We're just going to get her. Mrs.
Michelle, this is a friend of ours from

Wellington, Miss Julia Merrill. She's helping us out over the Bay. You know Dan and Tonie are away, don't you? Well, she's brick enough to suggest staying on till either Gran's better, or the gadabouts are back, but she was over for only a weekend, so she's in desperate need of some extra clothes. What have you got that would suit her? You want a sort of medium weight stuff, don't you, Ju? What about crimplene?"

Mrs. Michelle laughed. "For a horny-handed son of the soil, he's quite knowledgeable about women's clothes, isn't he?"

Julia went wicked. "I expect he's picked it up from his fiancée."

She tried for the cheapest possible, but he forestalled her on every count. "It's all right," he said, for the saleswoman's benefit, "I'll take it out of your wage-packet, but you might as well have something decent."

He was even outrageous enough to keep calling out, "Let me see you in that one," and said very naturally over a golden crimplene suit with an ivory jersey silk top beneath the loose jacket, "Why not just keep that on? It will save time, Mrs.

Michelle, you could just wrap what she was wearing, couldn't you?"

There were slacks, a skirt, two sweaters and a twin set in champagne wool, fine and embroidered with beads.

Julia said, "I'll just get myself some nightwear . . . you needn't pay for that. I've enough in my purse."

"Oh, I'll let you pick it yourself, sure, but it can be added to the account. I'll pay for the lot by cheque. Better save your cash. Look, I'll buy one of these cases and it can all be put in there, save wrapping," and as Mrs. Michelle went to get the case he said to her, "I'll hide it under one of the rugs in the back so Granny won't see it. You've got no idea how much you can conceal under a rug."

Julia turned away and bit her lip to stop it quivering. She did not want to laugh with him.

After the call at the Post Office they took the road to Blenheim, a road that wound, then straightened, that went past a deer park and through pastoral country till it came to Blenheim, a country town whose business centre was grouped round the river.

254

Julia found her heart racing a little as they got to the hospital. It seemed they were well known here and expected. According to instructions Phemy had rung to say they were coming.

Lydia was in a wheel-chair with an extended foot-rest, her leg in plaster, and not in a dressing-gown, but in a very smart lavender coat.

Adam grinned, "Hullo, Granny, we've got the flags out at Tupuna Bay." He turned a little to the girl at his side, saying to Julia, "Well, doesn't she look the part?"

Lydia emerged from Nathaniel's embrace to ask with interest, "What part, Adam?"

He grinned. "Oh, Miss Merrill knows her Bible. The moment we said you were called Lydia, she said, 'Oh, the seller of rich purple from Thyatira.' But I must introduce you . . . Granny, this is Julia Merrill, sister of a friend of mine in the North Island. You may have heard me speak of him. Name of Noel, lives at Omairangi, Castlepoint. The fact is Miriam walked out on us. No post-mortems, I don't believe in 'em. It's all washed up. So Noel told me his sister was just back from nursing her other brother's wife in Danne-virke and wanted a job in the country. Couldn't have been better. Our guardian angels must have been working overtime. She's a land-girl too. Cooks like you do, and while she gives us a bad time over cleaning the bath properly and wiping our feet and so on, she's not *too* finicky. I think you and she should get on fine. She's even been to Cape Cod and Boston and reads Joseph Lincoln."

The fine grey eyes surveyed Julia very keenly and apparently liked what they saw. She had a voice that still held a charming hint of an American accent. It gave Julia a warm feeling, remembering the kindness of those one-time strangers in Boston five years ago.

Lydia said, "Well, it sure seems as if you've been having fun, Adam, but have landed on your feet. My dear, I'm very grateful to you. I'm still fair exasperated with myself for breaking a bone for the first time in my life when the family were away. But my two men seem to have coped very well. We'll say nothing about Miriam now. I won't embarrass you, or be insincere either. You'd hate both, I know.

Now, if you call a nurse to work this contraption, they'll get me into the car. You can't think how I'm longing to see my own dear place again."

It was heart-warming to see the way the children greeted Lydia, with Phemy well in the lead. Then they had to decide how to get her into the house. She could negotiate the drive fine, but the big uneven beach stones were beyond her, and dangerous on crutches.

Julia said, "Adam, we can make a chair with our hands and carry her." She looked at Lydia. "You're very slight, and we'll be very careful. We won't drop you. You could keep your leg straight out ahead of you. It's no distance."

They managed it fairly easily and put Granny Dare into the big extension chair that tilted so comfortably and was almost as good as a bed.

Hine was there in the dining-room, setting out a sumptuous tea. The scones were piled with blackberry jam and cream, Hine had baked toast fingers crisped with beaten egg, cheese and bacon chips. "I thought it would be so easy to eat, half lying down." There was a sea-food salad, largely crayfish, served in the small Chinese bowls that Captain Ephraim had brought from some long-ago voyage, tossed in a tangy mayonnaise and served with a frill of lettuce.

"Oh," said Lydia, eyes suspiciously bright, "there's nothing like food served at home. They were very good at the hospital, but just as hunger is the best sauce, so is the dinner of herbs where love is. Luke, honey, don't touch the cat when you're eating. Whose cat is that, anyway? We didn't have a cat with a white shirt-front when I went away."

"It's Julia's," said Luke unguardedly.

Lydia started to laugh. "You mean you brought your cat right across Cook Strait with you?"

Luke's ears went red, poor lamb. He'd promised to keep the secret and now —

Julia said, playing for time and hoping for inspiration, "Well, not exactly, it was — "

Adam got in. "It was this way. We stopped on the top of the saddle for the view and left the door open and — "

Lydia said in a tone of utter surprise,

"I thought you came back in the early hours of the morning. You certainly booked for that."

"I intended to, but didn't think it fair to Julia to deny her a glimpse of the sounds. Hardly fair to take your first trip up Tory Channel in the dark, is it? So we came on the morning ferry, and we stopped, as I said, and this cat must have leapt in. Gave us a terrific surprise when we discovered it on arrival here."

Susanna got in, "We thought we'd have to butter its paws to make it stay, but we didn't have to. It just adopted us lickety-spit. Stood no nonsense from Esau. Gave him one good swipe across the chops — old Esau turned a real somersault — and that was it. We call it Jake . . . short for Jacob."

Lydia laughed. "We'll be fair stumped when it comes to naming the next generation, that's for sure, whether it's cats or children. We've taken a fair pick of the Biblical names. Because you couldn't saddle children with some of them. Still, we haven't had Lois yet, or Priscilla, but I don't think we'll have a Hepzibah or Nehemiah."

"Or Nebuchadnezzar or Hagar," said Phemy.

Esther's eyes gleamed with fun. "Or Zachariah or Ishmael."

Susanna chuckled. "Imagine being called Rahab!"

The conspiratorial adults breathed freely. Danger point was past. Hine's eyes met Julia's and they grinned at each other.

"Rahab . . . I know that one," said Luke. "She was a harlot, wasn't she? What's a harlot?"

Nobody rushed to answer that, then Lydia said casually, "A girl who's dead keen on chaps."

Luke left off stroking under Jake's chin. He sounded disappointed. "Oh . . . sort of soppy? What a clunky sort of thing to be. I thought it was kinda exciting. I thought it was *bad*."

Lydia's voice was very matter-of-fact. "Well, there's a silly sort of soppiness and a bad sort. I'll explain it to you some time tomorrow when we're on our own. Are you youngsters going to be ready for school next week? You'd better get your things out tomorrow, all of you, and I'll mend them if necessary. I won't feel so useless then. Hine, bring your mending over. I'll go mad if I have to sit and twiddle my thumbs, and that you can tie to."

Hine got away soon to give her own family their tea but said she'd leave Phemy there to help Julia. "You'll need to be inside more now, Julia. Phemy can help Adam outside. Oh, I nearly forgot. Ben's mother rang to say he'll be back the day after tomorrow. Well, I must be off."

At seven-thirty, they decided to get Lydia to bed. Nathaniel had the fire going in their bedroom by then, and the apple-logs and pine-cones added their own incense to the violets and wallflowers.

Lydia lay happily against the white embroidered pillow-slips Hine had put on the bed, and stroked the padded patch-work quilt she had brought with her from Cape Cod fifty years syne.

"Home!" she said, a wealth of love in her voice. Nathaniel was going to sit and read to her. They did a lot of reading aloud in this family. Julia knew he would say nothing to disturb his Lydia. If the bald facts had been told her in hospital she might really have been alarmed for the welfare of her great-grandchildren in the care of a scatty girl who had stowed away.

Julia tidied up the living-room, set the kitchen table ready for the breakfast, fixed a tray for Lydia with a thermos jug on it so Nathaniel could make her a cuppa before sleep, got the children off to bed when they'd seen their favourite serial and said to Adam, "I'm going to have an early night. I've found an old favourite in one of the bookcases — *Cranford*. All I want to do is lie and read."

He grinned. "You've earned it. It hasn't exactly been a relaxing day, has it?"

Suddenly he looked weary himself to the point of exhaustion. Julia shuttered her mind instantly to any thought of sympathy and went to bed.

8

SOMEHOW with the homecoming of Lydia, the days fell into a more serene pattern. Her extension chair became the pivot of the whole household. Luke spent a lot of time leaning against the arm of it, telling her small-boy things with a sort of loving earnestness.

Phemy waited upon her with a dedicated touch. Nathaniel still did an amazing stint in the paddocks for a man his age, but found twice as many excuses to come back to the house. Adam completely shed the moodiness that Julia knew had been quite natural after the shattering effect she had had upon his private life.

But Julia was becoming less sensitive about that now, because she was beginning to believe the writing had been on the wall long before she threw an additional spanner into the works. Heavens, she couldn't even think coherently these days . . . talk about mixed metaphors! No wonder . . . she was just a crazy, mixed-up girl, hardly daring to sort out her own feelings. She just went on with the tasks in hand.

They had to watch themselves that they did not give away any hint of how Julia had really arrived at Tupuna. Lydia was so sharp for her age. She said one day very casually, "Susanna must have recovered very quickly from the measles. And no one else got them. How odd . . . and how providential."

There was a silence, then Adam leapt in. "How did you know we'd had a scare? It was only a false alarm."

"Oh, Sybil Mortimer told me. Miriam's aunt had distinctly told her Susanna was developing them. I thought you must be sparing me any worry, so I didn't even ask one of the nurses to ring to find out how she was."

"That was it," said Adam thankfully. "Just as well we didn't, it would have been worry for nothing."

"But did she have a rash?"

The twins looked alarmed. But Adam grinned and said, "She'd had an unfortunate contact with a hairbrush."

Lydia's voice was amused. "Oh . . . is

that how you induce a measles-like rash? How very ingenious!" She turned and exchanged a smile with the twins that even in a woman well past the allotted span could only be described as a gamin grin.

The twins looked much relieved.

Lydia needed a lot of help, though every day she became more adept on her crutches. Julia and she pored over old books of Cape Cod and Boston, pointing out places Julia had visited during her mother's convalescence.

"We could have come home sooner, but this Mrs. March, who was on the hospital committee, and who had taken me into her own home, absolutely insisted we stay on. She said we might never again have the chance to see the States, and while she wouldn't tire Mother out, she'd like to think she returned to New Zealand having seen something of its beauties, and now, at this very moment, Mrs. March is spending the fall with my parents . . . yet it's spring here."

Julia too could spend more time inside now and she revelled in putting more spit and polish on the treasures of the old house. Not a lamb remained inside. All the fostering had been done successfully and things began to right themselves in the Dare household. After the children got back to school, Julia thought she'd ring Faith one night after the older folk had gone to bed and ask her to put another case of clothes on the ferry for her. Adam could pick them up at the terminal building, and Lydia would have no idea.

Letters were arriving from Daniel and Antoinette and from Adam's father and mother. In three weeks the younger ones would be home.

Julia and Lydia were sitting round the fire. Lydia felt the cold more, she said, since her accident. Julia said, schooling her voice to sound matter-of-fact, "When Antoinette gets back, she'll be able to take over here, won't she, Mrs. Dare? I mean, it's just across the paddocks, and by then you'll be getting round a little without your crutches."

Lydia said, threading a darning needle, "Why, my dear? Is there some reason you must haste back to Wellington?"

"Well, it was just a case of helping out in an emergency. You might be glad to have the house to yourselves again then."

Lydia looked at her over her glasses, then finally removed them to study her better. "And here have I been thinking up ways and means to keep you here! Antoinette works far too hard as it is. I don't want her to come back from the first really extended holiday she and Dan have had since their honeymoon, to run two households. Anyway, normally Nathaniel and I don't live here. Although that side passage opens straight into our cottage, we don't overdo things. I don't think in-laws should be forever on one's doorstep.

"Adam's mother was always marvellous. I recall when they were married Ruth offered to live in the cottage, and said she didn't like the idea of turning me out of this house. There was no question of building another. New Zealand farmers were just recovering after the depression, and a whole war and a few more years to boot lay between their marriage and the rise in the wool prices.

"But I wanted them to have a place of their very own, and not as small as the cottage. And I locked that door between and always came round to the verandah door and cooeed or knocked. What a girl

Ruth was! Adam is very like her. She had her two sons and carried on here, working like a man, while Paul was in the Pacific theatre of the war. They had Rebecca after he came back, and when she knew Adam was thinking of marriage, she made her plans, began to build that house in Picton, to serve Dan's children and, in time, Adam's."

Julia said, pain in her voice, "And she's to come back to find Adam's engagement broken and her withdrawal to Picton quite unnecessary. Lydia . . . oh, do forgive me . . . I mean Mrs. Dare — " she stopped in some confusion.

Lydia had flushed with pleasure. She leaned forward, patted Julia's hand, said, "Child, don't look so embarrassed. That's the greatest compliment someone a couple of generations younger can pay a woman of my years. That means you don't think of me as a grandmother but as a person."

"I do. I liked the sound of you from the very start, Lydia, the seller of fine purple."

Lydia snipped off her wool, looked for another hole in the thick farm socks and continued, "I would very much appreciate it if you would keep on using it. I've always had the greatest sympathy for Queen Victoria, who, when the Consort died, found the greatest trial of widowhood the fact that there was no one left who could call her Victoria. For me now, there are just one or two, Nathaniel, and the Guards. You see when I married Nathaniel, I left all my childhood friends behind me."

Julia was enchanted with her privilege, but — "Do you think Adam will object?"

"He won't," assured a voice behind her. Adam's.

Lydia said dryly, "I was about to say: just let him dare! But evidently I don't need to. Adam, can you spare a moment, it's so rarely we're alone."

Julia rose. "I'll go out and start getting the tea."

Lydia's hand detained her. "No, I meant rarely that the three of us are alone."

Adam and Julia looked puzzled, but Adam sat down.

He looked inquiringly at his grand-mother. She said slowly, "I sense in Julia a great uneasiness. Although she's a girl with a great sense of responsibility, she would prefer to leave us soon. I've noticed

269

when we're alone that the subject of Miriam and your broken engagement seems to have a sort of morbid fascination for her, as if she would like to act the role of mediator. Why?"

Julia expected Adam to push his chair back and leave the room, but not so. It did not seem an intrusion to him that his grandmother should so discuss his affairs. Julia began to understand . . . . till the last decade or slightly more, this had been a self-contained community. What affected one affected all. The same sort of thing that explained why they called a doctor only for serious illness. They were used to dealing with things themselves. The unhappiness of one member was the un-happiness of all. A caring concern.

Lydia repeated, "Why, Adam?"

He hedged. "Why ask me, Granny?"

Lydia's grey eyes opened wide. "Because I think you have the answer."

It was not often that Adam was at a loss for words.

"Well?" insisted Lydia quietly.

He shrugged. "Sometimes it's quite beyond a mere male to understand the torturous processes of women's minds."

Lydia looked at him scornfully. "What sort of answer is that?"

He burst out laughing. "None at all . . . but I hoped you'd not notice. I might have known."

Lydia pointed out that she was still waiting.

Adam said, "Exactly what is it you want to know, Granny? You think Julia is only staying because you need her at the moment. Well, we can't expect everyone to think that Whangatupana is the fairest place on earth and never want to leave it."

"But it *is* just that to Julia. She calls it the small Eden. I think she would like to stay but feels she must go."

"Why don't you ask *her* why, then?"

Lydia burst out laughing. "Do you really want to know why, Adam? Because I was intrigued to find out what lies you would concoct for me this time!"

The pair of them stared at her.

Lydia was wiping tears away. "I've not known anything so fascinating in my life. If you'd not come for me that day, Adam, I was going to set out myself in the ambulance. First of all telling me Miriam was doing fine on the farm . . . my goodness, if I hadn't been leg-roped like a wandering hog, I'd have found out a lot sooner. What was the idea?

"I'd had that visit from Sybil Mortimer, who, I'll say for Julia's benefit, is Miriam's aunt's neighbour. Mrs. Chillingham had told her in a state of great indignation that Adam, after exploiting her niece as a housekeeper, had turned up with a girl he'd smuggled into the bay in his car. Sybil had scoffed at the idea, knowing Adam, but Mrs. Chillingham showed Sybil a newspaper photo of you with this girl in Wellington." She turned to Julia. "You looked really beautiful with your hair on top. What a pity you hadn't kept it long. With your carriage it would be perfect."

Lydia turned back to Adam with a naughty chuckle. "It sounded so unlike you, Adam, but the photo did seem to prove you must have someone here. Then what happened? Oh, yes, Ben's brother came in to see me and told me he'd come over on the *Aramoana* with you that night. I asked had you brought a friend back — oh, so casually — he said no, that you'd chatted to him most of the time on board.

"I felt like Alice in Wonderland. It was getting 'curiouser and curiouser', but since Nathaniel was giving nothing away, much less Adam when I spoke to them on the phone, I bided my time. I knew something had happened, but that you probably wished to spare me while I was in hospital or that it was something you couldn't tell me on a party line.

"Then you told me you'd come over on the *morning* ferry with Julia. Oh, Adam, and you were such a truthful little boy! I don't know what your mother would say, I'm sure. Now, what *did* happen?"

Julia's mouth felt dry. Adam said, "What do *you* think happened, Granny?"

"I just haven't got your sort of imagination, but one thing I do know. You did not smuggle any girl in. Not while you were engaged to Miriam."

"Thanks, Granny. That's all I wanted — a vote of confidence. The confidence Miriam did *not* have in me."

He began, "That was what infuriated me so, she — " but Julia interrupted him. "Adam, you must be reasonable. Miriam didn't know you as well as your grandmother did. And it's in the very nature of the relationship between an engaged couple that it's easy to be jealous. If it hadn't been for that wretched photographer, it wouldn't have mattered. It was a cruel coincidence. And Miriam did it in the heat of the moment. She was probably all churned up the moment she saw the photo . . . and then to uncover the same girl . . . well! An apology from you over the telephone would have solved it all. But you were too pig-headed to — "

"*Apology!* What in tarnation do you think I had to apologise for? *I* didn't know you were under that rug . . . if Miriam had had any sense she'd have realised that before she got over the saddle. And for goodness' sake will you stop trying to whitewash Miriam's behaviour! Don't you realise what she's doing now . . . blackening *your* name, shooting off her mouth about me smuggling a girl in from the North Island. I'll go and see her and tear strips off her, believe me!"

"Well, before you do that thing, Adam," said his grandmother calmly, "I'd like to hear the explanation. I'm more confused than ever. Why *was* Julia hiding under the rug in your car? Why — " but as Adam started to rush into speech she held up one white hand. "No, I've changed my mind. This time I'm asking Julia. I can no longer believe a word you say . . . even if it seems to have been with the quaint idea of sparing my feelings. Julia? Begin at the beginning."

Julia told it simply and without frills and Lydia read between the lines, the girl's fear of having the whole thing publicised and laughed over, if nothing worse; her feelings at finding herself on the loneliest of roads with an unknown man; her complete mortification and remorse for what happened at the moment of discovery.

Then suddenly Lydia was giggling like a schoolgirl. "Oh, if only Ruth was here, Adam! She said once that emotionally you were the only uncomplicated member of her family, that you always knew where you were going and what you were doing, and while it made for a more peaceful existence, she hoped you weren't missing something. Oh, dear, oh dear, if only she knew!"

She sobered up. "Well, it would have been no laughing matter if — "

Adam's eyes glinted dangerously. "Go

on, Granny, go on. Don't give yourself any inhibitions at your age. You've never bottled things up. Go on, finish it."

Lydia's eyes flashed back. "All right, I will . . . I have a feeling nothing but candour will do. I don't want a bogey made out of this broken engagement. I understand now why Julia wanted to leave us as soon as I can manage for myself . . . because she feels guilty. Yes, I'll finish what I started to say . . . it wouldn't have been a laughing matter *if* you had suffered a broken heart as well as a broken engagement, but we all know that's not so. Now we can proceed from here. I've always been in favour of plain speaking. I — Adam, I'm talking to you! Where are you going?"

"Where do you think I'm going? To see Miriam!"

Julia's hand flew to her mouth to stop her bursting into protesting speech.

Lydia nodded. "Yes, very wise. You must scotch that story," and to Julia's great surprise grandson and grandmother grinned at each other. Despite the great difference in colouring, they looked extremely alike.

Adam was out of the door in a flash.

Julia looked and felt distressed. Lydia patted her hand. "The mad Dares!" she said. "Only till now Adam hasn't been as mad as the rest of us. Yet something was bound to happen. I'm in great favour of immunisation when young."

Julia looked at her uncomprehendingly. Lydia elaborated. "Adam was never one for the girls. He's an idealist, and fell in love with one with feet of clay. He was bound to take it badly, of course, but believe me, the disillusionment wasn't sudden . . . you only triggered it off.

"He met her in a glamorous setting. He was going for a holiday in Auckland, and my friend Sybil, hearing this, asked him if he would take a parcel up — something fragile — for Miriam's mother. He arrived to find her brother's engagement party in full swing. Let's admit it, Miriam is a beauty. She *looks* like an angel. It wasn't a long holiday, but he came home engaged.

"Miriam came down later, to her aunt's, to be near him. The rot set in almost at once. Against this background the flaws showed up. Oh, but it was a very good thing. Miriam decried all that Adam holds most dear. Nothing like bringing home goods on approval. You can see the shoddiness away from the flattering lights of the showroom. Well, that's the last of the socks. And we won't wait the evening meal for Adam. It's a fair step, though it won't take him so long by Rarangi."

Julia thought that the hands of Captain Ephraim's old clock had never crawled so slowly. Granny thought Adam had gone to scotch the story. Well, he had, she supposed, but who knew? When they met, it could take only one unguarded moment, one spark of what not so long ago they had felt for each other, and all barriers could be down. One look perhaps, and they could be in each other's arms.

They had dinner, washed up, looked at the news, and sat out on the quarterdeck verandah steps, gazing out over the harbour.

For once Julia found it hard to keep her mind on Nathaniel's stories. She was wondering just what Adam would look like when he returned. Would he have a spring in his step? Would he come home whistling? Would he look sad?

Adam didn't come home at all. He rang. They were all in the living-room and he spoke to Nathaniel who was maddeningly non-committal on the phone, giving away nothing of the conversation at the other end, merely saying: "Ay, ay," and nodding and asking him to be sure not to come home without some veterinary supplies. Fancy talking about drenches when a man's whole future was in the balance! Men!

Then to Lydia he said, "There's a film on he's always wanted to see and missed, so he's staying in Blenheim overnight. Do him good. He's not been off the chain for a long time."

To Julia's great surprise and exasperation, Lydia did not ask Nathaniel with whom he was staying, or in whose company he was going to the cinema. Of course she didn't need to. She'd get it out of Nathaniel (if she needed to) in the privacy of their own room later. Only Julia was left in this miserable uncertainty.

She spent a wakeful night and when she finally did drop off, woke resentfully to an unwelcome alarm clock, and from blessed oblivion to the painful knowledge that in all likelihood, Adam and Miriam had decided to forgive and forget.

Well, she couldn't lie here and dream

of what might have happened had she and Adam met in different circumstances . . . if he had never had that Auckland holiday . . . if he and Noel had met at that conference, and Noel had introduced his sister . . .

This was Saturday and the last working day before the children went back to school. They were all a little sad to be leaving the bay, even though they came home at weekends, and Adam had told them they need not go in on Sunday evening to the place where they boarded, if they promised to have their things packed and their books ready so he could take them direct to school Monday morning.

Lydia said, "I'll be so glad when the Picton house is finished — it should be in about six weeks' time, when Ruth and Paul come home. I mustn't fret about them, though, the homesickness never lasts because they love meeting their buddies again. But Luke is so small, and he's always dreadfully tired the first week or two back at school."

So today there was washing and would be ironing later, a vast stack of it, and she must get going. It wasn't till halfway through the morning that she gave up listening for Adam's car returning, because at morning-tea time, ten o'clock, Nathaniel volunteered the information that Adam had rung and he'd not be home till after lunch. He had an air of suppressed excitement about him, she thought. Why? After all, it was common knowledge that neither Nathaniel nor Lydia wanted the engagement resumed!

There was no gladness in the day for her, even though outside the almond blossom bloomed rosily and the apple-trees were unfolding pink and white buds. Julia hung the washing out against a background of sapphire bay and cared not for any fragrance, nor any birdsong.

At two-thirty she was putting a leg of wild pork into the oven and mechanically planning apple sauce to serve with it, roast potatoes and slices of deep orange pumpkin to go round it. If the worst happened and Adam brought Miriam back with him, there just must be a dinner calculated to wipe out the memory of that supercilious glance she had cast round the table, the disastrous day they had been dining off miscellaneous scraps!

Julia whipped up a huge bowl of a fluffy

pudding with a gelatine base that Lydia loved and pulped preserved apricots for a fruit mousse. She would pretty up the whipped cream with grated chocolate and blanched almonds and feel some satisfaction in achieving a dinner-table of which she could not be ashamed.

She looked down on her slacks . . . she had washed in them, scrubbed the back verandah on her knees, because no modern mop could cope with its irregularities, fed the fowls and a calf. She had hairs all over them from Esau and she felt really scruffy, even with the pale blue nylon overall she'd donned for the cooking. Oh, yes, Adam appreciated her help outside, but what was that more than a reaction from the exquisitive Miriam who had walked out on him? Julia decided to change.

She showered, happily conscious that the dinner, even though hours distant, was under way and would need little more doing to it. Also, that with the assistance of the girls, she could cope with all the ironing tonight. Julia brushed her chestnut hair till it shone, and belled up a little at the ends because she hadn't had time to have it cut since she came, and she even put polish on her nails, something she'd had no time or inclination for during lambing.

Finally she slipped into a slim-fitting frock of gulf green, so called because in some lights it looked blue, like the changing waters of the harbour below. It had wide revers of cream, stitched with the greeny-blue, and there were flaring cuffs to the short sleeves. Oh, what a lot of clothes could do for the morale!

She came back into the kitchen to put the kettle on and the door flew open . . . there in the doorway was not only Adam, but Faith and Noel!

It was such a relief not to see Miriam that it brought a sparkle of threatened tears to her eyes. Noel sprang forward. "Steady on, Sis . . . not tears . . . have you been homesick?"

Homesick? Nostalgic for *anywhere* when one lived in Eden? Oh, no, she hadn't been homesick for Wellington. It was just reaction.

She dashed a hand at her eyes, laughing at herself. "Oh, Noel, they're happy tears — what a wonderful surprise to see you and Faith." She kissed them both, then said to an Adam who was certainly not sad,

"But how did they get here? I mean — "

Noel grinned, folded his arms and looked down on his little sister mock sternly. "I got such an evasive answer from Faith here when I last phoned for news of you and was so peeved you'd not dropped me as much as a postcard, I simply left the men to it — we've finished tailing, so it's not too bad — and came down to Wellington last night. I was having tea at the flat when Adam rang to ask Faith would she send your clothes over. Oh, I'd already wormed the truth out of her. A good detective was lost in me. Fair go, Julia, you've excelled yourself this time. Wait till Robert hears! What Faith didn't know Adam filled in when he picked us up."

Julia put her hands behind her back in a defensive attitude and said, "Noel, I can't come back yet. I've got a job to do here. I must see it out. Until the children's parents are back and Adam's grandmother is fully mobile, I must stay. I've made enough mischief. Unless — unless — " she faltered and looked at Adam.

Noel stared. "What's the matter with you? I've never seen you hesitant before. Unless what?"

Adam said, quite gently, seeing her gaze was upon him, "Unless what, Julia?"

She felt her colour rise. "Unless — unless you've persuaded Miriam to come back?"

His turn to stare. "Are you quite, quite mad? Or do you think I am? When you knew the sort of mood I went to Blenheim in? I wouldn't bring Miriam back here under any circumstances. I value the happiness of Whangatupuna too much. Besides which, she's off to Auckland on the afternoon flight today."

Julia's turn to stare. She moistened her lips, said, "I don't suppose you know just what this is about, Noel and Faith. I — "

"Oh, but we do," said Noel. "I told you Adam filled in the gaps. Did you think he'd left out the most dramatic? It was very decent of him. I was very concerned about my little sister, you see." He grinned. "Well, mostly *you've* come to *our* rescue, but this time I wanted to make sure you'd not got into something sticky. Let's skip it, I'd like some tea, and that electric jug sounds as if it's going to boil over any moment."

Julia reached over and switched it off.

"You won't have very long, will you? I suppose you're getting the late boat back? But you'll be able to have dinner."

"Late boat nothing," laughed Adam. "They're getting tomorrow night's boat back. I invited them for the weekend. Faith brought your clothes. She can sleep in your room, and Noel can go in the spare room in the cottage. We have more than twenty-four hours ahead of us. Okay?"

Yes, it was okay . . . in fact everything was okay. Everything.

9

IT stayed that way. It was a golden weekend. The whole atmosphere after weeks of mistrust and wranglings and doubts, assumed a blessed ordinariness. Julia no longer felt the cuckoo-in-the-nest and she bloomed under it. She was needed here as a housekeeper to an old lady with a broken leg, and to cook meals for a man who didn't have time to cook his own. And he was a friend, even though so newly a friend, of her brother's and they were going to take whatever time Adam could spare to see something of the beauty of Port Underwood. Noel and Faith were as bemused with its beauty as Julia had been at first sight.

Noel and Faith. Might that be a solution? Hadn't Alison said, when she knew she wouldn't get better, that some day she hoped Noel would find someone to love him as much as she loved him, because she didn't want to think that he spent too many years alone, grieving.

After they had had their tea, Noel and Adam went out round the sheep and uttered a few words of praise for Grandpa Dare and Luke, who had coped so well.

Julia, accompanied by Lydia, showed them the treasures of the house . . . Faith fingered each one reverently . . . the French prints Camilla had brought with her from Sydney, the samplers, lovingly worked by Camilla's forebears. In one case, as Lydia pointed out, probably unwillingly stitched, seeing a little girl of six had done it. "She ought to have been out under the orchard trees of her home in Kent, playing, not sewing," said Lydia. "They were not always good old days."

There was the locket containing the picture of the little daughter Camilla had lost, with, in the back of it, under glass, a lock of her hair. It was the colour of Susanna's, who had been named for this little lost child of long ago. "They called it inflammation of the bowels," said Lydia sadly, "it would be appendicitis. It wasn't till Edward the Seventh had it that they operated for it. But even so, far from any medical aid in those early days here, the first Susanna didn't have a hope."

She sighed, "That's why that road out there, scarring the hillside, is the most beautiful of all scenery to me! Our Paul developed appendicitis. And it was a night of storm. We knew what it was, we had a very good medical book and were in touch with the doctor by phone. We had to put out in the launch. I'll never forget negotiating that bar, with Nathaniel as silent as Death itself, trying to hold that boat steady. I thought we'd never come about. And me with Paul on my lap, holding him as rigid as possible, lest such buffetings burst the abscess. But we got him there . . . the doctor and ambulance were waiting on the wharf at Blenheim as we came up the river . . . and he was operated on immediately. Oh, yes, that road is the most wonderful thing that's ever happened to the Bay of the Ancestors."

Paul. Adam's father. If Paul had died, there would have been no Adam and she, Julia, would never have found Eden.

Faith was fascinated by the photographs . . . the size of the families, the treasures the twins brought out, the white embroidered pinafores, the buttoned boots, the hats with face-veils, the butter moulds, the early paintings done by the family. Here was the harbour in every mood.

Julia said, "But do you know what I love best of all, Faith, even though there's no antique value attached to them — or almost none?"

"No, what?"

They were in the First Parlour now. The room that ought to have been called a library, because it's walls were covered with books, books that were shabby because they had been read and re-read by whole generations of Dares. Because here, with only the roads of the sea for access for more than a hundred years, books had been their greatest treasures, their strongest links with the outside world.

Julia sat down on the faded carpet, pulled out two or three books. "These were evidently great favourites because they're marked and underlined. Some of the underlinings and marginal notes are in Camilla's writing. It's so wonderful, like meeting her, to know she too loved these passages . . . Shakespeare, and Milton and Edmund Spenser and Keats. See here . . . she'd underlined this:

" '. . . Charm'd magic casements, opening on
    the foam
  Of perilous seas, in faery lands forlorn.' "

She looked up at the small-paned windows, casement ones too, of the First
Parlour. "I think she must have looked
out of here when she read that, sitting up
at that small table. They were perilous seas
here, all right, but I'm sure the last word
didn't apply. Once she got a garden growing it was a faery land, but not a forlorn
one. Oh, I love this library. The books,
so many of them, fall open at certain
places." She dipped into one that did. "I
like this. I wonder who said it . . . it's just a
quotation pencilled on the fly-leaf.

" 'Books are lamps that light our way to
    the heart of truth.
  He who reads widely lives well; he who
    reads deeply lives true.'

"And that's so right for here. They all,
even the children, read deeply."
  She looked up to find Noel and Adam
and Nathaniel in the doorway. She flushed
a little, but continued, "And one day a piece

of dried clover fell out. It had tiny daisies entwined with it too. I wondered if there was a story behind it. If it might have been before her roses and camellias took root and bloomed. If perhaps the only flowers Captain Ephraim could bring her for her birthday, or their wedding anniversary, were the field flowers, the little wild ones."

Lydia said to Faith, "Now do you see why we will not let her go? She's of the same ilk as Camilla."

A strange, talk-prohibiting silence fell upon them. Julia confusedly turned a few pages over at random. She must say something casual, something to bring them back to the present day. Why she felt that she did not know. She had just been paid the greatest compliment possible. Perhaps former ages had something . . . the women of yesteryear knew how to handle compliments.

Adam broke the silence. "Granny, we must give Camilla's diaries to Julia. She'll find the reference to the posy . . . yes, you guessed right. It was her birthday, and the ship that was bringing her present — the one Captain Ephraim had ordered, the old pink lamp on the piano, had been delayed."

Julia's eyes were astar. In the light of the westering sun, falling through the windows, there were golden flecks amid the hazel.

"You mean she kept diaries, you mean I can really meet Camilla in those pages . . . not just by hearsay?"

He nodded. "Yes, because Camilla wielded a vital sort of pen. I've been going through them, hoping some day I might find the time — and the skill — to put them into book form. But somehow it's not a job for a man. They're strongly feminine in style."

Julia said, "But if her style was so vivid, would they take much altering? I always feel New Zealand must have many fascinating records of pioneer days mouldering away in drawers for lack of someone to knock them into book form. Families always mean to do these things and never get round to it. You ought to have a crack at it, Adam."

"I know. But they need editing, despite her style. Camilla didn't write for other people's eyes, and she was no saint. She was exceedingly candid about some of the roystering that went on down below in the whaling station quarters, and in other parts of Port Underwood. Some of the most ungodly ones have descendants scattered round New Zealand, and some still local, who are upright citizens, known for integrity. The half of it can't be told. But I promise you, Julia. I'll work on them if you promise to help. How about it? It will be tough going. Some entries are very faded." His dark eyes held her, demandingly.

She was content to have it that way. It would be . . . heaven . . . working like that with Adam and it would be something she could do for this family she had come to love.

Noel said, "You've picked the right one, Adam. She probably won't tell you, she's too modest, but she's sure got the knack of writing. Her school essays were second-cousins to literature. Dad has it too. Julia has had several historical articles accepted by the broadcasting people. I'm always at her to put them into a more permanent form."

"Well, what about it, Julia?" insisted Adam.

She smiled. "I'd love to."

Lydia sighed a deep, happy sigh. "How wonderful, to have our family history put into lasting shape. We never know what lies round the corner in life, do we? Even in a life as long as mine. To think I lay in that hospital and fretted about what might lie ahead of me and Nathaniel! And all the time Providence was busy leading Julia to the wrong car!"

It was too much for them — they broke down. Finally Adam said, "Oh, Granny, Granny! There were a few moments when I thought the Devil had more to do with it. But . . . well, yes, I agree. I think Julia was meant to come to Tupuna."

It was just as well that at that moment Luke yelled out, "I say, when are we having dinner? I'm just ravenous. And I'd like a really big piece of crackling."

Julia got up, put the books back, said, "Well, thank goodness this was one day when I was forehanded. In the thick of the lambing, meals just happened when I could spare time for them. Faith, will you heat up the apple sauce while the girls set the table? Nathaniel, can you be washed up soon, ready to carve?"

Nathaniel, presently, at the head of his

table, beamed upon everyone. "I'm always glad to see an extra leaf in the table. I was one of ten, you know — the youngest, and the only son. It's a sad day for a family when the leaves get less and less."

Adam was full of plans. "We'll get round the sheep early tomorrow and get the milking done, then we're going to take Noel and Faith over to Cutter's Bay. And to Horahora Kakahu. Granny informs me that she's quite capable now of producing a midday dinner . . . just cold pork and salad. I brought some lettuces over from Picton and we'll have some preserved fruit and cream. No one is going to stay in and swelter over a big meal." He cocked a knowing look at Julia. "You can set the table while we're going round the sheep — the kids can throw the beds together, after they've fed the fowls . . . and we'll be off. Dinner will have to be a late one, say two o'clock, so we'll have a snack before we go. There's no very late boat on Sundays, it leaves at six, gets into Wellington at nine-twenty."

"That will be marvellous," said Noel. "Never before at this time of year have I ever managed a weekend off. But the men said they'd do fine without me." He looked at Julia. "The couple in the flat next door to Faith's are giving me a bed for the night and I'll leave early Monday morning."

Julia was very content to have it so. They covered the table with organdie throwovers, peeled the potatoes and washed the lettuce, and warmed up yesterday's scones for a mid-morning snack.

As they pushed off into the harbour, Adam said, "Julia hasn't really sampled life at Port Underwood at all yet. She's been confined to the farmhouse. That's not a true picture at all, for we're still very much attached to the sea, even if we no longer need to sail down the coast and go in over the bar to Blenheim. Julia's not even been to Rarangi by road. But she will soon. It's the loveliest run. White's Bay has the safest bathing beach imaginable. It was named for a Negro slave boy who swam ashore from an American ship and lived there for years, much loved by all. He had a great sense of humour and used to say he was the first 'white' man to live in the bay. His name was Arper Arthur Ainsworth, but he was commonly known as Black Jack White, a very trustworthy man.

You'll love bathing on that beach, Julia."

If she was still here when the bathing season started, she said to herself.

It was as still as a dream, only the speed of the launch blowing back the hair from their ears. The children were in fine fettle, pointing out various places of interest and sounding superior to these North Islanders whose world had never been bounded by these well-loved landmarks, islands and bays, till Adam abashed them by asking how much history did they know of, even, say Wellington, which had one of the most beautiful harbours in the world.

After they inspected the memorial marking the proclamation of Horahora Kakahu in 1840, they came to Cutter's Bay. Julia, of course, had heard of it from Nathaniel.

It was hard to believe that almost all traces of occupancy had vanished. Over at Tupuna and Kakapo the original homesteads were still lived in and cherished. Here, where Sarah Dougherty had lived in her thatched clay cottage, with priceless rugs on her dirt floor, with bush-covered hills about her, there wasn't even a crumbling ruin to mark the spot, only mounds in the turf to indicate where the walls of their cottage stood.

Her husband, Daniel Dougherty, had set up his own whaling station there. Nathaniel had said he was a handsome man in a fiercely-countenanced sort of way, with long black hair and violet-blue eyes. He had come from New Orleans, was of Irish descent, and his red-headed, grey-eyed wife, born Sarah McAulay, was of Irish-Scots origin and lived in one of the maritime provinces of Canada. Indeed, Daniel's and Sarah's first two children, Robina and Elizabeth, were christened in St. John's Presbyterian Church in New Brunswick. Daniel was a godly man who established his whaling station at Cutter's Bay to avoid the roystering of some of the other whaling stations. They were a mixed crowd with many ne'er-do-wells, convicts and deserters.

Sarah had loved her garden. Flowers just sprang to life beneath her coaxing fingers. She brought with her the runners of the famous New Brunswick strawberries right across the world with her. Many fragrant flowers bloomed beneath her arched whalebones, bleached by wind and tide. The whaling crews lived in thatched clay *whares* nearer the beach.

Sarah did not even quail before the mighty Te Rauparaha himself. When the great chief, from his nephew-in-law's boat, appeared at the station store, demanding rum, during one of Daniel's absences, he so terrified the clerk, he hid under the counter.

The young Sarah was summoned. She had been used to Indians, both friendly and hostile; and though she knew well his reputation, he was to her the old man her husband had cured of stomach-ache with castor oil and who respected her husband as a navigator as daring as himself.

Nevertheless, beneath her sweeping skirts, no doubt her knees knocked!

She called him by the name many *pakehas* used, unfamiliar with Maori pronunciation.

"Robulla," she said sternly. "I shall give you one tot of rum and one only. And you only get that on condition that you go *instantly* away from my house and my bay!"

Adam said, "Celia and Cecil Manson, in their book *Pioneer Parade*, have recorded that, 'Te Rauparaha looked at her with his glittering and sunken eyes, tossed back his rum and led his followers back down to the beach to his waiting boat.'

"Sarah was not to know the old chief was on his way to the Wairau Plains to tell the *pakeha* surveyors that they must not continue to put pegs into land he considered to be still his and his people's.

"In shocking weather some of the survivors struggled through dense bush and hill after hill to where Sarah Dougherty was rowed across two miles of storm-tossed waters to tend their wounds.

"As the indiscriminate slaughter of the whales had it's inevitable effect upon the supply, the industry dwindled, though some, of course, has continued to almost the present day — but not in Port Underwood. Captain Dougherty was offered the position of pilot for Wellington Harbour and sailed his wife and possessions across Cook Strait in an open whaleboat in 1849, just a few years after the Wairau affair."

Julia's eyes were adream. Brave young Sarah Dougherty, who had not quailed before Te Rauparaha . . . somewhere her treasures would still exist, the delicate watercolours that had adorned the clay walls, the historical and philosophical books, the fine rugs that had lain on the dirt floor.

She spoke the thought aloud. Noel said, smilingly, "I might be able to find out for you. At Castlepoint."

They all turned astounded eyes upon him. He laughed. "Little did I think I'd be able to add my quota to the stories today, but I can. It's all come back to me. Julia, you remember Blairlogie, on the road to Castlepoint? That signpost? You always say what a lovely name it is. Blairlogie Station was owned by Tom Telford, whose father had been a banker in Stirling, Scotland, and he named his station after his birthplace. He married a Sarah Dougherty too, just eighteen, the daughter of Daniel Dougherty in 1860, the fateful year when the war with the Maoris had broken out in Taranaki, and the Wairarapa District was declared a militia district. They had to ride over the Rimutakas . . . imagine it . . . and over hilly bullock tracks.

"Julia, you know where the Whareama River flows into the sea at Castlepoint . . . that magnificent piece of coastline that reminds everyone of Cornwall? Their furniture had been sent by schooner to there, and, as was usual, dumped on the banks of the river. Torrential rain fell, the river flooded and the furniture floated out to sea.

"But they were a young, gay-hearted couple, and a four-day journey on horseback before the birth of her first child, so she could be with her mother in Wellington, did not even daunt the young Sarah. Everyone for miles around who wished to go to the city decided to join in, and they made a picnic of it! She had a wonderful husband . . . Tom is still known for his soft heart. Sarah used to say he'd give the boots away off his feet, some day. A true prophecy . . . came the day when Tom turned up at home, bootless. He'd given his boots to a lone swagger, whose need, he felt, was greater than his own."

The children were thrilled. Luke said, "I'll tell it to Grandpa tonight. A new story from the old days, one he doesn't know."

They poked around happily. Faith said dreamily, "I feel as if every step is hallowed ground . . . it would be so different if this had become a bustling port like Wellington or Auckland. It would be hard to find a sense of stepping ashore to a brave new world there . . . it's all hidden under terminal buildings and bulk stores and skyscrapers . . . but this is just as Sarah stepped ashore, these rocks, the shellfish, the creek. . . ."

Noel was on a little plateau above her. He reached down a hand to her. "Come and see what I've found. A link with the past, I think."

Julia smiled to herself. Noel was going on with living again. Faith was helping. No doubt of that.

They all climbed up, though Adam had a fair idea what Noel had found . . . a bit of thick green glass, its edges rounded by rain and the sea-brine of many years, relic of an old rum bottle.

"There's quite a bit of that around over here. You can dig for something else." He caught up an old piece of rusted iron, dug down, and brought up some clods of sticky black earth.

Noel peered closely, then looked delightedly at Adam. "Not really ? Whale-oil ?"

"Yes, the whole place would be saturated with it."

Julia said, "These people of Port Underwood seem so real to me . . . I'm sure Sarah must come back here sometimes, on still, moonlit nights, dreaming of the happy times when Daniel Dougherty's ship was safe-harboured below, and she need not fear the drunkenness of the men on the beach . . . days when she tended her strawberry patch and played hide-and-seek with the children in the bush . . . nights when he would read to her from those wonderful books Lydia said Daniel treasured. I mean it wouldn't be all hardship and fear."

Adam said, "Her ghost would remember the day that Frederick Weld of Flaxbourne Station — later Sir Frederick — sailed across with Thomas Arnold, son of the famous Dr. Arnold of Rugby, and brother of Matthew Arnold. Frederick admired Sarah. He was horrified that sometimes she was left alone here, and gave her a Russian wolf-hound for protection. What a day that must have been! Thomas was most intrigued to find this New Brunswick woman and her pretty little daughters here. 'A cultivated and well-informed woman', he wrote home."

Julia was enraptured. "Oh, I wonder if she ever read Matthew Arnold's poems? But perhaps it was too early for that. They might not have been published then. But there's a very old set of Matthew's poems over home."

She turned away quickly and said, "Oh, a sea-anemone . . . look, what a beautiful colour," and hoped desperately that no one had noticed she had said "over home" instead of "over at Tupuna". She must watch this tendency of hers to identify herself with this small Eden . . . the forebears of the Bay of the Ancestors were not *her* forebears!

Adam was rounding up the children. "Come on . . . don't go any further up that hill. We've reached the point of no return as far as time is concerned. I'm fair clemmed. We're done with ghosts and poets and whalers for the moment, and for all the beauty of ships under sail, I'm glad an engine can take us quickly across the harbour to our cold pork and salad. Right . . . scramble down."

Lydia was beaming with pride that she'd been able to free them for their exploring.

She had hobbled round her garden and picked Faith a posy of wallflowers, daffodils and hyacinths and somewhere in the middle of it she had tucked a sprig of orange-blossom to scent it all. Nathaniel's offering was a box of fresh brown eggs for her, a jar of thick cream, and giant Meyer lemons fresh from the trees.

The day had been one of accord, not a jarring note. Lydia allowed the children to go over to Picton with them to see the ferry steamer go out. They stood for quite a long time watching its graceful passage, down the serene blue sound, between Mabel Island and the Snout.

They stopped on the saddle for the matchless glimpse of the two worlds, the indented, fretted outline of the sounds, and the sheltered harbour on the other side, Port Underwood, running out into the open sea. Far back in Picton, they heard church bells ringing.

Lydia, proud of her increasing independence, had a late tea ready for them. The children then put the last of their things in their suit-cases, turning a little sober because it was the end of the spring holidays and the beginning of the last term of the New Zealand scholastic year.

Lydia said, "But it doesn't tear the heart out of me as once it did, sending my boys and girls off to boarding-school, knowing if they were ill, and the sea was stormy, I might not be able to cross the bar. Or when my grandchildren had to go. Daniel and Rebecca just loved boarding-school, but Adam never really got over his homesickness. Even when — and it was his own idea, to fit himself more for the farming — he went on to Lincoln College, he felt he was an exile returned from long banishment when it was over."

As no one was within hearing, Julia said, "I can't imagine Adam homesick and forlorn. He seems so — so — self-confident."

"Don't you believe it. He's sure good at hiding his feelings — too good. He bottles things up. Oh, well, when we say good-bye to the children tomorrow, we know they'll be back Friday night. And by the end of the term, they'll have settled in with Ruth and Paul some time."

"You mean that Adam's father and mother will still retire to Picton even though he's not now getting married?"

"Just that, honey," said Lydia lightly.

"Ruth wants to do this for her grand-children, and Antoinette. So whatever happens, when my leg is completely healed, don't be running off. You say you prefer keeping house to typing. I don't think I could quite cope now with all these rooms plus the cottage, and cook for Ben and Adam."

Her voice was as smooth as cream. Julia decided she must not take it too seriously. "Anyway, I'll stay till Antoinette is back. Perhaps she could give the men their meals at the new house and even assist a little over here. After all, she'll only have the children at weekends. But I won't leave you till you're quite nimble."

After that came an interlude that under-lined for Julia the former self-contained state of Tupuna Bay. They were in the old parlour and the children were bathed and in their pyjamas. Julia wanted to laugh when she saw Esther under Captain Ephraim's picture and Susanna under Camilla's. Adam followed her gaze and saw her lips twitch.

He said to her in a low voice, "Fantastic, isn't it? I always want to shave the Cap-tain's beard off to discover if his chin really is the same as Esther's. And with Susanna's hair brushed out like that, she's Camilla all over again. Yet it's Phemy who has Camilla's voice."

Nathaniel reached out for a Bible on the shelf beside him. "We missed going to church today. So we'll ask a blessing on us as we go our ways apart tomorrow. Will you read us a Psalm, Adam?"

Adam thought for a moment, then said, "I always liked it when you read this one the night before we went back to school, Grandpa."

He began to read it. Yes, a Psalm that gave one a sense of security.

"The Lord is thy keeper; the Lord is
    thy shade upon thy right hand.
The sun shall not smite thee by day,
    nor the moon by night.
The Lord shall preserve thee from all
    evil; he shall preserve thy soul.
The Lord shall preserve thy going out
    and thy coming in from this time
    forth, and even for evermore. Amen."

Nathaniel's prayer was so natural Julia felt she would never forget the essence of it. He prayed for all men everywhere, but also that all who were under the shelter of their roof-tree that night would take into the larger world of tomorrow, a sense of God's perfect fatherhood. That the ones who had lived here and now were in Europe and in the sea-lanes of the Pacific would know that their dear ones would be remembering them in prayer at this hour. Nathaniel thanked God that in recent days they had been so well guided, and so blessed in one who had come amongst them but was no longer a stranger. And he asked that the children would be wise enough to take full advantage of the chances of education and the way it would enrich their lives.

The children got up, kissed their grandparents, coming to Adam too, and Julia, then trotted off to their rooms. Esther looked back over her shoulder. "You will come and tuck us in, won't you, Adam? In about a quarter of an hour."

Lydia smiled. "The twins are always scared we'll think them too big for tucking-in. It may not last much longer, I know, but I'm glad they're not at the blasé stage yet."

Julia said a little unsteadily, "I don't think anyone could be blasé . . . in a household like this."

While Adam was doing the tucking-in, Lydia said to Julia, "I wonder if you would mind helping me to bed now? I've been on my leg rather longer today, and I'm feeling it a bit. I don't want a setback, because the sooner I have this plaster off, the better. You've no idea how the wretched thing itches."

Nathaniel twinkled. "I have. I saw you the other day having a great poke down it with a knitting-needle."

Julia had an idea Lydia was putting it on a bit. Especially when Nathaniel announced that he too wouldn't be long following Lydia.

She didn't go back to the First Parlour. She slipped out on to the quarterdeck verandah and leaned on the rail. She was living her happy day over again. There might never be another quite as perfect.

A big orange moon was sailing out from a bar of cloud over Fighting Bay, and in its beams she could pick out headlands and dark havens. Away south all was darkness.

An elbow joined hers at the rail. She had heard him coming but had not spoken. "My favourite spot too," said Adam. "I always used to come here my first night home. Just lean here and exult in being home again and to revel in the fact that every solitary thing in the bay belonged to us and I'd break no rules wherever I went."

Julia straightened up and put her hands on the rail, moving away a little, unnoticeably, she hoped.

Adam said, "You said you were sure Sarah must have come back on moonlit nights to wander round her strawberry patch . . . I've always thought of that here, on nights like this. Mother felt it too and had a poem in her scrapbook. Oh, it wasn't about Port Underwood, it was written of North Otago, I believe, but it gave homage to the pioneers. The last verse fitted us."

Julia had noticed before that all the Dares quoted poetry as if it were as natural to them as breathing . . . something that came of years in a close-knit and isolated family circle.

" '. . . And sometimes in the owl-light,
    when phantom breezes stir,

I hear strange whispers rustling the groves
   of birch and fir;
Oh, welcome to my garden, dear ghosts of
   yesteryear,
Come where your flowers still scatter
   their sweetness on the air,
And grant to those who follow the gratitude
   that knows
You made the swamp and tussock to
   blossom as the rose.' "

Julia said, "They are here, the ghosts,
I'm sure of that."

Adam looked up at the moon and said,
"Do you ever have a strange feeling of
slipping back in time? As if it must be the
same moon and the same hour that Captain Ephraim and Camilla knew?"

Julia caught her breath with the sweetness of that. Oh, what a place this Bay of
Ancestors was . . . how conscious one was
of those who had gone before. . . .

Adam said, "It makes me think of that
bit from *The Merchant of Venice* — a
symbol of timelessness, our master called
it. Do you remember it?"

" 'The moon shines bright; in such a
   night as this

When the sweet wind did gently kiss the
   trees
And they did make no noise, in such a
   night
Troilus methinks mounted the Trojan walls
And sigh'd his soul toward the Grecian
   tents,
Where Cressida lay that night.'

"Remember, Julia, how Jessica and
Lorenzo recalled other moons, other
loves?"

Julia was spellbound. She said dreamily,
"Those passages were marked in Camilla's
Shakespeare, weren't they? Oh, Adam, I
do hope Captain Ephraim had his romantic
moments too. I hope he didn't take her for
granted once he was sure of her."

"Oh, he didn't." His tone was so sure,
Julia was astounded.

"But how could you know?"

"That underlining wasn't Camilla's.
Didn't you realise that? Hers are all
light. The Captain's are very heavy. I'll
show you some of his logbooks some
time."

Adam continued, "In the same scene
he'd marked:

315

'How sweet the moonlight sleeps upon
   this bank!
Here will we sit, and let the sounds of
   music
Creep in our ears; soft stillness and
   the night
Become the touches of sweet harmony.
Sit, Jessica. Look how the floor of
   heaven
Is thick inlaid with patines of bright
   gold:' . . .

"Don't you think Ephraim must have
been marking some night when he and
Camilla sat out here?"

He waved to the right where indeed the
moonlight lay softly on the bank; where
mosses and ferns cushioned it.

Julia felt strangely shaken. She said
lightly, "But the sounds of music are
missing. Our musicians are all in bed."

At that moment the morepork hooted.
Adam laughed. "Not all . . . Solomon is
out."

Julia was only too aware of the effect the
moonlight — and Adam — were having on
her. She must keep talking, bring in the
family, anything to dispel this too-close,

too-intimate atmosphere of a world of two. "I envy you having a grandfather like Nathaniel, Adam. I only knew one of mine, and that not for long. And to-night — " she stopped, suddenly shy.

Adam prompted her. "And tonight?"

She continued, a hint of embarrassment in her tone, "I mean his prayer tonight. It — was like nothing I ever heard before."

She heard Adam swallow. Then he said, "I know exactly what you mean. His prayers, even aloud and with all the family present, are so natural. I — I believe what I believe, because of my grandfather's prayers."

Julia lost all embarrassment. "Yes. Exactly. It got me completely. I had a sudden thought: That he ought to have been called Enoch."

Adam turned his head quickly to look at her, as if to ask why, then before he could frame the words, it came to him. "Of course . . . 'and Enoch walked with God'. . . . That exactly describes Grandpa. I think of all the descendants. Grandpa harks back most to the Pilgrim Fathers. Only perhaps in a more gentle mould. He's a true Cape Codder."

317

Julia's voice held a touch of wonderment. "I don't think I ever talked to anyone like this in all my life before."

Adam said, "Of course you haven't. Neither have I. That's what Port Underwood does to you. Well, that swing seat is just behind you. They may not have had them in *Merchant of Venice* days, but they must have sat somewhere . . . 'Soft stillness and the night become the touches of sweet harmony. Sit Julia!' "

She said breathlessly, "No . . . I'd rather stand here, watching."

Almost imperceptibly she moved a little away. Adam straightened up, moved too. His hand found Julia's on the rail.

Idiotically, as if *she* had touched *his* by accident, she said, "Oh, sorry," and moved away.

He chuckled. "What are you apologising for? I did it, not you. Did it purposely." He put his hand over hers again. Julia held her breath. This was sweet, this was heady, but . . . well, less than three weeks ago he had been engaged to Miriam.

She said quickly, "Why has Miriam gone back to Auckland?"

His voice was reproachful. "Julia, you

are without doubt the most maddening girl I've ever known. You're deliberately reminding me that I was very recently engaged to her and ought not to be holding another girl's hand yet. As if time had anything to do with it!"

She said stubbornly, "Adam, I think you ought to put me in the picture."

"Of course, who has more right to know?"

She would not let herself read too much into that. He must mean because she had been the cause of the rift. "Then, what *did* happen in Blenheim, on Friday?"

Certainly he must be an adept at hiding his feelings even as his grandmother had vowed, because he actually chuckled and said, "Believe it or not, but I arrived to find her in the arms of another!"

Julia was outraged. "I expected a sensible answer, a truthful answer! No wonder Lydia made *me* explain the other day."

He swung her round to him. Both his hands gripped her upper arms. He loomed over her like Captain Ephraim himself. In the light of that extraordinary moon his eyes smiled brazenly into hers. "Julia, I *am* telling the truth. Look, everything that happens to us is fantastic. Just remember how you felt when you were trying to convince us you'd got into the wrong car. I'm not going to paint the lily at all. Miriam's aunt's house has a drive edged with close-set shrubs. It winds round to a side-door with an open porch.

"I came up to that porch, mad as hell that she was spreading a yarn like that and was so busy going over exactly what I was going to say to her and her aunt that I hardly noticed a low murmur. But I stopped dead level as I got there, because on the porch were a couple absolutely locked in an embrace. It was quite obviously a dramatic moment. I was appalled — embarrassed. One was Miriam, and in a moment that chap was going to lift his head and see me. I melted clean back into the rhododendrons and silently pushed my way through them till I got to the back door, thinking I'd still try to see Miriam's aunt. Luck was with me. She was in a sort of little potting-shed they have.

"She looked completely horrified on seeing me and said: 'Miriam hasn't seen you, I hope. Oh, you can't come here. Not now. She'll never make it up with you, I can tell you that. You must go, and without them seeing you.' "

Adam grinned. "It was about the first time I ever liked that woman. She was practically human. I said, 'I know. I saw them in a clinch on the porch.' Then I went on to tell her quietly why I had come. That it had been a madcap prank of yours and that I wouldn't have your good name smirched."

A rush of joy flooded over Julia's heart. He wasn't worrying about his own reputation.

"Then she told me Miriam had only got engaged to me on the rebound. A chap she had truly loved had gone away without declaring himself and, piqued, Miriam had decided she'd flaunt a diamond ring in his face when he came back to Auckland. He was overseas.

"Apparently someone had made mischief. He came back long before he was expected, had gone to see Miriam's mother, who told him her daughter was in Blenheim and didn't mention the engagement, seeing it was all off, anyway. He'd not been there more than twenty minutes. Talk about timing! Her aunt felt I'd best disappear.

She promised to say nothing more about the stowing-away — she'd only said it to Mrs. Mortimer, anyway, who's as safe as houses — so I folded my tent like the Arabs, and silently stole away. I was never so relieved in all my life." He chuckled. "That's not, I know, a gallant thing to say of an ex-fiancée, but by the shade of Captain Ephraim, whose yea was yea and whose nay was nay, it's true."

Julia said bewilderedly, "But why — could you really fall out of love like that?"

The pressure of his fingers tightened. "Of course I could. It was just a mid-summer madness. It wouldn't have lasted half as long as it was if it hadn't been we were so far apart. Very easy to feel enchanted still with all the length of the North Island between you. A courtship carried on almost entirely in letters is dangerous. When writing letters you're almost always in a good mood. Gauzy sort of stuff. Nothing homespun about it. Engaged couples should always, in my opinion now, see each other in the worst of situations so the corners can get rubbed off. If they're incompatible it will show. Letters can be a false world of two. You can't live life in that sort of isolation. Other people come into it and have to be considered too."

Julia knew a searing moment of jealousy. She thought of all the letters Adam must have written Miriam. Love-letters. Adam was an eloquent man, and would possibly be more so in letters. She shook her head a little.

Adam said, "What is it, Ju? Am I hurting you? Sorry, I hadn't realised I was gripping you so hard."

Julia said, "It doesn't matter."

"No, it doesn't really . . . what matters is you *must* understand how it was. A man doesn't always bring his brain to bear upon matters like these. Stupid but true. Well, I'm sure Miriam's mother knew we were not right for each other. She insisted that Miriam gave up her position and live with her aunt in Blenheim so we could see more of each other before getting married. It was fun, at first, I used to go into town frequently. Then the rot set in.

"She deliberately set herself out to get her own way about building another house. I don't think I'll ever forget the night she actually said that the best site in the bay was where this one stood and hadn't the time come to have it demolished!"

"Oh, Adam!" a cry of real anguish was wrung from Julia.

He smiled, the dark face softening immediately. "I know . . . desecration. That really finished it. Only I was in the very hell of a fix. Granny in hospital, Dad and Antoinette away, my parents on the other side of the globe, and the kids home on holiday. I thought I'd have to play it along. I'd realised love wasn't enough. There had to be respect too, and liking and friendship. And Tupuna is a family home, we're bound up in it together. I'll never forget how unhappy Granny was. When she was first in hospital she developed a chest infection and I got it into my head she would just relinquish her hold on life and slip away. That she knew her days at the bay were numbered, anyway.

"I felt no end of a cad, knowing I'd have to terminate my engagement, but decided as soon as the kids went back to school, I'd do it, that even though Ben was off work, Grandpa and I would manage somehow. It was funny about that short conference. I felt I shouldn't go, but Miriam urged me.

What I didn't know — in fact Grandpa has just told me now — was that Miriam wanted the opportunity to tell Grandpa that she felt they ought to move into Picton with Mum and Dad, that we'd decided to use the site of this house to build a new one.

"Fortunately Grandpa stoutly refused to believe it. He told Miriam quietly when the children were in bed — the night before I came back — with you — that she couldn't be aware of the situation — that I am only heir to the house and that, legally, the land is well tied up between him, Dad, and me. And he said to her that as soon as I got back he was going to ask me, outright, had I any such plans? No wonder she was in a stinking mood that morning!"

He looked down on Julia who was standing very still. "So you see you didn't have to have that load of remorse on your conscience. Oh, Julia, I could have twisted your neck many a time when you kept trying to put things right. What you thought was right! But now you have it all straight, haven't you? And we can go on from here?"

Julia was trying to cope with too many

emotions. She said confusedly, "Where to ?"

Adam laughed, "To here, I think," and tilted up her chin and brought his mouth down on hers, gently drawing her to him.

There was a very long sensation of magic for Julia, till, slowly, she withdrew. They looked at each other, she uncertainly, he confidently, then she said, "Adam, you go too fast. You don't learn, do you ?"

He made an impatient sound, then seemed to control himself. "I forgot. Till now you've regarded me as Miriam's fiancé, temporarily estranged. And besides, two people, even kindred spirits, don't necessarily proceed at the same pace, are not geared the same."

Julia made a hopeless gesture. "Adam, for the length of time we've known each other we're being too serious-minded by far. The trouble is, I was pitchforked into your life, there's been no gradual getting to know each other. Everything has been too dramatic, larger than life. No ordinary living. For goodness' sake, let's just go on as if there had been no clashing of personalities, as if I was indeed what you told

Lydia to start with, someone who came in to help. I'm going to bed. Good-night, Adam."

10

TILL now Ben had been still convalescing. Adam had insisted on that as he was terrified the changing winds of spring might cause complications. Having him back helped tremendously. He was so gorgeously ordinary and always around. It meant that even if Lydia pretended she was tired, or her leg not so good (Julia was sure it was pretence) and went to bed early, there was always someone else there.

When the tailing came along Julia was pressed into service, with Lydia vowing she could manage the meals with the children away.

Julia didn't mind the tailing at all. She knew from experience that the lambs found the restriction of the rubber rings uncomfortable for no more than half an hour, then frisked round as happily as ever. In time the tails dropped off and there was no infection to be dreaded, and it saved them much discomfort, even pain, and uncleanliness later.

She liked working with Adam. He was swift, efficient, but had no impatience with the animals. Julia was glad of this. If he had been callous and unfeeling, she'd have had to admit it was a flaw in his nature, one she could not bear in men or women.

When it was over, Lydia brought up the matter of Camilla's diaries. She had no intention, she informed them, of having that put off again. "We've been saying for years and years it ought to have been done. Two or three writers through the last decade or so have turned up and asked if they could see them and use extracts, but I felt I didn't want Camilla's flesh-and-blood entries just sandwiched into historical records. I wanted a book written about the Dare family."

"I think this is right, Lydia. Port Underwood, for instance, deserves a book to itself some day. This one, I'd like to be a book about the Bay of the Ancestors. I want to read up the Maori history that caused it to be called that, or find it out somehow."

They were working this night, Adam and Julia, at the big table in the living-room under the centre light, because the entries, some of them, were faint, and Ben, Nathaniel and Lydia, were watching TV. It isolated the two of them in a world of their own, a world that had nothing to do with jumbo jets and world news via satellites.

Adam said, nodding towards Lydia's back, "She's almost slave-driving us. You don't think," dropping his voice, "she's got any ideas that — that her time might be getting short and she wants to see it in print before too long?"

Julia's denial sprang to her lips because she couldn't bear the thought. "No, I think it's just that she wants me to get it done before — "

He looked at her as she stopped. "Go on, Julia, before what?"

She moved their notes uneasily. "Oh, I think she knows I won't be needed here much longer."

"Don't talk such rubbish. Don't throw a spanner in the works when Mother and Father get back by presenting them with alternative duties . . . either looking after us here or going into Picton to make a home for the children — something Mother has dreamed of for years. As for going back to

Wellington . . . your boss has another secretary. It would mean hunting for a job, and there's one going right here!"

"I thought by now Noel might let me go up there."

Adam said slowly, "You would be very ill-advised to do that."

"What do you mean?"

"You'd fill a need for him. A man likes his comfort, his meals ready when he comes in from the paddocks. He could slip into too contented an existence with you at the helm. Oh, don't be so blind, Ju. With you not substituting for Alison, he might turn to Faith."

"Yes, that's a point."

"And as far as here is concerned you — "

"Look, Adam, let's get on with this. We've got to the part where she's making candles because they were short of kerosene. For Jonathan and Mary. Isn't it odd to think we're talking of the cottage Lydia and Nathaniel live in?"

They slipped back into the less compli-cated yesterday.

They turned another page, then two pairs of eyes gazed at each other in delight.

Adam said, delight and triumph in his

voice, "There, what did I tell you? That was a horrible thing you said the other night, that it just might have been a marriage of convenience, that women — decent ones — were scarce here, and that Captain Ephraim might almost have forced her to marry him. That she might never have loved him, but thought that this way she could stay here, with her brother. Read that, Julia . . . read it again and admit you were wrong."

The two heads bent over the book again. The young Camilla had written: "Lieutenant Bross of the HMS *Penguin* came in tonight. He said that the *Solander* is just across the Strait in Port Nicholson, that he had had speech with Ephraim. It has another captain now, Ephraim has merely worked his passage back as he said he would. The Lieutenant said that Ephraim told him to tell me that before two more sunsets come and go, his ship will be anchored in Port Underwood. Oh, it has been so long, so long! That he has bride-clothes in the hold for me and has persuaded a clergyman from there to come across with him. Oh, I so hope he will not find me too much changed. I must wash my hair tomorrow night, and do my hands up in grease and gloves. And what shall I wear when I greet him?"

"The eternal feminine question," said Adam, laughing. "So you can let yourself go, Julia. This was high romance, no question of that."

She said, "Is it too much to hope she would record the meeting?"

Well, Camilla hadn't recorded it in full, but she had written:

"Ephraim couldn't believe we had achieved such a garden in the time he has been away, but then everything grows so quickly here, in this fertile, rich, virgin soil. John has been so good in sparing the trees I could not bear to see felled . . . those lovely trees of the native bush whose names I do not yet know fully. But I will. My violets were in bloom and we walked down the shell path they border. There was a full moon above the over-harbour hills and the sounds of revelry from the beach were not so raucous last night. Ephraim brought me a letter from his mother. I do so hope we may sail across to meet her some day. She has sent me a beautiful bureau . . . we haven't got it over yet, but Ephraim has described it and there are some crocheted doyleys and the christening robe used at Ephraim's baptism."

"I don't suppose you have seen that yet, Julia. Get Granny to show it to you. I was christened in it . . . so were all the others."

The TV programme ended and the other three returned to the fireside. Adam said, "Well, back to a prosaic world, but remember, Julia, that there is another one."

Ben was laughing. "What a yarn that was on TV. Beats me how they keep thinking them up. What a stupid pickle those two on the box got themselves into. It would have taken about two words to have straightened it all out. Well, one question, one answer. But it went on for three-quarters of an hour after that. It was terribly aggravating!"

"But without those complications there'd have been no story," pointed out Adam, "and you'd have missed some great entertainment, judging from what I heard. You were laughing fit to kill yourself. And don't think those things don't happen in real life. We can get into incredible muddles. Like Julia and me."

Julia said hastily, "I'll put the supper on."

Lydia said, "Could you warm up those biscuits, dear? It's just what I feel like."

Lydia still called scones biscuits and biscuits cookies, and Julia herself was falling into the way of it.

Julia lay awake a long time that night, not tossing and turning, just thinking. They were thoughts she was reluctant to think, but must. This was a strange set-up, very clannish. One in which family was all important. What had the girls said? That Adam had been swept off his feet. Didn't every girl wish to be loved like that?

She could imagine Adam calling at that Auckland house with his parcel, being asked in and included in the gay gathering. There would be his first sight of Miriam, tall, queenly, confident . . . a glittering sort of personality, even if it had been ice that had made the glitter.

Adam . . . returning home still in that bemused state, writing his love-letters. Again the stab of jealousy. Then Miriam's coming south and the consequent dis-illusionment. The intrusion of the everyday

335

into something that was just stardust and gossamer . . . Miriam's incompatibility with the life of Tupuna.

Into this situation Julia had erupted. It brought it to a head. Now Adam had to face the fact that Miriam had just used him to salve her pride. Julia supposed that could harm a man's ego. But what of a girl's ego? The girl to whom he was turning with a sort of quiet deliberation, with nothing of a headlong falling in love here . . . Adam had most likely said to himself that next time he went courting, he'd pick a girl who loved the bay, who could lend a hand at lambing and tailing and shearing . . . someone who, like himself, felt there was a place for former generations within the family circle still . . . who revered ancestors, loved history and poetry and books . . . and here *she* was, Julia, right at hand. And, if his mother was to realise her particular dream, he needed a permanent housekeeper at Tupuna! And what more permanent than marriage?

Oh, a sensible wooing this one would be, with already the seal of Lydia's and Nathaniel's approval upon her. Someone his brother's children loved too. He would think of the way tough little Luke had bawled when he'd thought Julia was going away with Miriam, and put another mental tick beside her name. Oh, yes, it all added up to *suitability*!

Julia didn't know what she was going to do. She loved Adam, with an intensity that had nothing to do with *his* suitability as a husband, even though there was that also. A kinship of spirit. But she wanted more than that, to be loved as she loved him, without rhyme or reason, as well as for the other things. Julia decided she'd just have to let time take care of it . . . poor silly, impetuous Julia who could never decide when to act upon impulse and when to look before she leapt. Oh, what a devilish thing life could be! Well, she'd held Adam up that night on the quarterdeck verandah and gone in for delaying tactics again tonight . . . she'd keep that up. She would not fall into his lap like a ripe plum. Julia's mouth twisted wryly . . . she'd always despised girls who played hard to get!

Adam had said of the love-letters: "Gauzy sort of stuff . . . nothing homespun about it."

It was unfortunate he had used that

word. It had made her remember the song Adam had sung the other night at Lydia's request. There had been something lovely about it, yet a little poignant . . . for Julia.

After he'd sung it Julia had noticed Lydia give a little nod to Nathaniel, who had nodded back. The next morning Julia had gone to the stack of music and looked up the words again. It was called *The Choice*.

"O Lilith, she wears tinselled shoes upon her dancing feet,
And Lilith has such shining curls, all honey-gold and sweet;
But Mary's steady brogues were meant for rough and ready going,
Her smooth brown tresses toss and stir with every free wind blowing;
So, as I need a homespun mate to tramp the hills and heather,
I'll put my ring on Mary's hand and we will walk together;
For whatsoever way I take, there will be shine and shadow,
'Tis sturdy brogues are needed on the road to El Dorado;

Yes, Mary's heart will never quail whatever
  wind or weather . . .
So here's a ring for Mary's hand, and we
  will walk together."

Julia found it haunted her. Lilith? Wasn't
there some legend about a Lilith, who had
been the real serpent of the Garden of
Eden? A siren of a woman who had caused
Mother Eve much jealousy? Did any
woman ever want to be regarded as a
homespun mate? Didn't she rather want to
be adored for herself alone? Did a woman
have to be content with knowing she
provided other needs for the man she
loved? Julia could find no answer.

Oh, well, the children would be home
tomorrow, and the house would be full
of joy, not tension. What appetites those
children had, and the Watson children
came over a lot then too. Miriam's biscuits
had long since gone. Julia came to the
conclusion that she must have a horrible
nature to be so glad they were finished.
They were so perfect they put her own
slapped-up cookies in the shade. It served
her right that she somehow never found

enough time to do extra to put in the bags and store in the deep-freeze. It was quite enough to do to keep half a step ahead of the demand as it was.

The twins would want her to set their hair. Luke would insist on help with his collections . . . his room overflowed with them, cards out of cereal packets, pressed leaves and grasses, shells, rocks, stamps . . . oh, there was no doubt Luke would become a scientist. Lydia was sure of this. An uncle of hers in the States had been an authority on such things.

It turned out much as she expected. Luke came home hugging a huge and tattered book someone had given him, on shells.

They had very strict rules about clambering round the seashore at Tupuna, due to some tragedy of long ago. Adam said, "Yes, we'll make time to take you to Shelly Beach past Ruddy Jack's Point, but not this morning. I might manage it about four this afternoon. I've got a bit to do in the smithy. Not much, but while the fire's hot I'll do a few other small jobs. Julia, you might like to come."

But by three Luke was very impatient,

and the girls were over visiting Phemy. Julia got into some old slacks and wandered over to the smithy with Luke. She always liked to pay a visit there, watching the bellows and seeing the sparks fly.

"Adam, say I go to Shelly Beach now with Luke? I think it will turn cold later and it would be fun for him tonight, having new shells to identify."

"Okay, only stay away from the edge of the cliff at this end of Shelly Bay, it's very crumbly and eaten away. Stick to the path and you'll be okay. The shells are thickest at the far end, anyway. It will be just as well if you go now. The tide will be in later. That beach is never cut off, but you get more shells when it's down. If you don't get all you want I'll go down with Luke tomorrow afternoon. Make sure he stays beside you."

Luke was an engaging companion, talking madly in his pleasure at having a grown-up to himself. They had an idyllic time, poking round in their old sandals in the rock pools, watching small fish darting, sea-anemones opening and closing, crabs scuttling away, and in getting their basket full of shells.

"I don't know the names of half of these," said Luke, "but I will soon now I've got that book. Only some of the words are too big for me."

"We'll look them up in the dictionary and see how to pronounce them properly," promised Julia. "Luke, we'd better make that all."

Luke scooped up two or three more and trotted after her quite happily. It was a lovely path and led through patches of native bush. It climbed a little, though not steeply.

Julia said, "Oh, look, another fantail. Aren't they friendly?"

The fantail fluttered ahead of them, pirouetting and flirting with them, and they watched it till Julia, intent on its flight, bumped into a tree.

She rubbed her forehead and laughed, "I'd better watch where I'm going." Luke was ahead of her now. Julia took the basket from him. "You're swinging it too much. You'll drop some."

She stopped and scooped the shells more into the centre of the basket, heard a yell from Luke, a soft crash . . . and the next moment he just wasn't there, but a crumbling and a rumbling was going on and a cloud of dust rising.

Julia let the basket go and stared in horror . . . there was a hole in the track and . . . good heavens, it was a huge cave-in . . . oh, imagine if it kept crumbling . . . Luke could be buried! She found herself edging forward on her knees, gently, not to do more damage, and was reassured by a muffled yell from below, "Julia, I'm in a hole, a big hole!"

She lay down and peered over the edge and said into a cloud of dust, "Are you hurt, Luke? I can't see you yet."

"No . . . I'm not hurt, but — b-but I don't like it much."

The dust thinned. Julia's nostrils felt clogged and her eyes were stinging, but she peered in. It was a colossal hole like a cave, sort of triangular, wider towards the direction of the shore. She could see tree roots dangling into it, like stalactites. Some of them must have loosened the earth under the path.

Then she realised something that made her heart lurch against her ribs. It was deeper than she thought and tremendously hollowed out. Luke could not clamber out

343

and she wasn't going to be able to reach down to help him. In any case she dared not lean too far over this hole . . . if any more broke away these saplings would crash in and perhaps bring larger trees to follow them.

But she didn't think he was in any immediate danger. She said in the most casual tone, "Luke, I'll just have to go to get Adam to get you out. He's got a longer reach than me and he'll have you out in no time. Now it's okay, it'll be a grand yarn to tell the twins. They'll be green with jealousy. Adam's so near, just in the smithy."

She tried to peer further in. Oh, there were rocks on the far side, smooth, very black, and it appeared as if the roof over them was rock too. "Now listen, Luke, get over on those rocks, it's much less dusty and horrible and nothing more can fall on you there. This moment, Luke."

Protesting, Luke retreated. "Please, Julia, can't you get me out? Look, I'll bring some of these boulders over and pile them up. I could try to reach your hands then. Don't go, Julia!"

She made her tone an extremely firm, no-nonsense one. "Don't be stupid, Luke.

This is all crumbly and your weight would just pull me in too. You get right over there and I'll run for Adam. He may even bring that light ladder. Now listen, you're not to try — " she broke off, because something had happened. Her eyes had been getting accustomed to the gloom below, but suddenly all was darkened. Like a cloud going over the sun. But there was no sun in there. And there was a sound too . . . a sound that had been there faintly all along, but now was intensified. Just as Julia realised what it was, Luke screamed in panic.

"Julia, don't go! *Don't* go! It's the sea, it's coming in . . . a big wave . . . this is a cave, and it's covered the entrance. *Julia!*"

She forgot about the danger of the crumbling surface, the other menace was too horrifying, and leaned in and yelled, "Back you go . . . back . . . right to the far edge of those rocks. No, I won't go . . . back you go . . . it won't reach you there!"

There was the sound of a desperate little boy scrambling up and the horrible surging, sucking noises of the sea . . . it swirled up, up, up . . . right to the very edge of the rocks, then drained away, leaving a greenish-white fringe of dirty foam.

Luke screamed, "The next one will get me, the tide's coming in. Julia, don't — "

He didn't finish it because there was a thud as Julia leapt in, landing in sand that had been dry when Luke had first fallen in, then she was up on the rocks with him, clutching him to her, "Luke, I'm here, Julia's got you. It's all right."

Her eyes were darting about, straining into the far edges of the cleft for signs of high-water mark, for a ledge, for anything that might tell her they could get out of reach of this tide. But when she looked up at the hanging roots her heart failed her. They had been washed clean. That was what had been undermining this cleft or cave . . . tide after tide coming in. A process of decades, she guessed.

Luke said, his eyeballs showing white, "What can we *do* ?"

Julia looked towards the shore end. There was the cave entrance, a very low one, and the water had ebbed to it but had not left it completely dry. It was more shingly there, she thought . . . but quite soon the tide would completely cover the arch. It was a hideous thought.

346

She said quickly, "We must use our brains, Luke. You can swim, can't you?"

He nodded, his eyes fixed desperately on hers.

"Well, this wave that is coming now won't reach us here. We'll let it go out, then as the next one ebbs, we'll rush to the entrance, in its wake, dive down through the arch, and we'll bob up on the other side. We'll be on the shore, on the home side of Ruddy Jack, I think. And we'll scramble up from the rocks. Quick . . . that one's just going. Off with your jersey and your trousers . . . you'll swim better without."

She got them off him with incredible speed, managed to yank her own bulky jersey off, but had no time to get out of her trews. But they were fitting and wouldn't hamper her much. That wave came up so far they were terrified. If forced them back and back. Then it receded. They ran down, dismayed to find the floor of the cave shelving steeply so that the water deepened horribly. Julia was almost demented with the fear that it might fall away suddenly . . . then she realised they were near enough.

She caught Luke up with a sort of superhuman strength, and, keeping hold of the waist of his briefs, plunged down with him with a terrific thrust that she hoped would carry them under and out.

They came up into light and the open bay. They rested on top of the waves for a moment, to get their breath back, then lest they be sucked back into the cave, Julia thrust Luke ahead of her, to the left. He struck out quite strongly. She kept saying: "I'm here, I'm here, keep going."

She saw evil-looking kelp reaching out menacing tentacles and said "Veer left, Luke," and was glad to see him obey implicitly without question. They rounded some rocks, jagged and cruel, and got tossed about for a moment or two with some swirling current, then into slightly calmer waters, but Julia was sick with dismay. They were certainly not on the home side of Ruddy Jack and — she saw some rocks that looked as if they joined the shore, said, "Get up on those rocks. They'll hurt, but it doesn't matter . . . on you go!" He was still a little ahead of her. She dared not lose sight of him. His arm flung up, his hand scrabbled, clutched, held. He panted, turned his head to see where she was, slipped back. Julia gave the most frantic and cruel push and flung him on to the rocks, grabbed a ridge, and came up beside him, sharp fragments and barnacles scraping her legs and arms and hands. She pulled him to his feet and gazed in despair.

This was the tiniest of bays, but it was half circled by the steepest of cliffs, not high ones, but high enough. In fact just too high, just too sheer. Certainly they could scramble over this reef of rocks to the beach, but in no time at all there wasn't going to be any beach, she thought.

Julia's eyes raked every inch of cliff, gauging the lowest point, the least steep, the part where the tumbled rocks on the beach were highest . . . and all the time that hungry, roaring tide was coming in.

They were so near to safety, yet so far. Luke gave a little whimper, then clapped his hands over his mouth. A wave surged up and over the reef of rocks, then drained away. The rocks they'd have to cross were lower, unfortunately, but they could make it before the next. She grabbed Luke. "Never mind your feet, we've got to run for it."

They negotiated them with a speed and skill born of desperation and reached the tiny strip of shingle beach beneath the cliffs. The first wave reached them, just the shallow fringe of it. Luke and Julia, straining their eyes up at the cliff, noted the high-water mark at the same time. She couldn't hide it from Luke, he was a child of the sea. Her eyes roved on and she realised something.

Her voice became full of confidence. "Luke, from my shoulders you could reach the edge . . . right here. These rocks go up a bit, and there's a bit of root leaning out . . . that might help you . . . you must get on my shoulders and reach for it. You must scramble over, then go for your life for Adam. You're my only hope, understand? Go up the headland, and over the grass. I'm sure it's only grass. But anyway, take the easiest way, it'll be the swiftest if not the shortest. There's a rope in the smithy. He's going to need rope. But he must hurry, I'll cling on here."

Luke gave a shudder, not for himself. . . . "What if the tide comes in too quickly? What — "

"I'll swim for it. I may not be able to

swim round the Point, though I'd try, but I'll keep afloat all right. I'm a good swimmer. . . . Up, Luke!"

She knelt on the shingle as the next wave subsided, felt him scrambling up, and steadily with Luke clutching her forehead, raised herself up. It was an anxious moment when Luke had to let go to get himself upright, but there was a boss of rock he could cling to, then a gnarled *ngaio* root. Then his voice saying, "I can't — quite — reach." Then before she could answer. "Oh, Julia, can you wiggle, very slowly, to the right? There's a bit of iron sticking out there . . . I think it's very firm."

Very slowly, with that weight on her shoulders, she inched along, felt his weight lessen a little, heard him say, "Got it . . . it's driven right in . . . Julia, could you take my legs and give them a terrific push when I say when?"

He said: "When!" She thrust with all her might and saw a small bottom in saturated briefs disappear over the top.

One more second and he was reversed, his face looking down on her. "I'll go like hell . . . hang on for your dear life. See if you can get a bit of rock to stand on and try to reach that mooring ring. I'm off."

Julia felt the nausea of relief sweep over her. She had been so terrified he might sway back, fall. At least, whatever happened to her, Luke was safe. His parents would not come back to a little empty bed, to the lifelong regret that had they not left their children it might not have happened. Luke was safe, safe!

A wave splashed viciously against her, drenching her, but worst of all was the force of the suction as it retreated. A few more like that and she'd have to swim for it. If only, if only she could get further up the cliff. If only that loop of iron were a little further down. Oh, no, if it had been, Luke couldn't have reached the top.

She willed herself not to panic, but to concentrate on getting higher, somewhere, somehow. As the wave receded she saw a rock on the shore wobble, then settle. She rushed to get it, trundled it back to the cliff edge. It was big enough for a base. In frantic haste she gathered others, each time waiting till a wave ebbed. Sometimes the incoming wave helped her bowl the larger ones along. She chocked them with smaller stones to keep them firm, though how much suction they would stand she did not know. The gnarled root would be of no use to her. It had barely held Luke, bits of clay had fallen from it immediately he grasped it. It would have to be the iron ring.

She tugged and heaved and rolled, battered by the waves. She was beginning to shiver. The sun was dropping and the wind was chill and she was lost in an enormity of sea and sky and pitiless cliffs and diabolically hostile waves. She'd have liked just one more rock, but now the waves were not receding so far, and almost tumbling her over . . . she mustn't get swept out. . . . She braced herself against the next onslaught, hated the drag of the wave round her feet, with the fine shingle scouring out under them . . . she must get up now. What was it about every seventh wave being bigger than the others?

It was hard getting up on to the top one, but that was good in a way, because it meant the pile was pretty high . . . she just might reach that mooring-ring driven into the cliff face in a crack. It had bits of seaweed clinging to it, so must be submerged by high tide. Steady, Julia Merrill, keep your mind off that. It won't help. Surely

Adam will be here before high tide. You can hang on to that ring for some time, so you just be grateful for that. She straightened up and found she could reach it.

Oh, what a relief! It must have been driven in here in the whaling days. Could they ever have needed to tie boats up to here? This was far too difficult of access with that reef of rocks and that swirling current.

She had her feet firmly on the rock at the top. She must not keep fearing the little chocks would get washed away and that if the rocks fell she would be left dangling. If they did, how long could she hold on? Her hands would numb. As it was now, it wasn't too bad because she was not hanging from it . . . it was for all the world as if this relic of the whaling days had been inserted here to save her life . . . but it wasn't really a perfect ring, one side of it was quite flat.

What if Adam had left the smithy? Nathaniel had been away up the hill tending the graves, she knew. What if Luke had had to run on to the house where only a lame old lady was? But Lydia would know what to do . . . she would beat that gong by the door as it had not been beaten for years, beat it ceaselessly till Adam and Nathaniel came running. Then she would ring Phemy's father, and Orewa would come round the far point by boat. She'd only have to keep on swimming. The trouble was she was already frozen.

Meanwhile, there was this loop of iron. Julia changed hands, careful not to shift the top rock with the movement, because if she knocked it off she couldn't get down to retrieve it. There was no beach left now. She brought her other hand up and brushed some of the seaweed away. She was deliberately concentrating on that mooring-ring. She must, because she dared not look down, mustn't get dizzy over these swirling green waters . . . what a very peculiar mooring-ring. The flat piece was so symmetrically flattened. And a sort of edge fitted against the rock, driven hard against it . . . and the bit beyond it was curved. She could see that because on this side the rock became crumbly and there was clay in it. It wasn't like a straight spike driven in, it was curved, like a knife-blade.

The truth hit Julia between the eyes . . .

it was Captain Ephraim's cutlass! This was where it had lain all these years . . . driven into a clay-filled crevice of this cliff . . . her heart surged up. This was providence, this was meant to be — oh, the ghosts of the Bay of the Ancestors were never very far away. Captain Ephraim was here beside her, saying, "Hang on, lassie, hang on . . . my cutlass was once the strong right arm that defended my Camilla from the lasciviousness of the whalers . . . now it will defend you from the cruel sea!"

She even imagined a warmth flowed from it into her chilled white fingers. A wave dashed against her, the spray this time reached the back of her head, and with it, reviving her, an idea she was sure came from Captain Ephraim himself. Her trews had a belt. A belt that was purely ornamental . . . and tough. It was made of nylon and nylon had a terrific breaking strain.

She managed to unbuckle it with one hand, to grip it firmly lest it go from her grasp and drew it out of the loops. She tied one end round her left wrist, during a few anxious moments when she had to let go the cutlass. She slipped the buckle end through the handle of the cutlass and fastened it firmly. Now, even if the rocks slipped she would be held there with one wrist and could cling to it with her other hand. Oh, Captain Ephraim, thank you, but bring help quickly. Please, please! The next wave was the fiercest yet, and hit her with a sickening force. She spun a little. . . . Oh, Adam, Adam, hurry, hurry!

Then she heard it, faint and faraway . . . a voice, a voice that neared, became a shout, "I'm coming, Julia . . . I'm coming, Julia . . ." over and over again. Oh, wonderful and blessed sound!

Then she heard Adam roar: "Now keep well back, Luke!" and the next moment he was looking over at her. She would never forget the expression on his face. The overwhelming relief . . . it was like seeing a bit of granite crumble!

He said gaspingly, "Thank God! Don't leave go now . . . don't leave go. There's a tree here, I'll get this rope round it . . . don't leave go."

She said, shouting against the wind and the spray, "I *can't* leave go . . . I'm lashed. I've lashed myself to the cliff with my belt.

Get it really firm, that rope, won't you? Take your time. I can't let go."

He said urgently. "What are you lashed to? Will it hold? I'll only be out of sight for a moment. I've got a rope ladder too." He was straining to see what she was lashed to.

She said, and Adam looked aghast, thinking she was wandering in her head, "I'll be all right . . . *he'll* never let me go. Not *Captain Ephraim!*"

Adam said something unprintable, disappeared from her sight, and in no time a rope ladder . . . the most beautiful sight in the world . . . was sliding over the edge of the cliff towards her. She had to wait to grasp it while a huge wave dashed at her, tried to tear her from the face, retreated foiled.

She said to Adam, "Just hold it steady. My fingers are frozen. I must get this buckle undone."

He said, "Don't be ridiculous . . . I'm coming down. Just hold that ladder steady . . . hold it. Your fingers will be so numb you might fall back. And I'm so tall, I can steady you . . . have you got it? Good."

They waited till after another wave had

come and gone, receding only to her waist, then he was over and down, swinging round the back of her, steadying himself on her rocks by one foot, but the other on a rung of the ladder in case his weight was too much for the pile.

Luke's terrified face appeared above them. He was lying down, steadying the ladder. Adam roared at him to get back.

Luke said simply: "I won't!"

Adam knew he had met the nay of Captain Ephraim and wasted no more breath.

He was warm against her . . . a bulwark between her and those dashing waves. His hands were warm too, as they unfastened the buckle.

She said, "We can come back some day at low tide for it, can't we? With pickaxes and crowbars."

"For *what*?"

"For Captain Ephraim's cutlass . . . it saved me," she said.

Adam took one incredible look at it, said, "My God! But up you go . . . I'll be just one step below you. You won't slip, darling. You can't, with me behind you. Luke, hold it steady!"

So short a distance. So near, yet so far. The margin between life and death. They were over the edge and sprawling, and Luke flung himself on them both, sobbing. "You made it . . . you made it . . . you made it!"

They sat up, Adam pushing Luke off and grabbing Julia, folding her to him roughly. "Oh, Julia, Julia, oh, Julia!" His hands came to the back of her head, fondling it. His mouth clung to hers, stifling speech.

Then he held her off a bit, surveyed her, said, "Oh, if I'd lost you . . . Julia, Julia!"

She pushed back sodden elf-locks of hair. Her fingers scratched and bleeding from the rocks, made ghastly smears across her wet face. She said, "Oh, I believe you *do* love me!"

"*Love* you?" He bellowed it. "Love you? Of course I love you . . . the minute I saw you in Camilla's nightgown I knew I loved you!"

Julia peered up at him incredulously and collapsed into the giggles. Adam didn't laugh, but when Luke said plaintively, "Do we *have* to talk, I'm frozen!" they came to themselves.

Adam peeled off his enormous jersey and enveloped Luke in it. Then off came his shirt, a warm checked one, and he pulled it over Julia's head. Not till then did she remember she was only half dressed. She huddled into it gratefully.

Adam unroped the ladder from the tree . . . the only sturdy tree on the headland, the rest was just scrub, and the three of them, still gasping occasionally, but so thankful, trudged up the hill.

They talked as they went, in staccato sentences . . . Luke managed to get more than his fair share of the conversation, explaining exactly where and how it had happened, for he had gasped out only the bare essentials to Adam in the smithy.

They came up the quarterdeck verandah steps, through the front door, down the passages and into the warm living-room where Lydia was laying the table and the girls discussing what they'd make for tea, seeing Julia wasn't back yet. Nathaniel was entering with a huge pile of driftwood.

The three of them stood there inside the door, but only just, dripping wet, grinning slightly, Julia in jeans plastered to her legs and Adam's huge shirt flowing out behind;

Luke looking like an orphan of the storm in a jersey that reached to his ankles, both of them covered in blood, and Adam clad only in singlet and trousers.

"Wal, I swan!" said Nathaniel, entirely unreproved for once, and dropped his bundle of driftwood.

11

LYDIA found words first. She said, staring. "What on earth have you been doing?"

Julia's eyes danced. "Finding Captain Ephraim's sword," she announced.

They all kept on boggling at her. This was just one sensation after another.

"Finding Captain Ephraim's sword," repeated Nathaniel, but there was no conviction in the words.

"Ay, we did," said Adam, "but it's very firmly embedded in the cliff at Ruddy Jacks Cut. We'll have it out at ebb-tide tomorrow. But it saved their lives . . . Julia's and Luke's." All of a sudden he grabbed a chair and sat down and put his head between his knees.

Lydia said sharply, "Nat . . . the brandy!"

Nathaniel had it there very quickly. Adam's colour came flowing back.

Luke said, "Gosh! Just look at that, will you? It was Julia and me who nearly got drowned and *Uncle Adam's* gone and flaked out!"

Adam growled, "I have *not* flaked out. I only nearly did. Julia, you must have some too."

"I bet they won't let *me* have any," said Luke in a gloomy tone.

Lydia said, "Give Luke something sweet, girls. Raspberry cordial, and for goodness sake tell us what happened."

Luke beat them. Adam and Julia exchanged the faintest of smiles and let him have it. Actually, he told it very well.

He said, finally, "Julia acted like greased lightning . . . she had my jersey and trousers off like that — " he made an expressive gesture — "and her own jersey. She didn't have time to get her jeans off. We had to go down with the next wave."

Julia interrupted with a giggle. "Just as well, at a moment like that you don't think about the subsequent rescuing."

Luke got hold of the conversation again. "She just threw me on to the rocks, then yanked me up, rushed me over the sharpest barnacles you ever saw, across the reef, with the waves just drenching us, and got to the shore. But the cliff was too high and

364

too steep to climb. She got me on her shoulder. I grabbed a root, then the handle of the cutlass. Gee, I wish I'd had a closer look, I thought it was an old mooring-ring! Then I was over the top. Only just made it. If I hadn't grown a lot this year I couldn't have! Jingo, Uncle Adam, I was scared stiff you'd have gone back to the house."

Adam took up the tale. "It was the most appalling decision of my life. Luke gasped out the bare essentials very graphically, very concisely, but he was screeching at me to come quickly. I thought if Julia had got washed into the sea, I ought to be getting the launch out, and rushing to the cliff would be so much time lost. And I wanted to send Luke belting up to the house for more aid . . . but I was terrified I wouldn't find the location without him. And all the time I was running I was wondering if I'd made a decision I'd regret all my life.

"And I got there, and there she was, perched up on rocks she'd somehow trundled there, buckled to Captain Eph-raim's sword handle. Not that I knew that then . . . I got the rope-ladder tied to a tree as firmly as possible and Luke held it steady . . . he made a magnificent job of doing it. Luke, you deserve a medal."

"And everyone," decreed Lydia, "deserves a hot bath. Girls, get Luke into the bath in the cottage. Adam . . . the shower. Julia, come with me."

Luke went scarlet. "I will *not* have those girls bathing me!"

The twins burst out laughing. "It's all right, Luke. Granny didn't mean that. We'll just get it ready for you. Grandpa can bath you. It's only that after an experience like that, you might feel dizzy. Come on, you look blue!"

"Well, they didn't give *me* brandy," muttered Luke as they led him away.

Lydia was managing very well with a stick, the best she had been yet. She got Julia fresh clothes — oh, how good they felt. Julia towelled her hair; good job it always dried so quickly. She took the old whalebone hairbrush and brushed it till it turned up at the ends, glinting gold amidst the chestnut.

Before she got into a dress Lydia carefully placed sticking-plaster on the worst scratches and dried up the others with peroxide. When Julia picked up the frock of gulf green, Lydia shuddered. "No, not the colours of the sea tonight."

Julia smiled. "It was just that it's a button-through, Lydia, so easier to slip on over these scratches. Luke's toe-nails want cutting!"

Lydia took down one of Antoinette's frocks, still in Julia's wardrobe. "Wear this. I think Antoinette would be glad to think you were wearing it. If you hadn't jumped into that cave after Luke, her son might have — " Lydia could not finish.

Julia said lightly, "I love this frock anyway. It's just gorgeous."

It was coral, with a self-coloured embossed stripe through it and butter-coloured revers and cuffs stitched in coral, with a huge chunky brooch on one lapel. Julia went across to the bureau that Captain Ephraim's mother had sent Camilla and picked up the coral necklace that went with it. Lydia had once asked Julia why she did not wear it. The girls had brought it over, but Julia had said she felt she was wearing enough of Antoinette's belongings.

She looked down at the sticking-plaster

patches adorning her legs and showing up clearly through her pantie-hose and giggled. "How glamorous," she said.

They arrived in the living-room to find them all assembled. Julia became aware that she was ravenous. "Nothing makes you so hungry as dangling from a cliff," she vowed.

Esther said. "We've heated up that soup. Can we dish out now? And we've got stacks of hot savoury toast in the oven. All sit down, please."

Nathaniel used the grace Captain Ephraim had always used when he came back to harbour. It was very fitting and nobody took it tonight as just a family custom. It was a giving of thanks not only for daily bread, but for deliverance.

Had ever anything tasted as good as that vegetable broth? When they were satisfied they went over and over the adventure. Discussed what they would do about the cave-in.

Adam said, "Of course I've not seen it yet, but it sounds to me as if we'll have to get bulldozers in to uncover it. To deepen the whole cut, otherwise it will continue to erode and present a real danger. And the track must take another course."

He turned to Luke. "You'll be able to write a real good essay on this, young feller. Doesn't your teacher always set you one on what you did in the holidays?"

Luke pointed out it hadn't happened in the holidays, but added, his eyes lighting up, "But sometimes we're allowed to pick our own subjects. Gosh, nobody else will have an adventure like this to write about. And finishing up finding the family treasure . . . oh, beaut!"

Adam caught Julia's eye and grinned. She knew why he was doing it . . . if Luke could see it as a recountable escapade, he was less likely to turn and toss in nightmare that night — and other nights — recalling that quite horrible moment when they dived under the water in the cave-mouth. When they felt the gurgling and sucking and surging of the waters just before they gained the surface. Worst of all, when they realised the sheer inaccessibility of the cliffs for climbing.

Involuntarily she gave a little shudder, instantly repressed. Adam's foot came across the table to hers, exerted a little pressure. It said as a handclasp would have done. "I know. And I love you."

Her heart was singing. It was a crazy, glorious, mixed-up old world, but soon, soon, she and Adam would find themselves blessedly alone. And tomorrow they would tell the family.

Luke began going over the various bits he would put in his essay, all of them watching him with tender indulgence and the girls forbearing to correct him for anything.

He was sitting beside Julia. He suddenly looked up at her, bit his lip. "Ju, will I have to say in my essay how scared I was?"

She said candidly, "It wouldn't ring true if you didn't. Nobody would think you could be anything but scared. I was just about petrified, Luke. And I was sick with fear when you were scrambling up off my shoulders in case you slipped back off my head in that moment before you clutched the cliff-edge. And you must have been too. But you concentrated on getting up, clutching at the frailest things. . . . It was the bravest thing I ever knew, and you kept your promise and didn't look down. And you must have gone like the wind to get Adam back so soon."

Luke basked a little in their combined praise, then he thought of something. "I'll put in about us rushing up to the house and about Grandpa dropping the wood . . . but I won't say anything about you and Julia on the cliff-top, Uncle Adam . . . that'd be soppy."

Adam dropped his rock-cake, in the process of being conveyed to his mouth, clean into his tea!

He said hastily, "Now look what you've made me do! And I guarantee that's a clean cloth! Sorry, Julia, you get enough washing as it is."

As a diversion it was a complete failure. Lydia said in a tone of extreme interest. "Soppy? Soppy, Luke?"

"Yeah. Like anything." He swallowed the last of his chocolate biscuit while Julia and Adam sat petrified and said, "Girls are mad, quite mad. She started asking him if he really loved her . . . on top of the cliff. *And I was cold!*"

Julia wasn't cold at that moment. Neither was Adam.

It was too much for Nathaniel. His

curiosity vanquished all his finer feelings. "And what did Adam say?" he asked.

Adam made a convulsive movement, pushed his chair back, started to say something, but his grandmother rapped his arm. "Be quiet, Adam, be quiet."

Luke said distinctly, "It was a really clunky bit of talk. He said he'd loved her ever since he saw her in her nightgown."

Well, this time Luke really had made a sensation. Four pairs of eyes positively boggled at Adam and Julia.

Luke took the opportunity to secure another chocolate biscuit.

Julia and Adam both started to speak at once. Both stopped, then Adam waved Julia down. He said: "Luke means Camilla's nightgown."

Lydia said, in a strangled sort of way, "*That*, of course, makes it quite respectable!"

"It's not as bad as it sounds, Granny. It was the night the owl busted Luke's window. The first night Julia was here, and she had no night-clothes with her. You might say . . ." he was beginning to grin, "that Luke has been in it from the start. From Alpha to Omega. But Luke, if you put one word of this in any essay, I'll tear you limb from limb!"

Julia felt like a demonstrator in a shop window, with the world peering in on her.

Adam was helpless with laughter now. "Oh, if only you could see the looks on your faces! I'll let you have the lot now. She sort of bowled me over that night. I knew she was the girl for me, the girl for here, but she gave me the hell of a time, always trying to heal the breach between Miriam and me. I nearly went mad. I don't reckon any other chap has ever been involved in a situation like mine before. Then later she seemed to think I was a real off-with-the-old, on-with-the-new-sort of guy. But — " he looked across at Julia, "from what she said, on the cliff-top, I'm inclined to think it really didn't matter. Just as well. I'm no Jacob, serving seven years for his Rachel . . . I'm far too impatient."

There was a rapturous squeal from the girls, held till now in a most unnatural silence. "Then you're engaged . . ." and they flew round, both of them, to Julia.

"Oh, my gosh," said Luke, "*more* kissing."

Julia said faintly, "I don't know about engaged — I — we — Adam ?"

Adam said firmly, "Adam didn't get time to ask you, besides, he took it for granted. He had a small demon of a nephew wailing that he was freezing. Talk about moonlight and roses . . . when I think of the settings we could have had here in — "

"In this small Eden," said Julia, looking at him completely frankly for the first time. "Adam, if this is a proposal, I'm warning you I'm accepting. I couldn't bear to leave Whangatupuna, or Lydia, or Nathaniel, or the children . . . I'd snatch at any chance of staying here permanently."

"You've got it all wrong," said Adam, grinning. "You really mean you couldn't bear to leave *me*."

Lydia got up, walking stiffly, and bent over Adam, taking his face between both her hands, and kissing him.

"I don't need to wish you happiness, Adam, you've got it. Oh, how thrilled Ruth will be when I tell her it's come off."

Adam was startled, "Come off? What can you mean ?"

"Oh, your mother knows all about it. I wrote and told her that you'd met the right girl this time. I thought she'd enjoy her last few weeks of England just that more if she knew you and Miriam had broken up."

Nathaniel was kissing Julia, "All I can say is I'm mighty thankful Adam has at last stopped behaving like a damfool."

Adam took it as a compliment.

How prosaic to come down to washing dishes. Nobody wanted to look at television tonight. Today's events had eclipsed anything on the screen. Julia had a hard job keeping the girls off wedding plans.

"You'll be the first to know the date and where and how. Adam and I have, after all, just got to know each other."

"Only just?" said Susanna. "Gosh, we thought you were slow! We could have told you from the start — almost — that this was bound to happen. I mean, Uncle Adam was himself again. Not like when he was engaged to Miriam — phew! I said to Ess once, 'Well, if this is love, I hope I never catch it!' "

Esther said anxiously, "You won't expect us to call you Aunt, will you? I mean I just couldn't. And I'm sure Susanna couldn't. You see, you're just like us . . .

you get into pickles even if you are — " she stopped.

"Even if I'm what?"

"Even if you are grown-up. And you're so right for Adam. He'll never have a dull moment now. Like Captain Ephraim with Camilla. Julia, *how* did you take so long . . ."

Julia said, "Long? You must be daft. There's going to be gossip . . . it's no time since he was engaged to Miriam. People will say at best he doesn't know his own mind, and at worst . . . well, if any hint of the stowing-away gets out they'll think Miriam had a lucky escape!"

Susanna giggled, "And think of the scandal if Luke goes round saying Adam fell in love with you in your nightgown!"

"He won't," said Adam behind them, making them jump. "Now, you two, you've had a fair innings. I've just tucked Luke up and underlined my earlier statement that the nightgown incident is taboo. Off you go and kiss Granny and Grandpa good-night. And not another peep out of you till morning! And yes, I've decided you two and Phemy can be our brides-maids. Satisfied?"

Susanna gasped: "*You've* decided! Oh, Uncle Adam, you'll ruin this romance too if you aren't careful. It's the bride's privilege to say who'll attend her. Julia will want Faith."

Julia smiled, "She can be my maid-of-honour. You three can be junior bridesmaids."

The girls gave her rapturous hugs, came one each side of Adam, reached up and kissed his cheeks, went on their way. Susanna turned at the door. "Are you sending Granny and Grandpa to bed too?"

He made a threatening move towards them. They retreated, then Esther said over her shoulder, "Aren't you the lucky ones? Ben's spending the night at Uncle Oliver's."

And they were gone.

Adam said, "Julia, let's give Granny and Grandpa a little time with us first. Grandpa is bursting with it all. Then we can be alone."

She nodded. "Yes, I'll come now. No, Adam, don't kiss me . . . I think the twins are hanging about out there."

Adam flung wide the door, said: "Scram!"

They gave Lydia and Nathaniel a very happy hour, discussing, planning. As soon as all the family was home, they would be married.

So it was much later when Adam led Julia into the First Parlour. He'd suggested the quarterdeck verandah where the moonlight was still sleeping sweetly on the bank, but Julia had said, "I'd sooner it was the First Parlour, where *they* are."

He had understood.

Adam's eyes crinkled up when he saw the fire of driftwood, burning with flames of blue, green and sulphur. "Grandpa had the same idea as you." He added, "Don't let's bother with electric light. Say we light the old ship's lantern?"

She was enraptured. "I'd love that."

Had it stood in the Captain's cabin the night that wrathful man had discovered his stowaway? Had it shed its soft light over other, more tender scenes? Had it watched as Captain Ephraim brought Camilla the little posy of clover and daisies? On an impulse she stooped to the row of books and pulled that one out, fingered the dry stalks, looked up at Adam and smiled.

He came across to her, took her hands, held her off from him a little, smiling, looking his fill of her. He nodded at the pictures, "They may not be *your* forebears, Julia, but they will be your descendants' forebears." He grinned as she blushed a little. "This is the place where our children will grow up and our grandchildren, where a new story will be told over and over again, of another stowaway, an unwilling one, who crossed the Strait and brought rare happiness to the Bay of the Ancestors, and who, in a time of great peril, was saved by Captain Ephraim's sword. It will be brought up and cleaned and put in a glass case I shall have made for it, between Camilla's picture and his."

Adam said, "Before we settle to sign and seal this engagement properly . . . I think we should clear up one or two things. By the way, do you want a formal proposal? I mean the dinner-table was frightfully public . . . sorry about that. Will you feel cheated?"

Julia's eyes were dancing. "Adam, you idiot! Heavens, man, you've just been talking about our grandchildren!"

"Well, I just want you thoroughly convinced that from the moment Miriam fled in her car, I had no intention in the wide, wide world of making it up with her. It was the most maddening thing to have you trying to do it. Oh, you were wilful and persistent and blind! Times without number I could have wrung your neck. That night you followed me down the shell path I'd gone to try to analyse my feelings towards *you*.

"You see, having fallen out of love with Miriam, so soon after she came down here, I hardly trusted my own judgment. I tried to resist you. And you followed me down full of sympathy and plans for healing the breach. I can tell you, you really turned the sword in the wound. My conscience was giving me hell. I'd allowed Miriam to resign from her position . . . oh I felt a faithless swain all right. Time and again I told myself you just couldn't care, the way you went on. Then that day you wanted to go off with Miriam . . . I could have murdered her that day, anyway. I hadn't told you about the road being clear because I was plumb scared you'd be up and off. I had to keep you here by fair means or foul to give you a chance, the merest chance, of falling in love with me. With a twit of a chap who didn't know his own mind, who had no discrimination — till he met you! Oh, my gosh, I took a risk when I grabbed you that day and held you by brute force and reckoned I was the luckiest chap in the world when my grandfather stood up for me. All I could think of was I must have time to try to make you care."

Julia laughed. "You complete chump! I was already head over heels."

"When?" he demanded.

"The night you overheard me on the verandah saying I was glad, just the same, that I'd come here."

He looked incredulous. "I thought it was just that you loved Whangatupuna so much . . . the scenery. And you wasted all that time, didn't give me a hint of encouragement. Why, you little — "

She said, soberly enough, "Adam, I had to be sure. You see I thought you were so incensed about Miriam's reaction to the age of this house, to its traditions, that you were ready to fall for anyone who loved those things too. I thought it was not so much me as for the way I fell for your grandparents, the children, this bay, this small Eden! I had to be sure it was *me* you loved!

"Then you sang that song . . . about Lilith and Mary. I felt . . . *too* homespun, *too* made to order. I felt so sad, thought you were going to ask me to marry you because I'd fit in here, because Lydia and Nathaniel and the children found me a kindred spirit, and it would free your mother and father to live in Picton.

"I'd been told Miriam had swept you off your feet. I wanted to be loved like that too. I thought you'd never feel like that about me. Every girl likes to think she's bowled a chap over . . . that's why I couldn't let myself hope. I wanted to be loved for myself . . . romantically!"

Adam gazed at her as if she'd gone mad. "Romantically! Honestly, Julia, you must be nuts! There was precious little romance about Miriam and myself, after that first week in Auckland. But, suffering catfish, did the glamour wear off quickly down here! Miriam wasn't one for standing on the quarterdeck looking at the moon, believe me. She did nothing but pull the house to pieces . . . and wanted to do it in actual fact too! Heavens, girl, don't you realise what it was like? Nothing but discord. Just because she was called Miriam, I thought I was going to follow in Grandpa's footsteps. When he met his Lydia, he said it was foreordained.

"How *can* I convince you!" His face lit up. "I know. I've got the perfect answer." He dived off, and came back with his own diary, began thumbing it over, then paused, with a finger between the pages.

"Before I show this to you, let me tell you I never dreamed I'd have need of it. But I can't bear that you should ever suffer one jealous pang over what I felt so briefly for Miriam."

She smiled. "It's all right. It's gone, never to return. I do understand, Adam, because it happened to me too. I nearly drifted into an engagement, then realised in time that it was nothing more than friendship, a habit — we'd partnered each other to so many things — but something was lacking, the sort of thing poets have written of. We didn't have it, so we finished it. So I do understand, after all, Adam."

"Thank goodness! But I'll show you this just the same. Camilla loved Herrick's poems. That night you found me packing

Miriam's things up, and nearly stabbed me to the quick telling me the estrangement couldn't last, I came back to my room and hunted up this poem and copied it into my diary.

"Remember you were wearing that gorgeous thing of Antoinette's? A filmy sort of turquoise robe. I'm going to ask her to give it to you when she gets back, or buy you one just the same. It floated out from your shoulders to your feet. Listen, here's what Herrick said — wrote — to a Julia centuries ago. He died in 1674.

" 'Whenas in silks my Julia goes
Then, then (methinks) how sweetly flows
The liquefaction of her clothes.

Next, when I cast mine eyes and see
That brave vibration each way free;
O how that glittering taketh me!' "

Julia looked down on Adam's black positive writing and saw the "my" was underlined. *His* Julia. Oh, yes, yes.

She gave a cry, "Adam!" He looked into her eyes and knew she had no doubts left. He drew her close.

It was quite some time later that she

stirred in his arms, lifted her head and laughed.

"What are you laughing at now?" he demanded. "No wonder those twins love you. You're as big a giggler as they are — and every bit as mad. I have a feeling that all my life I'll have to fight for a fair share of your company against my family."

"I was thinking of the way stories are handed down in this family. Some of ours can never be passed down. You just think of it, Adam. You fell in love with me in Camilla's nightie, and quoted poetry about me when I was wearing Antoinette's negligée. Really! Shame on you!"

He laughed with her. "Well, it's all over. We've had such a stormy courtship it doesn't seem possible it's taken place in so short a time — talk about time being measured not in hours, but in heartbeats! But at least this time I didn't have stardust in my eyes. I started off absolutely loathing you, and in about forty-eight hours, I couldn't think of anything but your face and your voice when I went to bed. Your chestnutty hair, your hazel eyes, your pepper-pot freckles, and there was nothing to blind me. No complications this time of a name fitting into the family tradition. Curse Grandpa and his foreordaining! Now what's the matter? What's so funny about that?"

Her eyes had crinkled into slits of laughter. "Oh, Adam, Adam! I was terrified the twins would find out what my second name is. They would have thought it foreordained too. They were match-making enough as it was."

He was staring at her. "I saw your initials on the back of that letter you wrote to Faith. It's J. E. Merrill, isn't it? What's the E. stand for? Some Biblical name? Let me see . . . Elizabeth? No. Well, Eunice? No — well, what?"

She could hardly get it out for laughing. "The most obvious one of all, idiot! Come on, come on, dimwit? No . . . I was named for Father's mother, who was called *Eve*!"

Adam gave a great shout of laughter and folded her into his large embrace.

Above their heads the firelight flickered on the glass of the two old portraits. Although neither of them noticed, it seemed as if for a moment Captain Ephraim nodded across the chimney breast to Camilla, and she nodded back.

And down on the lonely shore the embedded cutlass waited. After all, it had bided its time for more than a hundred years. One more night didn't matter.

THE END

ROMANCE TITLES IN THE ULVERSCROFT LARGE PRINT SERIES